EVE SILVER

BODY
OF SIN

Otherkin: Torn between
loyalty and desire…

Forbidden alliances…and inescapable desires.

Collect three more volumes in the darkly sexy and
seductive Otherkin series from

EVE SILVER

and HQN Books.

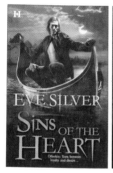

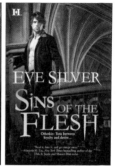

Available in stores today!

HQN™ HARLEQUIN®
www.Harlequin.com

PHES0911IFC

EVE SILVER

BODY OF SIN

HQN™

Recycling programs
for this product may
not exist in your area.

ISBN-13: 978-0-373-77592-7

BODY OF SIN

For Michelle Rowen.

Vegas, baby!

Acknowledgments

This book would never have come to be without the help and support of many people. I appreciate each and every one of them.

Thank you to my editor, Tara Parsons, and the entire team at Harlequin. To my writing pals: Michelle Rowen, Ann Christopher, Caroline Linden, Kristi Cook/Astor, Laura Drewry, Lori Devoti, Sally MacKenzie. A special thank you to Nancy Frost and Brenda Hammond.

Thank you to my family. To Dylan, my light; Sheridan, my joy; and Henning, my forever love.

And a huge thank you to my readers, so many of whom let me know they couldn't wait for this book.

Dear Reader,

The first time I met Lokan Krayl, he was standing in a bar, taking a long, slow pull on his beer. He set the bottle down, turned his head and pinned me with eyes the color of faded jeans. My breath caught. Despite the pretty color, there was something dark in his eyes. I stood in the shadows and watched as he met someone besides me that night. A woman, Bryn Carr. She changed his life. She changed his future. He just didn't know it yet.

The next time I ran into Lokan, he was trapped in choking darkness. No scents. No sounds. Nothing, except the mind-numbing edge of his panic and the knowledge that he had sacrificed everything in order to keep his daughter safe. He was brave. He was smart. He was dead sexy. And he was...dead.

And dead he remained as I wrote the stories of his soul reaper brothers in *Sins of the Heart, Sins of the Soul* and *Sins of the Flesh*. But I couldn't let go of Lokan. I couldn't leave him trapped in a prison without bars or walls, condemned to an eternity of loneliness and loss. Enter Bryn, the woman he allowed himself to think of only as his daughter's mother. She's duped him in the past. She's the last person he's likely to trust. And now, she's his one hope for salvation.

This book had my pulse pounding, my eyes tearing up, and once or twice, it had me laughing out loud. I hope you enjoy reading Lokan and Bryn's story as much as I loved writing it.

Happy reading!

Eve Silver

BODY
OF SIN

CHAPTER ONE

Miami, Florida
Seven years ago

"So…WHAT'S YOUR SIGN?" Bryn cringed inside as the words left her mouth. She should have thought of something better. Would have, if she had any real idea of how this was supposed to go down. But she wasn't experienced at this sort of thing.

Her last three efforts had been a total failure, and four was the magic number. Get it right or lose the opportunity. She would never have this chance again.

The man leaning against the gleaming black bar was blond and tall, and his clothes looked good on him. Not too tight. Not too loose. He had muscles, but he wasn't bulky. So far, she'd only seen him in profile, but it was a nice profile. Straight nose. Strong jaw. She supposed it didn't hurt that he was handsome, but really, what he *was* mattered far more than how he looked.

He was a supernatural of some sort. She could feel the air tingling and sparking with his power. Maybe he was some sort of lesser demon or a high level psychic.

He wasn't a walker, like her. Walkers were always female, and they didn't emit a supernatural vibe, which he definitely did. Two important points that proved he was something else. She just didn't know exactly what. The very fact that he was standing here meant he could go Topworld, and the really strong ones were confined to the Underworld. She knew that much. She wished she knew more. But her brothers had kept her sheltered and untutored. They'd figured the less she knew, the easier she'd be to control.

And for a while, they'd been right.

"What's my sign?" He turned his head, pinning her with an amused look. His eyes were an interesting shade of light blue. Like her favorite pair of well-washed jeans. Comfortable and soft and warm.

A shiver coursed up her spine.

Who was she kidding?

This guy was not soft. Or warm. There was something dark in his eyes, no matter how pretty the color.

But he was her one hope, and that kept her from backtracking and walking away.

"Next you're going to ask me if I come here often." He took a slow pull from his beer.

She wet her lips, more from nerves than anything else. But his gaze dipped to her mouth, and she felt the first spark of optimism that maybe, just maybe, she could do this.

"You…um…you come here often?" she asked, happy to oblige.

He blinked then laughed, the sound rich and warm against the pounding of the music. "Aren't those supposed to be my lines?"

"Your lines? Why? Do you use them often?" She was practically screaming to be heard over the music.

He laughed again. "You *are* kidding, right?" He stared at her until she felt like a slide under a microscope. Then his eyes widened, and she saw a flicker of surprise. "You're not kidding. Okay. I'll bite. Do *you* come here often?"

"Oh, all the time. I—" She blew out a breath and opted for the truth because, really, what was the point of lying? "No." She'd never been to this club before. Just as she'd never been to any of the clubs she'd tried for the past six nights. She'd only known about this place because her brother had mentioned it more than once; he liked to come here when he was in Miami. Since he tended to frequent clubs with other supernaturals, she'd figured it was a good bet that there'd be others like him here.

As a rule, she wasn't a party-all-night kind of girl. Except for three times in the past year when she'd managed to evade her brothers and had spent a week each time going through these same steps, hunting for the opportunity to do what she had to do.

This was her last night. Her last chance. All the previous failures wouldn't matter if she could just get it right this time.

She *had* to get it right this time.

He was still looking at her.

"It's my first time here," she admitted at last.

His gaze flicked over her, from the top of her head to the tip of her toes and back again. She resisted the urge to look down and check her T-shirt for stains.

He reached for her, and she jerked back, taken by surprise. He froze for a second, then carefully pulled the covered elastic from her hair, freeing her ponytail and sending her straight brown hair tumbling over her shoulders.

"It's sexier down," he said. "Always a bonus if you're trying to pick someone up." Then he turned to face the bar once more, lifted the bottle in front of him and drained the last of his beer.

"I could buy you a drink," she blurted.

The look he sent her spoke volumes. "I'm waiting for someone," he said, a blatant dismissal, but at least he didn't walk away. He just kept leaning against the bar, studying her as if she was a puzzle he was trying to figure out.

"Well, I could still buy you a drink. While you wait. And you could drink it." Desperation dripped from every word. There was no denying her ineptitude. She didn't have a second's doubt that she sounded like something out of a bad movie. But she had his attention, and that was exactly what she wanted. There was no one else for her, not in this entire, massive club. And, so far, not in this entire city.

She'd heard that supernaturals liked Miami. And Vegas. But Vegas was *not* a possibility.

So she'd opted for Miami and this was the seventh—and last—night she'd spent prowling the club scene, searching for a male supernatural. The guy standing beside her was the first one she'd found. He was her one shining chance.

Either she got pregnant tonight or she never would.

And if she didn't get pregnant, she could never be free.

"Maybe I'm the someone you've been waiting for," she said before she could think better of it. Actually, she thought that sounded pretty good. Emboldened, she tilted her head, thrust out one hip and tried to look sexy.

He blinked. Then he did a slow perusal of her pose and shook his head. "Seriously?" He lifted his head and looked around with narrowed eyes. "I feel like I should be looking around for the camera."

"Camera?"

"Yeah. What is this, some reality TV show? A new version of *Candid Camera?*"

"What?" She shook her head.

His gaze flicked around the club once more, the flashing lights dancing across his skin. She was losing his interest. Any second, he could walk away.

She sidled a little closer.

He sidled a little farther away and studied her, his gaze intent. "Did Mal put you up to this?"

"Mal?" Was Mal a woman? Someone who'd know exactly what to say to lure a man like this. Frack. Bryn's heart sank. "Who's Mal?"

"My brother."

Relief was sweet and smooth as honey. "I have one, too. A brother," she clarified. "Three of them, actually. All older than me. By quite a bit."

"Yeah?" He looked around again, a bit of his amiable humor disappearing. "They here?"

The very thought made her ill. "No. Thank heaven. I mean—" she waved a hand "—I don't know if there really is a heaven but it's an expression. So, um, yeah…"

His attention snapped back to her, and he smiled, an easy, slow curve of his lips that made him look almost…nice. "Three brothers, huh? Guess we have that in common, then."

"You have three brothers? Well, you already said you have one. Mal, right? Are they older than you, too?"

"You talk a lot," he observed in a lazy drawl. "And ask a lot of questions. You always like this?"

She opened her mouth, then paused, considering her answer. She *was* always like this. A friend—well, more of a paid companion her brothers had hired— had once told her she had no filter. And she tended to ramble to fill any silence. "Yes."

"Honest—" he quirked a brow "—and strange." He shook his head, and the corner of his mouth lifted in a wry smile. "A combination that I wouldn't normally find attractive." The way he said that made her think that maybe this time, he did find it attractive.

He lifted his empty beer bottle and gestured to

the bartender. "Another, thanks. And my new and lovely friend here will have—" He lifted his brows.

What to ask for? She didn't drink alcohol often. She didn't really like the taste. And she'd read somewhere that pregnant women shouldn't drink. Did that apply to hopefully-about-to-be-pregnant women, as well?

Both the bartender and the blond supernatural were looking at her expectantly. She put her hand on his arm and nearly jumped at the tingle that shot through her. Warm skin over smooth, hard muscle.

"I'll have...*you*," she blurted.

He stared at her for a moment longer, but she brazened it out, holding his gaze.

Finally, he took one last glance around the club, apparently didn't find what he was looking for, and shrugged. "Why the hell not?"

LOKAN HAD NO IDEA WHY THE GIRL in front of him was so hot to climb down his pants. Not that he didn't attract his share of attention, but she seemed too eager. Almost desperate.

She was pretty enough. Brown eyes. Dark brown hair that hung in a shiny curtain past her shoulders now that he'd pulled it free of her ponytail.

He thought she might have an Asian ancestor somewhere in her background. Japanese maybe? Hard to say. It would account for the gorgeous color of her skin, the shape of her eyes. The delicacy of her features.

She had full lips. Kissable lips.

Funny, he hadn't noticed that until this second. When she'd approached him, he'd been amused, then wary, thinking that Mal was playing some bizarre trick on him. Now, he was feeling open-minded.

There were worse ways to spend a few hours than having sex with a pretty, if utterly strange, woman. And since Mal and Dagan seemed to have ditched him, he just happened to have some hours available. He sent them a text to say he'd left the club, then he made a sweeping gesture with one hand.

"Lead the way, sweet thing," he said and watched the sway of her ass as she did just that. Nice figure. He hadn't noticed that before, either. She seemed to get more attractive as the minutes passed.

Maybe that was because he found her...interesting. She was definitely different. Despite the fact that her expressions and body language made her pretty much an open book, he got the feeling there were layers there. Strange and possibly fascinating layers.

She shot him a glance over her shoulder, as though worried she might have misplaced him, and he looked deep into her eyes. It was a soul reaper thing, the ability to see the Ka—the soul. Hers was pretty and shiny and...

Whoa.

It was as if she slammed a door on him.

He saw her eyes, dark brown, fringed in dark, curling lashes. And he saw nothing else, nothing deeper. The soul he'd been looking at was completely shuttered.

He'd heard about the rare human who could mask their soul from a reaper's senses, but in the centuries that he'd been doing Sutekh's bidding, he'd never actually encountered one. Until now.

So, yeah, definitely layers.

Outside the club, she paused by the curb and looked up and down the street as though confused about which direction to choose.

"Your place or mine?" Lokan asked, not at all convinced that she'd choose either. He half expected a group of giggling friends to jump out of the alley and say that it had been some sort of dare. Because this girl just didn't seem like the type to pick up a one-night stand in a club.

She looked at him now, her gaze lingering on his face for an instant before sliding down his body. She took her time taking in the details. For some reason, he felt as if he was being measured for a suit rather than sized up in a sexual way. It was a little unnerving. And it made him curious. How long would it take him to find her buttons and push them just right? He was always up for a challenge.

"You're very handsome," she said, an observation, not a compliment. "Not that it matters."

He laughed. "Do you ever censor what you say?"

She slapped her palm over her lips. "I'm sorry," she whispered. "I don't mean that the way it sounds."

"Right. Because you're not after my face and

body, but rather my vast intellect and scintillating wit, both of which you've discovered during our lengthy conversation."

"No. Yes. No." She shook her head. "I just want sex."

He laughed. He couldn't help it.

Her brows drew together, and she looked both perturbed and adorable. He wanted to reach out and smooth his fingers along the twin little lines that marked her frown. But he had a feeling that if he touched her, she might bolt. And, oddly, he wasn't ready for her to bolt.

"How about we start with a name?" he asked. "Mine's Lokan. Lokan Krayl." He offered his hand.

She stared at it for so long, he almost withdrew it. Then she pressed her palm to his and said, "Um… Bryn…Carr… No. I mean, Carrie."

"Which is it? Bryn or Carrie?" He didn't know why, but he'd expected her hand to be cold. Maybe because she seemed so nervous. But her skin was warm and smooth, and almost without conscious thought, he found himself tightening his grip just a little when she made to pull her hand away. He ran the pad of his thumb over her knuckles. Soft skin over delicate bones.

"For tonight, I was supposed to be Carrie." She looked down and stared at their clasped hands, no longer trying to pull away. He slid his thumb along the inside crease of her wrist then up to the center of her palm. She took a quick, soft breath, then said, "But you might as well call me Bryn."

"Okay. Is Bryn your real name?"

"Does it matter?" Her gaze flashed to his. There was a hint of humor there now and more than a touch of self-awareness. She knew what a hash she was making of things.

"You were planning to use a fake name."

"I was. But I'm not good at the cloak-and-dagger thing. Or at—" she shook her head and made a vague gesture with her left hand because her right one was still trapped in his "—this."

"This?"

She flapped her hand back and forth between the two of them. "This. Us. *This.*"

"Oh, you mean picking up a guy in a bar." He was finding this conversation, such as it was, highly entertaining.

She lifted her eyes to his. They shimmered under the streetlight. Pretty, pretty eyes. And the smell of her hair, her skin. He leaned in a little and breathed deep. She smelled good. Better than good. He wanted to put his lips against the pulse at her throat and lick her.

"You smell like a fresh baked cookie," he murmured. "And I have a fondness for sweets."

"I didn't have any perfume. I don't usually wear it. But since I was coming here, it seemed like I should wear something. I read that you can use vanilla extract." One sentence ran into the next, as if she was racing to get them all out. She shrugged. "I like to bake. Cookies. But not eat them. The cookies, I mean. Just bake them. I don't really like sweets."

He wasn't sure he followed that little monologue, but he liked her voice. It was soothing. Smooth. Soft. Like her skin.

"No? I like sweets." In fact, he and his brothers made a habit of popping candy to satisfy their half-god metabolism with a quick hit.

Taking a step forward, he closed the gap between them. Her head tipped back, and she took a small, gasping breath. Her eyes widened, and he saw her pupils dilate. Fear? Desire? He'd like to think it was the latter, but he wasn't taking her anywhere until he was certain. Her reaction to a kiss would tell, and right now, the sweet he had a hankering for was her.

Slowly, he lowered his head, giving her plenty of time to change her mind, to stop him. He breathed deep. She did smell like vanilla. And something else equally delicious.

"Strawberry shampoo?" His lips were a breath away from hers.

"Yes. It's called Strawberry Blast. I was looking for coconut but they were sold out and the strawberry was on sale so I bought two bottles. I—"

He kissed her, stilling her words. Her lips parted in surprise, and then he was the one surprised. It was as if he'd flicked her "on" switch. She didn't just let him kiss her. She took over. Coming up on her toes, she molded her body to his and flicked her tongue over the seam of his lips. Then she pushed inside, her tongue darting to meet his before slipping away.

A taste. A tease.

He wanted more.

Lust kicked him with unexpected force.

For a second, he forgot where they were. He just fisted his hand in her long, silky hair and pulled her head back, feasting on her.

She rocked her hips into his. She snuggled her breasts against his chest. She slid her palms up his arms and along his shoulders, then tangled her fingers in his hair. She wasn't subtle. Instead, she let her passion free in a wave that rolled over him and through him. The girl was definitely all-or-nothing.

As he slanted his mouth on hers and took the kiss deeper, harder, she made the most gorgeous sound, somewhere between a sigh and a moan.

She was one hell of a contradiction, little Miss Bryn. And she was hot as beach sand under the July sun.

He skimmed his hand along her hip, the curve of her waist, and then he stopped, reminding himself where they were. On the street. Out in the open.

Keeping one arm around her waist, he asked again, "Your place or mine?"

Seconds ticked past, then she drew back and stared at him, her pupils dilated, her lips wet and pink. He had the feeling that she was steadying her thoughts, and then she finally said, "Yours," and her gaze dipped to his mouth.

It was all the invitation he needed. He kissed her again, the taste of her delicious, the soft sound she made as she opened to him only fueling the heat. She fisted his shirt, dragging the hem from his jeans before thrusting her hands underneath and digging her nails into his back. Her eagerness made up for what he suspected was a lack of experience.

No worries. He was more than happy to offer tutoring services. When he kissed her, she melted in his arms. When he stroked his hands down her back to cup her ass, she mirrored his move and pressed her hips to his. She was an unexpected combination of sweet and spicy, and he was startled by how much that turned him on.

He drew his lips from hers, and she sighed. Her lips were a little puffy and wet from his kisses. Her eyes were heavy lidded and glazed. Her hair was mussed.

She looked sexy as hell, but somewhere in the back of his mind, a warning bell clanged. Because she'd shown up at the club with her hair in a conservative ponytail and little makeup except for some pink lip gloss. Because she was dressed in a simple pair of jeans and a T-shirt under a denim jacket—not exactly the come-do-me outfit most women would sport if they were on the prowl. And because, despite her eagerness and interest, it was blatantly obvious that she wasn't very experienced.

Add that together, and he had all the ingredients for a beware-and-be-careful cake.

Dragging her up against him, he lowered his head and kissed her again. He'd never quite gotten the hang of being careful. Political, yes. Careful, no. What would be the fun in that?

MALTHUS KRAYL GLANCED AT HIS phone. The text from Lokan made no sense. He hadn't planned on meeting his brother in Miami. Whatever. Lokan had probably meant to text Alastor or Dae.

With a shrug, he shoved the phone back in his pocket. Then he slapped his palm against the side of the plane. Balance was a bit of a challenge as the Cessna plunged, pilotless, toward the ground.

Lifting his head, he studied the pilot, who was standing directly in front of him. Well, not exactly standing; more like hanging around.

"Where were we?" Mal asked with a grin, enjoying the rush. "Right. We were about to get down to business."

He dragged his hand out of the man's chest, his fingers tight around the heart. The body slumped to the floor of the cabin with a dull *thwap,* then slid forward, pulled by gravity.

Mal dropped the heart into the leather pouch he wore slung across one shoulder. Then he squatted and shoved his hand back in the hole, all the while watching as the trees reached up toward them. He had seconds. Only seconds.

"Gotcha," he said as the darksoul curled around his wrist and slid up his arm.

His timing was a bit off. The underbelly of the plane scraped the tips of the tallest trees just as Mal straightened and opened a portal to the Underworld. Black smoke surged toward him and an indescribable chill.

He stepped through the dimensional hole just as the Cessna erupted in a giant ball of flame.

Adrenaline rocked him, a nice rush. He'd have to try that again sometime. Maybe wait just a shade longer before he got out.

He really did love the razor's edge.

CHAPTER TWO

THE LOBBY OF LOKAN'S HOTEL WAS deserted except for two men behind the front desk who were more interested in their conversation than in anything going on around them. Lokan rested his forearm across the open elevator door and held it as Bryn scurried in and moved to press her back against the far wall. She watched him, dark eyes wide and wary, quiet for the first time since he'd met her.

Well, except for the moments when he'd been kissing her.

His gaze dipped to her lips. She pressed back against the wall.

"It smells like apples," she said. "But sort of chemically. I think it's an air freshener. I didn't see a potpourri in the lobby. I think if you're going to put apples in a potpourri, cinnamon is—"

"Do I make you nervous?" He still held the door of the elevator, and he made no move to step inside. They'd walked here from the club, and she'd talked the whole time, mostly about baking. Which actually made him hungry. He did have a thing for sweets.

She stared at him, pressed her lips together, then

said, "I always feel like I have to fill the silence." Her eyes widened, as though she'd caught herself unawares with that admission.

"Okay." He stepped into the elevator but stayed at the opposite end. "Talk away."

"Really?"

"Yeah. I like listening to you talk."

"Really?"

He laughed. "Yeah. Why does that surprise you?"

Something flickered in her eyes. Then she shrugged, "I guess I talk so much, people sort of tune out what I have to say."

"Their loss."

The look she sent him then wasn't teasing or sexy. Assessing maybe…speculative. As if she was startled to find more there than she'd expected. It made him feel odd.

He gave his head a mental shake. She amused him and befuddled him. For a woman who had come right out and said she wanted sex, she wasn't doing much to nudge that along.

But her behavior wasn't the oddest thing in the mix. No, it was his reaction to it that surprised him. He liked listening to her talk. He liked her voice. There was no subterfuge in her. He was used to listening to conversations with a focus on deciphering the true meaning behind every word.

With Bryn, what you heard was what you got. No artifice. Just recipes.

He had the fleeting thought that after the sex was

done, he just might want to get to know her a little. Or a lot. He just might want to sample a few of those recipes over time.

And that was dangerous. While a one- or two-night stand wasn't out of the question, he made a point of avoiding relationships of any kind with human women. Too complicated. At some point she'd want to know more about him, things he could never share. At some point, she'd notice that he hadn't aged, while she had.

At some point, he'd run out of ways to lie.

Despite his invitation, she didn't talk now. She only stood there staring at him. The elevator started to rise. Her eyes widened; she looked more than nervous. She looked scared.

"Hey," he said, stepping closer to brush his knuckles along the curve of her cheek. "No pressure. This doesn't have to go anywhere. We can just—"

He never got to finish. With an inarticulate sound, she launched herself at him, her fingers tangling in his hair, her mouth on his, demanding a response. Her tongue touched his, tease and retreat. Lust kicked him, racing through his blood, straight to his groin.

Zero to sixty in under four seconds. Damn, she was smoking hot. And she didn't even know it. Maybe that was part of the attraction.

He backed her against the wall, his thigh between hers. She made a gorgeous little sound, somewhere between a gasp and a moan. He took over, took the kiss deeper, nibbled on her lower lip, then sucked on it gently.

She worked the buttons of his shirt until it hung open, baring the front of his torso. Her hands shook as she touched his naked skin, her nails raking down his belly.

"We're in an elevator," he pointed out when her fingers got to the button of his pants. A part of him was screaming that it didn't matter. That he could hit the emergency stop, yank her jeans down and take her right here, against the wall.

Except, he didn't want to rush this. He wanted her completely naked, a banquet he could feast on, and his suite was only a minute away.

Behind him, the elevator doors slid open. A glance over his shoulder revealed an empty hallway. He swept her up in his arms, a romantic gesture that wasn't usually in his repertoire, but it fit the moment. She buried her face in his neck and ran her tongue along his skin, and then she bit him, just hard enough to feel good.

"You smell good," she whispered. "Like lime. I love baking key lime pie. Getting it just right. The mix of sweet and tart and—"

He turned his head and kissed her, hard, demanding. She didn't complain. Her fingers curved against the base of his skull and drew him closer still, her mouth open and so fucking sweet under his.

"Key card, right pants pocket," he murmured against her lips.

Her hand snaked into his pocket, her fingers brushing his cock through the thin material. Her breath hitched. "Oh."

"Yeah." He couldn't help but smile. "That isn't the key card."

Her fingers dipped deeper into his pocket, and she came up with the card, then inserted it in the door. A flash of red light, then green. She pushed the handle down. The door swung open.

Once inside, he kicked it shut behind him and let her slide down the front of him. Her arms looped around his waist. One hand settled on his ass and the other climbed under his shirt, her palm flat against his lower back, skin to skin, urging him closer. She tipped her head back and offered her mouth, so lush and tempting, her lips already swollen from his kisses.

He took what she offered.

He undid her jeans and slid his fingers under her panties. She was wet and hot, and she bucked against his hand as he ran the flat of his fingers against her slick folds.

"You're gorgeous. So fucking gorgeous." His blood roared. His cock ached. He wanted to be inside her, right now, right here. He'd get her naked later. He'd take his time with round two. And three.

Then she shoved her hand down his pants and took hold of his cock, and he mentally added round four.

BRYN FELT AS IF SHE WAS ON fire. She couldn't stop
moving—her hips rocking, her back arching to press
her breasts against Lokan's chest, her fingers tightening around the smooth, hard length of his shaft,
hot and thick in her grasp.

She had one hand pressed flat to his chest, his
muscle hard beneath her palm, his heart racing.

He groaned against her mouth and dragged his
lips from hers to graze his teeth along her jaw, her
throat. She cried out when he withdrew his hand
from her panties, wanting that contact so badly she
ached. Then she felt her jacket slide down her arms
and heard it hit the floor. She felt cool air on her skin
as he yanked her T-shirt over her head, forcing her
to let go of his cock.

"Please," she whispered, not even sure what she
was asking for. She wanted to touch him. She wanted
him to touch her. She wanted to get on her knees,
take him in her mouth, suck him and bite him. So
she sucked on his tongue.

"Bryn," he rasped. In that second she was fiercely
glad that she'd told him the truth about her name.

He bit her throat. He bit her shoulder. Heat tun-
neled through her, leaving her trembling. His lips
pressed to the curve of her breast, just above the lacy
cup of her bra. She bit her lip to keep from crying
out as a wave of desire crashed over her.

Lifting his head, he stared at her, denim-blue eyes
gone dark with lust.

"Let's slow this down a little." He held her gaze as

he pushed her jeans down over her hips, her thighs. She used her heel to push one leg down to her ankle, shifted her weight to get the foot free, then repeated the awkward little dance with the other leg.

One side of his mouth curled in a dark, sexy smile. She felt that smile ignite a spiral of heat low in her belly, like a gas stove flaring to life.

Reaching out, he dragged the tip of his index finger along her bra strap, then down over the swell of her breast to where her nipple peeked through the lace. She gasped and arched into his touch, then gasped again when he let his hand fall away.

"Pretty bows," he said, and shook his head. "Why does that not surprise me? I almost expected them to be white."

She glanced down at her lacy lavender panties and matching bra with the little dark purple bows. "You don't like bows?" Was that her voice, so raspy and low?

His finger moved again, down along the outer curve of her breast to skim her waist, then lower, until he was touching the little purple bow at her hip.

"Right now, I fucking love bows."

Lowering his head, he caught her nipple through the lace and bit her. Not hard. Just a graze of his teeth. Just enough pressure to make her cry out. And when he stopped, she whispered, "Do that again."

He didn't. Instead, he used his teeth to drag the lace edge of her bra down, baring her nipple. Then he took her in his mouth, his tongue stroking her, and she fisted one hand in his hair while the other clawed at his shoulder.

His fingers replaced his mouth, and he moved to the other breast, baring that nipple, taking it in his mouth.

Her back arched.

"I want—" She gasped as he gave a hard, sucking pull, her words lost, her thoughts lost. There was only him and the need he ignited. There was only the feel of his mouth on her breasts and his fingers easing between her legs. He didn't settle for light stroking now. He pushed his fingers up inside her, the heel of his palm pressing against her clitoris. She bucked against him, on fire.

She ran her hand over his back, down to his ass. Frantic, she shoved at his pants, her fingers hooking the waistband of his boxers. Everything slid down with a faint shush.

Sliding her hand between her own thighs, she let her fingers tangle with his. Then she closed her fist—wet from her own body—around his shaft and pumped from base to tip. He grunted, and she felt his cock throb beneath her touch.

He didn't bother to take her panties off, just pushed the scrap of cloth aside, lifted her and closed his hand over hers, holding her fingers against his shaft as he positioned himself.

The feeling of him, full and hot, pressing against her opening, stretching her, made her gasp. He pumped his hips just enough to push the broad, smooth head of his cock inside her, and she let her head fall back against the wall, her teeth clamping on her lower lip. It felt good. Better than good.

Her breath escaped her in a rush as he sank himself in to the hilt.

"Fuck." The word was low and hard and pulled from him, as if he didn't want to let it go.

He moved then, slow, deep thrusts that stretched her and filled her and made her boneless. He eased his hand between their bodies, clever fingers moving in perfect rhythm until she couldn't think, could barely breathe.

The pressure inside her built until she felt as if she was going to scream.

She moved into each thrust, taking him deep inside her, forgetting everything about her quest and her goal. In this moment, there was only the feel of his body and the response he wrung from hers.

"So sweet. So damned, fucking sweet." His fingers stroked a little faster, and his cock was so hard and big inside her.

Fisting her hands in his hair, she yanked his mouth to hers and kissed him, bit him, frantic, hungry.

She felt like a wind-up key was twisting her tighter and tighter and—

With a cry she spiraled over the edge, her body shaking and flying and scattering into a thousand pieces, her muscles taut, her back arched, and him, there, inside her and around her.

He made a dark sound low in his throat and thrust

hard into her, once and again, and then she felt him pulsing inside her, his body going tense beneath her hands, his breathing harsh against her lips.

For a second, she closed her eyes and just let herself enjoy because this was far different—far *more*—than she had ever expected.

"Bed," he murmured and carried her there. And with feathered kisses on her breasts and gentle strokes between her thighs, he started all over again.

Hours later, she rolled over and found Lokan sitting on the edge of the bed, naked, the glow of the bedside lamp painting him in gold tones and light. For a long moment, she only stared at him, dazed by what had passed between them. Such intimacy between two strangers.

"I like your nose. I thought it was perfectly straight, but it's not. It's got a tiny bump at the bridge." Reaching up, she traced her finger over the bump. He stayed very still, his expression unreadable. Had she offended him? She rushed to say, "I didn't notice that at first. I mean, I saw your profile before I saw your whole face, but I didn't notice the bump. It's a good thing, not a bad thing—"

His brows rose at the same time as he frowned. She hadn't imagined that expression was possible. It made her laugh. Which made him frown harder.

"I've offended you. I didn't mean to. You're very handsome. Really. I thought right away that your profile was nice, but full-on, well, you're…" She let her words trail away as she ducked her head, embarrassed and appalled.

He was beautiful. There was no denying that. His body was lean and hard and sculpted with long muscles and smooth skin.

"Frack," she said on an exhale.

He laughed, a low, rich sound that wove through her and invited her to join him, and made her feel a little rush of pleasure. "You are one of a kind, Bryn. Definitely one of a kind."

"I have this habit of running on. My brothers always make fun of me."

"I like it," Lokan said.

I like you. The second the thought formed, she thrust it away. She didn't dare like him, didn't dare ever see him again. That wasn't what this night was about.

"I like you," he said, his tone warm and amused.

Her head jerked up, and she saw something flicker in his eyes.

"When you look at me like that, I feel like I'm having a warm bubble bath," she whispered, snared in the moment.

"When you look at *me* like that, I feel like climbing into a warm bubble bath with you." He leaned in and kissed her, his mouth gentle, his lips and tongue teasing her. He ended the kiss slowly, then straightened and held out his hand. "Bathtub's this way."

She stared up at him, wishing she could take a picture, a memento of this moment and the way he was looking at her. Then she put her hand in his and let him draw her to her feet.

LOKAN WOKE WITH A SMILE ON HIS face. The room was dim, but through the crack in the drapes he could see sunlight.

Rolling over, he reached for Bryn. Innocent, sweet, hotter-than-hell Bryn. She'd definitely proven to be a surprise. He'd had her in the bathtub, then against the wall and on the bed. Then the floor because she'd laughingly danced away from him, and when he'd dived for her ankle and dragged her down, they'd both decided the carpet was comfortable enough. He had rug burn on his ass, but it had been worth it to have her astride him, her head thrown back, her body riding his.

He figured that another round in the bed wouldn't hurt.

So it was disappointing to find that she wasn't there.

He pushed upright, swinging his legs over the side of the bed, and glanced at the bathroom door. It was open, the lights off.

He rose, dragged on a pair of sweatpants, then padded barefoot into the sitting room, expecting to find her there. She wasn't, but the door to the balcony was partially open, the sheers waving in the breeze.

Nice. Morning sex on the balcony overlooking the ocean. He was up for it. In more ways than one.

He was about to head outside when a knock at the door stopped him.

A bellboy stood in the hall with an enormous white cardboard box tied with a lavender bow. The smell of vanilla dusted the air.

"Mr. Krayl? This was delivered for you to the front desk."

Lokan's gut sank. It was the lavender bow that did it. "You see who delivered it?"

"Yes, sir."

"Male? Female?" But he already knew.

"Female."

Lokan didn't even glance at the balcony door now. She wasn't there. He felt oddly deflated by that thought. And he wondered how she'd managed to sneak out without waking him.

He reached over, snagged a wad of bills from the console table behind the door and passed a couple of twenties to the bellboy. "Can you describe her?"

"Dark hair. She was wearing it in a ponytail. Red T-shirt. Black knee-length shorts." The kid paused. "Or maybe navy. I'm not sure."

The description was enough to confirm her identity. Bryn had been a busy girl this morning.

"What time is it?" he asked, scrubbing his palm over his jaw.

"Four o'clock, sir."

Which meant she'd been a busy girl this afternoon.

He gave the kid another bill. The kid passed him the box. And then he was alone.

That bothered him, though he couldn't think of a single reason why it should. Great sex was great sex. What the hell was wrong with him that he'd thought even for a second that it might be anything more?

What had he expected? That they'd hang out indefinitely?

Not likely, given that his "indefinitely" was a hell of a lot different than hers.

He leaned down and sniffed at the box. Vanilla. Chocolate. Maybe a hint of coconut. He pulled the trailing tail of the lavender bow, and it fell to the sides. Then he opened the box to find dozens of cookies—chocolate chip, coconut, white chocolate and macadamia nut. Fragrant. Tempting. Still slightly warm.

Lying on top was a simple white card with two words written in flowing feminine script.

Thank you.

"Well, fuck me raw," he muttered, stealing his older brother Dae's favorite expression. Because it suited the moment. He'd been fucked. And he'd been left. And he felt inexplicably pissed off about that.

He hadn't been finished with her yet. Not just for the sex, which had been admittedly and unexpectedly spectacular. He'd liked listening to her chatter. He'd liked the way she smelled. He'd liked that she made him smile. He'd liked…her.

Absently, he lifted a cookie, took a bite and paused midchew. Damn. He closed his eyes, letting the flavors melt on his tongue.

He polished it off, ate another and then a third. And with each bite, the feeling that he'd been cheated grew. Good as the cookie was, it wasn't an adequate replacement for the woman who'd baked it. The woman who'd spent the night in his bed.

How the hell had she snuck out without him noticing? How the hell had he let her go?

In that second, he made a decision. He wasn't done with her yet. He would hunt her. And he would find her.

He was a soul reaper. How hard could finding one human woman be?

CHAPTER THREE

I have hidden you from those who are upon the earth...

—The Egyptian Book of Gates

Detroit, Michigan
Present day

"NO LIGHTS, BABY." BRYNJA closed her fingers loosely around her daughter's wrist as she reached for the bedside lamp. A pink lamp with white cats printed on the shade, exactly like the one they'd had to leave behind once before. A lucky find at a garage sale. Or maybe not so lucky. The way the night was shaping up, it looked as if they'd be leaving this one behind, too.

"I don't like the dark," Dana whispered.

Guilt congealed in the spot behind Bryn's breastbone, an ugly, tight knot.

"I know. But the moon's bright enough." Masking her edginess, she kissed Dana's palm, then turned her hand over. "Bright enough that I can see your pink nail polish." More than bright enough. The moon was a luminescent ball hanging low in the sky, sending light leaking through the edges of the drawn shade. Frack. Tonight of all nights, some cloud cover would have been nice.

Dana stood by the bed, unnaturally still, a golden-haired doll painted in shadow and night. Was it only short months ago that she'd laughed in the sunlight while her father pushed her on a swing? Back then, she hadn't been afraid of the dark. She hadn't been afraid of anything.

"Socks and shoes, now." Bryn dipped her chin toward the child-size dresser, forcing herself to betray none of the fear and urgency that crashed through her like breakers in a storm. What she wanted to do was grab her daughter, thrust the shoes onto her feet and run. Hide. But letting panic win and rushing headlong into the night was a sure recipe for more mistakes.

Worse, it would terrify Dana. Better to let her think this was just another practice run.

Maybe it was. Maybe Bryn was overreacting.

But the air felt electric and wild, sending a shiver crawling up her spine. She knew that sensation, recognized it for the threat it was. There was someone— or some*thing*—out there.

Turning, she peered through the narrow sliver left between the edge of the blind and the window frame. The house they were renting—a straight cash deal with no signatures and no contracts—was on a pie-shaped lot at a bend in the road, which meant she had a clear view in either direction. The neighbor's fat, orange cat prowled across her lawn, but other than that, nothing moved.

It didn't matter.

They were out there. The power and menace of their presence vibrated in the air until she felt as if her skin was stretched tight enough to split. She didn't know who *they* were, and it didn't matter. She had no illusions. She and Dana stood alone against pretty much everyone else.

"We need to practice." Bryn forced herself to smile as she spoke, because Dana would hear the smile and, hopefully, be pacified by it. She would do anything to keep her daughter from being afraid. Dana still woke up most nights, crying about bad men and closets. Crying for her daddy. Bryn couldn't do a damned thing about any of that other than leave the closet light on all night long, gather her baby girl close and hold her and rock her while the horrific memories played out.

She hadn't been able to protect her daughter when the events had actually unfolded, when she'd been pried from her father's side, kidnapped, locked in a closet in a dingy motel room. An acid truth. One that ate at Bryn like a cancer. As did the questions of why Lokan had been killed, and how, and why they had taken Dana. Were they hunting her even now? Was that who was out there? The ones who had murdered Dana's father? Or was it Bryn's secrets that were rearing their serpentine heads?

"Again?" Dana gave a heavy sigh, then, "Can't we practice later?"

"No. Practice now." Bryn shot a glance over her shoulder and offered what she hoped was a reassuring smile. "But we can get donuts later." Turning back to the window, she stared at the tree across the street.

There. Was that movement?

Adrenaline slammed her with the force of a train.

"With sprinkles?"

"Wha—" Right. The donuts. "Absolutely." She lost the battle to keep the tension from staining her words. "Socks now. Quick as a bunny. Donuts later." Much later. After they'd left Detroit far behind. She regretted the fact that they had to run again; she'd begun to like it here.

There was a beat of silence, then Dana offered a wary, "Okay."

Watching the road, Bryn willed her daughter to hurry. The movement across the street was just branches swaying in the wind, but the next shadow that shifted might herald something far more sinister. And once whoever was out there decided to make a move, things were going to slide straight to hell at rocket speed.

Behind her, a dresser drawer opened, then closed, soft, just as they'd practiced. Nothing to give them away. Only this wasn't a practice run. They needed to get out of this house. Now.

"Black socks," she said. To go with the black pants and sweater and coat and shoes. Everything to blend with the night.

"Pink ones." Dana's tone slid toward belligerent.

Unbidden, unwanted, a memory of Lokan's voice snuck up on Bryn and wormed its way into the moment. *You want me to argue with a six-year-old? I'll lose every time.* He'd been so good with Dana. Never losing his temper or his calm. Maybe it was easy to be that patient when you were just a part-time parent, one who was around almost exclusively for fun and games. She'd tried to convince herself of that many times because she hadn't wanted to admit he had a right to be in Dana's life at all. He wasn't supposed to have been. He was supposed to have been nothing more than a sperm donor.

She's mine. The first time he'd seen Dana, he'd made that claim, and his voice had been tinged with wonder, incredulity. Certainty.

He'd never had a doubt.

From the second he'd set eyes on his daughter, he'd known. Bryn hadn't had a hope in hell of convincing him otherwise, not when Dana's features were a childlike, feminine version of his, and her golden hair and denim-blue eyes marked her as his daughter, standing in stark contrast to Bryn's own dark hair and brown eyes. She'd resented him for insisting on holding a place in their lives, and now she thought she might hate him for it because, by claiming his daughter, he'd put her straight in harm's way.

Except he didn't have a monopoly on that. Bryn had put Dana in harm's way just by giving birth to her.

Such a tangled mess. They were both guilty of lying and evading, of hiding dangerous truths. She couldn't help but wonder if things might have turned out differently if they'd both chosen honesty.

Probably not. In fact, things might well have turned out worse.

She clenched her fists, then forced her fingers to uncurl, squashing the thought that she was equally responsible for the way things had gone down. She couldn't exactly play the righteous injured party when she was the one who'd been lying to Lokan all along.

"The black socks with the pink hearts at the top," Bryn said softly. A compromise. The hearts wouldn't show, and they'd keep Dana feeling as if she had some control. She needed that. If she was to have any hope of coming out of this without bone-deep scars, she had to feel as if she had some control.

Silence. For a second, Bryn thought she was about to face a mutiny. She exhaled in relief when Dana said, "Okay."

"Need help with your shoes?" She didn't take her eyes from the view of the street. Branches swayed. A cloud moved across the moon. And the prickle biting at her skin wormed deeper.

How many were out there? How soon would they make their move?

An exasperated sigh from behind her. "I don't need help, Mommy. I'm doing it myself."

"Double knot," Bryn said. Dragging laces would slow them down.

"Done." Dana's tone became uncertain and wary as she asked, "Can I take my backpack?"

Again, guilt slithered through her. The last time they'd had to move in a hurry, Dana'd had to leave everything behind. Toys. Clothes. Even Flopsy, the stuffed cat she'd had since she was less than a month old. Bryn could still remember the look on Lokan's face as he'd—

No. She would not think about Lokan Krayl or how very much he had loved his child. She would not acknowledge the fact that a part of her missed him horribly. He was dead. He was gone. He was never coming back. And he was the reason they were being hunted.

"I'll carry your pack." She turned from the window and scooped up the small black backpack that Dana stuffed with treasures each night before bed, just in case they had to run. "Got your spare inhaler?"

Bryn carried one of Dana's asthma inhalers, and Dana carried one, just in case. When she'd been kidnapped, she'd been taken without her inhaler, and Bryn had been terrified she'd have an attack.

Dana nodded. "But I don't need it anymore."

"Just in case," Bryn said. While it was true that Dana hadn't had an asthma attack since before those terrible days when she'd been taken, Bryn wasn't counting that as a sign she'd never have one again.

She glanced at the window. How the hell had they been found? No one had managed to find them in nearly seven years…except for Lokan. And since Dana had been kidnapped, Bryn had been so damned careful. She'd done everything Roxy Tam had told her to do and a few things Roxy hadn't thought to tell her. And still, it hadn't been enough.

Don't think about that now. The reasons didn't matter. What mattered was getting her daughter somewhere safe, somewhere she could disappear, one small human child in a sea of humans.

Because despite what her parents were, Dana was utterly and completely human. At least, for now.

The stairs didn't creak as they made their way down. Bryn had taken care of that first thing when they'd moved in with a few well-placed nails each driven in at an angle. She'd oiled the doors and the windows. She'd planned exits and alternates. She'd done everything she could think of to plan for the time when things went south. She'd even set up safety deposit boxes with money and new identities in a dozen cities. All they needed to do was make it out of here tonight.

Doubt uncurled like a poisonous seed sprouting in fertile soil. She'd made so many mistakes—

She gave a sharp exhale. This was the worst possible moment for her to loosen the chains of her self-doubt. Whatever mistakes she'd made in the past, she had to let them go for this moment, trust that she'd make the right choices tonight. She was all that stood between Dana and those who would take her, harm her, use her for their own ends.

She strangled the urge to tighten her hold on her daughter's hand, to bolt through the house, to run and run until their chests screamed and their hearts pounded against their ribs. Running wouldn't do them a damned bit of good. Because whatever was out there was faster.

Bryn needed to be smarter.

They'd expect her to take the back door.

Instead, she led Dana down a second set of stairs to the dark basement. She pushed open the basement window, lifted Dana and helped her crawl through. Then she scrambled after her and together they huddled in the clump of bushes that grew thick and tangled by the side of the house. Bryn closed the window behind them. She would leave no clues if she could help it.

Directly ahead was the street. To the left of the house were the driveway and her car. She wasn't interested in the car. It was too risky to take it. They needed to leave behind everything that might identify them. To the right, separated from her yard by a simple chain-link fence, was a wide, winding path through a thickly wooded area of evergreen and oak that bordered an industrial park. The path led from her street to the local elementary school three blocks over. A shortcut with lots of places to hide. And lots of places for those who hunted her to hide. It was a calculated risk.

Lifting a finger to her lips, she motioned Dana to follow as she began to inch along the side of the house. Six feet, four feet, two…they were almost out of cover. Another few steps and they'd have to make a run across thirty feet of lawn under the ivory glow of the moon. She glanced at Dana's sun-bright hair, wishing she had thought of a hat. She felt a flash of anger, directed at herself, but she forced it back into the pit it had crawled out of because that anger would breed mistakes.

As a makeshift solution, she pulled up the hood of her own black sweatshirt, relieved when Dana mirrored her and lifted the hood of her jacket, hiding her hair. Not perfect, but better than nothing.

The supernatural energy vibe that had sent them out into the night in the first place was muted now, as though whoever was out there was purposefully hiding it.

Crouched low to the ground under the cover of the shrubbery, Bryn scanned up and down the street, letting her gaze pause on each front yard. Nothing moved. But the night breathed, heavy with expectation. She couldn't see the threat, but it was here.

She felt it now.

She surged to her feet. They'd been found.

The Underworld

I WOULD DIE FOR HER.

Dana. My daughter.

I did die for her. But I can't remember exactly how or why. I know that I let someone kill me in order to keep my daughter safe. Which makes no sense. The thought drifts away and, with it, all other thoughts and hopes. This is my eternity.

I float in a place that is nowhere and nothing. I have neither shape nor form. The agony of that—of losing myself and having lucid flashes where I know what has been done to me and what I have lost— is indescribable. The moment fades, and with it all knowledge.

Who am I? I don't know. Fear chases through me.

An instant—or a century—later, I blink and stare straight ahead. I've been in the dark so long, I've forgotten what it is like to know light. Except there, a pinprick, so bright it hurts. Not just my eyes. My arms, my legs, my heart.

Pain drags awareness with it. Flash to a memory: I have three brothers. I must warn them, save them.

Urgency fades to confusion. Then I have only darkness.

A vortex of pain brings me back, incredible suction, like a giant vacuum pump pulling on my limbs.

Words, foreign and confusing, are on the tip of my tongue.

I hear myself speak as though the sound comes from a place far away. "Guardian, watch over my body. Let it not be slain. May it not be destroyed forever."

Hot pokers skewer me. Knives slice my flesh. The pain is more than I can bear, tearing me apart, barbed talons digging into my bones. The not knowing is even worse, and with the pain come embers of understanding. I reach for the agony. I welcome it. Embrace it. Because the knowledge that comes with it is the ultimate prize.

Memories fly at me, bright sparks and snaps. I know now what I am. *Soul reaper. Son of Sutekh. Eternal. Immortal. I cannot die.*

But I am dead. Murdered. By Sutekh. My father.

My daughter is at risk with only the blood oath of my murderer to keep her safe.

I look down at my hand—my hand—and know that somehow I have form once more. I can think only that my brothers have found a way to reunite my body and soul. How? I do not know, and at this moment, it doesn't matter. I clench my fist, reveling in the sting of my nails digging into my palm.

There is no way to put words to the emotions that rush through me. Relief, rage, regret and so much more. I am no longer dead.

I am alive. My name is Lokan Krayl, and I am alive.

EAT THE FOOD OF THE DEAD AND he could never leave; it was an inviolable rule. So Lokan Krayl stared straight ahead and forced himself to walk past the platters of delicacies: rice with raisins and saffron, spiced lamb, tender, grilled vegetables.

The smells assailed him, mouthwatering and so tempting he almost gave in to the urge to sink to his knees and shove fistfuls of food into his mouth. He was starving, hollowed out, as though a red-hot poker had burned his insides away and left him an agonized shell.

His half-human, half-god metabolism demanded inordinate amounts of energy, and that left him smack-dab between a rock and a hard place. If he didn't eat, he would fade and grow weaker. If he did eat, it would be the equivalent of locking the door and throwing away the key. One bite of the food of the dead and he'd be trapped here for eternity—wherever *here* was.

The food of the *dead.* Wasn't that a kicker?

Lokan couldn't die.

He was a soul reaper. Son of Sutekh.

Sutekh. Set. Seteh. Lord of the desert. Lord of chaos. The most powerful of the Underworld gods. He went by many names. The one Lokan had called him was father.

So he couldn't die, couldn't be killed.

But he had been.

He'd been murdered, his body hacked to bits. His soul had been banished to a null zone, a place between the Topworld and Underworld, a place that was his prison. His every attempt at escape had met with failure.

Then something had changed. Somehow—he suspected the intervention of his brothers—his body had been returned to him. He had substance and form once more. But he was still trapped in a null zone. At least, he thought he was...

Reaching out, he laid his hand on the stone. He *felt* it, cool and rough beneath his fingers. He didn't want to dare hope, but it snuck up on him nonetheless. Maybe he'd found a way out, at last.

He turned and stared down the corridor. It appeared to be endless. Just as his time in the null zone had been endless. Immeasurable. He had been adrift, unaware of who or where he was. He had lost himself, lost his memories of his past and his hopes for his future. All that had been left to him were brief moments of lucidity and the gnawing desperation that had accompanied them before everything drifted away once more like smoke on the wind. Save for those brief seconds of clarity, he had known nothing of his past.

But with the return of his body, some memories had come back to him. His daughter. His brothers. Bryn. His recollection was incomplete; there were still patches of gray, soupy haze, and the gnawing certainty that there were important things he had forgotten. But they were coming back to him in bits and parts.

He remembered the name and face of the soul reaper who had killed him, and the true face of his ultimate betrayer: Sutekh. His father.

His murderer.

He *knew* those things, and that meant he was no longer completely lost, that he had taken a step beyond the confines of his prison. His past and present had been returned to him. He only had to figure out how to salvage his future.

He needed to warn his brothers about Sutekh's betrayal. He needed to know why his father had done it. And he needed to make a plan for payback in full measure. Blood for blood.

But now wasn't the time to contemplate vengeance. Not yet. That would only fragment his efforts.

His number one priority was his daughter. He'd given his life for the promise that Dana would not be harmed. But that promise had come from his father. The same father who'd had no qualms about murdering his son. He couldn't count on Sutekh to keep his word.

So first up, Lokan would see to the safety of his daughter.

Then he would see to his father.

Problem was, he had to find his way to Topworld to do that, and so far, his efforts had been a bust.

He took a step, stumbled, his palms slapping stone as he struggled to keep himself upright. His vision swam, and the platters of food danced before him.

Damn, he was weak. A shadow of himself. Yet another reason to hold thoughts of vengeance at bay. He would need his full strength and more than a lion's share of cunning to best Sutekh and make him pay for what he'd done.

Sheer will kept him moving, one foot in front of the other, his eyes trained on the walls rather than on the seductive platters of food. The massive blocks of gray stone were painted with hieroglyphics and figures. He recognized them. There was Anubis. And there was Ra. And there was Ammut, the Devourer.

He walked until he thought he could walk no more, and then he realized that the scenery had changed. Before him the hallway widened and a cordon of dead souls—corporeal here in the Underworld—stood rank on either side. They wore simple cotton wraps about their waists, and their chests were bare.

These were the first other souls he'd encountered. There had been no one else in his dark and empty prison. Only him, his incoherent thoughts and the false images of those he conjured from his memories.

"Who are you?" he asked as he drew abreast of the first man. The words caught in his throat, his voice rough and dry with disuse.

The man lifted his head and looked at Lokan but said nothing. His eyes were pure white, opaque and eerie. Etched in the wall behind him were depictions of rows of men bowing to the Sun God, Ra. Similar to the rows of men who stood before Lokan now.

A prickle of premonition crawled across his skin. "Where am I?" And in the face of the man's silence, he ordered, "Speak."

"The Gate to the Gates. The antechamber," came the reply, the words echoing off the walls.

The sound made Lokan freeze in place. When he had been locked in his hallucinations, he had been like a ghost with neither substance nor form and no true voice. When he had spoken, no one had answered, except in the echoes of his memories. The man before him answered. Another bit of proof that this was real.

"Whose antechamber?"

"The son of Geb. The son of Nut. He who is king of the living and king of the dead. The lord of silence."

"Osiris," Lokan murmured. Well, didn't that just make his day perfect?

He was in the Territory of Osiris. Or perhaps merely at the gate of that territory. He didn't recognize this particular path, though in his position as his father's ambassador to the other Underworld deities, Lokan had visited Osiris before. But that meant nothing. This could be a back door. Every Underworld Territory had multiple entry points.

Problem was, Sutekh was no friend of Osiris, and the enmity was mutual. So by extrapolation, Osiris was no friend to Lokan.

Then again, given that Lokan wasn't exactly on his father's favorites list right now—and vice versa—Osiris just might turn up as an ally. A way out. What was that human saying? *The enemy of my enemy is my friend.*

Sutekh had made himself Lokan's enemy when he'd hacked him to bits.

"And you are what? Guards? Ambassadors?" he asked.

"We are here for you."

"Good to know. Don't mean to sound ungrateful or anything, but in what capacity?"

Silence answered him.

Lokan tried a slightly different tack. "How do you know that you are here for me?"

"It is written." Turning, the man gestured at the wall and the detailed paintings depicted there.

The ancient Egyptians—those who had created these works—believed that if you wrote it down, it would become reality. That belief had been so powerful that it became fact.

Lokan got it now. These souls were here because of him, bound by the powerful magic that imbued the Book of the Dead, and that meant they could leave only if he left.

"You're locked in as surely as I am." They weren't here to lead him. They were here to follow.

Fucking A.

As he drew abreast of each pair, one to the right

of him, one to the left, they bowed low at the waist and held their positions as he walked on.

To his left, the dark water of an endless river rippled as he passed, his reflection and the reflections of the souls who bowed to him flickering and dancing as the water lapped softly at the gray stone on which they stood. It was only then that he realized he was naked. His brothers might have found a way to return his body to him, but they'd neglected to figure out a way to send clothes with it.

Probably because it had been in pieces at the time.

The last pair in line held out their arms as they bowed. One held a white linen strip of cloth, neatly folded, and the other an intricately beaded hammered gold necklace. Lokan wrapped the cloth around his waist. He almost refused the necklace but changed his mind before the words left his lips. He had a feeling that ceremony was an important part of what would see him clear of this place. So he took the heavy gold and jeweled piece and settled it around his neck. It fanned out over his shoulders and the top of his chest.

Before him was a boat manned by two oarsmen.

Of course. It just had to be a boat.

He had a moment of unease, a terrifying memory unfurling in his gut of a red river and a boat and a ferryman with hands of bone that were denuded of flesh. The memory sharpened and grew clearer. He could almost reach out and touch it. There had been a woman there. He remembered her. Her skin had been milk pale, her hair coal dark, her eyes a mix of pale blue and gray.

Seeing her had made him horribly afraid, not for himself, for someone else. He stopped in his tracks, shook his head and tried to remember.

Damn. That woman had been Bryn. He'd seen her in his phantasmal conjuring of the River Styx while he had been trapped in the null zone, and he remembered that seeing her had left him afraid for his daughter. Because if Bryn was in the Underworld, who was protecting Dana?

He closed his eyes and cleared his thoughts. Logic. Reason. Those were his sole allies in this trek.

Bryn couldn't protect Dana, not against this. She was a great mother, but she was entirely unequipped to deal with the supernatural. Hell, she didn't even know what he was. He'd never told her. She thought he was some Mafia don's son. She thought he was human.

If Sutekh went for Dana, Bryn's ability to protect her would be about as effective as a tiny cocktail umbrella against a monsoon.

And the woman he'd seen couldn't have been Bryn. While the image might have looked like her, the coloring had been all wrong.

Bryn wasn't in the Underworld.

She was alive, and she was Topworld, caring for his daughter. She had to be. He'd called her that night. He'd warned her: Trust no one but the Daughters of Aset. His enemies. The only ones who would be powerful enough to help her keep Dana safe. The only ones with a dark and deep enough hatred of Sutekh to risk his wrath by doing so.

The image of Bryn that he'd seen in that hallucination hadn't been real.

Was the boat before him now real? The possibility that it wasn't chilled him.

Narrow and long, the vessel could hold only a handful of men in single file. It was made of tightly packed papyrus reeds that narrowed toward the prow and stern, where they curled up in traditional fashion. There was an oarsman at the front and one in the rear, their torsos bare, their hips wrapped in linen.

"Where will this boat take me?"

"To the mouth of the Twelve Gates," came the reply.

"The Twelve Gates of Osiris?"

A nod, then, "The Gates of coming into day."

Hope seeded in the barren soil of his desperation. Here was an opportunity to enter not only the Underworld Territory of Osiris but the Topworld. That's where the Twelve Gates led. Back to the world of man. Back to his daughter.

And these souls in the boat were his guides.

All he needed to do was pass the Twelve Gates. His pulse kicked up a notch as adrenaline surged. But nothing ever came for free.

"What do I need in order to pass these gates?"

"Purity of heart," came the reply.

Not good. He harvested hearts; he doubted that left his own anywhere near pure. "And?"

"Magical strength."

Strike two.

"Knowledge."

Strike three. He wasn't carrying a handy copy of the Book of the Dead to guide him. He had no spells or potions. And whatever soul reaper power had been his was depleted by starvation and location. His half-god metabolism might have allowed his soul and corporeal form to unite once more, but it was also starving him. He was weak. Sheer will alone was keeping him going.

All things considered, he had the nasty suspicion that this might not end well.

Fuck. He had this one chance to escape the hell his father had consigned him to, and he was going into that chance tethered by cluelessness.

Not a nice feeling for a guy who went into every situation with at least three backup plans. But going forward was a far better option than either going back or standing where he was. So he stepped into the boat.

It rocked and swayed beneath his weight. The men at the prow and stern dipped their oars, and the boat began to move, gliding smoothly through the inky-black waters.

Lokan studied the etchings and paintings on the walls as they passed: gods and goddesses, flames, stars. A golden sun. And snakes. Lots of snakes. One in particular, far larger and more menacing than the others, caught his eye.

The only sounds were the faint splash of the oars as they dipped and his own breathing. A glance over his shoulder revealed only an endless dark tunnel, the water narrowing to a thin, smooth ribbon in the distance. The walls were gray and damp, curving in an arc over his head. If he extended his arm and reached up, his fingertips would brush the surface.

Around them, a hissing sound grew and swelled, echoing off the walls. The man in the prow stopped rowing, tension lacing his frame. To the left, the water shifted, and with a splash, a reptilian head broke the surface, then sank into the depths once more.

"Is there some particular significance to the snakes?" Lokan asked, watching the ripples disappear.

Neither man answered. As far as guides went, he wouldn't say he'd recommend them to the next guy in line.

Again, the rowers dipped their oars. The boat moved on, the surface of the water obsidian and smooth, and then something—a sound, a flicker of movement—made him look up. He froze, his attention snared by what was before him: a massive square opening, trimmed in blue and gold, bordered by markings. He was still too far away to read what they said, but he suspected that they were warnings.

As one, both men stopped paddling, and the boat

grew still. The river was utterly calm; there was no current to move them along.

The rock face that surrounded the gaping maw of the entry was twisted and gouged, appearing to flow in an undulating wave, as though lava had poured down the face and solidified.

"Speak the name," said the man behind him.

Lokan caught glimpses of scales and slitted eyes in the water.

"Speak." There was urgency in the man's tone now, and fear.

"What name?" Lokan had no idea what he was supposed to say. And before he could ask, the lava moved, rippling and heaving all around the gate.

He tensed. Not lava.

More snakes.

And every last one of them was now looking straight at him.

CHAPTER FOUR

*He hath decreed for them a place, the Hidden
Mountain, which consumeth men, and gods...*
                                    —The Egyptian Book of Gates

Detroit, Michigan
Present day

BRYN'S HEART SLAMMED AGAINST her ribs. The fear was
paralyzing, and she couldn't allow that. She needed
to stay sharp. She needed to get Dana to safety. And
for all her talk about being smarter, now was the
moment to—

"Run," she ordered and tightened her hold on her
daughter as she suited her own actions to words.

The bushes clawed at them, and Dana cried out
as one tangled in her jacket, drawing her up short.
Bryn grabbed the cloth and tugged. It held fast.

Panic clogging her throat, she yanked harder.
There was a sharp tearing sound, and they were
free, feet pounding against the night-cold ground,
the scent of damp earth turning up with each step.

She didn't hear footsteps behind them, and that
was worse than hearing them. Whoever was out

there had to be toying with them, a predator batting at its prey.

They needed to get to the industrial park, to the body shop and the second car she paid the owner to store for her. And they needed to lose their pursuers before they got there because a speeding vehicle was no guarantee of escape from those who hunted them. Some supernaturals were faster than cars.

There was only one option left to her.

And it was going to hurt like hell.

Centering her thoughts, Bryn gritted her teeth against the pain as she ripped a part of her soul free and tore herself in two. She held half her life force tethered to her body, scattering the rest into a mist that settled like a massive umbrella over her mortal shell and the precious body of her daughter.

This was her legacy. *This* was her power. She was a walker, able to leave her body at will, ostensibly to act as a guide for the dead. But her soul was supposed to remain intact. She was breaking every natural law and rule by splitting herself into two parts of a whole that was never meant to be divided. For Dana, she would do this. For Dana, she would do anything.

Panting more from agony than loss of breath, she ran on, holding the bubble that was a part of her soul close around them, a cloak and a shield.

In this, she had an edge. Whatever was out there was expecting a human mother/daughter pair. They certainly weren't expecting Bryn. Her particular skills might be of little benefit in an all-out battle, but they were perfect for stealth maneuvers.

Hand in hand, they angled across the lawn, into the cut-through. The gravel path was a pale ribbon before them. Bryn dragged Dana toward the trees. They could hide there. They'd practiced. They knew the layout, while those who followed didn't.

But those who followed had supernatural sight and hearing and—

No. She needed to hang on to her optimism, no matter how thin and worn that thread got.

Bryn skidded behind a massive tree, the trunk thick and sheltering. Chest heaving, she pressed her back to the rough bark. She bent, wrapping her daughter in her arms, scanning the area for those who followed. She measured the darkness and the odds. Not good. Not good at all.

But not terrible. They had a chance.

"I'm scared," Dana whispered, the words clawing at Bryn's heart like talons.

So her subterfuge had failed. Dana knew this was no pretend run.

All Bryn could offer was a nod and the press of her lips to her daughter's forehead before she leaned out to scan the perimeter once more. The supernatural vibe she'd felt earlier was no stronger, no closer. Didn't matter. She couldn't trust that. She couldn't trust anything.

Damn Lokan. Damn him for insisting on being part of Dana's life. Damn him for dying and leaving Dana with only Bryn for protection. She was a walker, not a warrior.

But for her daughter, she'd *be* a warrior. She'd be whatever she had to be.

"We aren't practicing, are we, Mommy?"

Bryn opened her mouth, ready to lie. Then decided against it. Dana already knew the truth.

"We have a good head start," she whispered firmly. "And you can run faster than the wind. No one can catch you." Resting her lips against her daughter's ear she whispered, "You remember the number?"

Dana nodded.

She'd drilled it into Dana's head that if ever they were separated, if ever she was alone and scared, she should call the woman who had come for her once before. Weeks ago, Bryn had followed Lokan's instructions and phoned the Asetian Guard. They'd sent a woman—a soldier. Her name was Roxy Tam. She'd found Dana and brought her home.

Though she barely knew her, Bryn was convinced that Roxy would be willing to step in and save Dana again if the need arose and not just because it was her assignment. There had been an obvious bond there, a connection. When Bryn had asked Roxy about that the night she'd brought Dana home, the other woman had shrugged and muttered that she knew all about the dark side.

Bryn hadn't pried, but she took that to mean Roxy's childhood had been tough, and that she understood up close and personal how rough Lokan's death and the kidnapping had been on Dana. But much as Bryn had liked Roxy and respected her, she hadn't dared trust her with the truth. She'd presented a flutter-brained, purely human facade, because letting Roxy suspect that she was something other than human was too dangerous.

"Don't leave me." Dana's tone was both fierce and frantic.

"I won't leave you, baby. It's a precaution. You call Roxy if you need her. No one else. Just Roxy." Because, hard as it was to trust a woman she'd met only once, Bryn knew there wasn't any option. There was no one else.

Lokan had been clear during that last, tense phone call. He'd given her emergency numbers long ago and instructions to phone his brothers if she ever needed help and he couldn't be reached. But he'd never brought his brothers to meet Dana and never taken Dana to meet them. Bryn had always had the impression that he'd prefer to keep Dana separate from everything else in his life, and that had been fine with her.

Then, during that final call before his death, the one where he'd told her Dana was in danger, the one Bryn wished she could relive just to say… Well, it didn't matter now what she might have said. What mattered was Lokan's sudden about-face and his insistence that she *not* call his brothers. He'd told her not to trust them. Not to trust *anyone* from the life that had been his. Call only the number he gave her that night—the Asetian Guard.

Odd that he felt he could trust only those who were the enemies of his kind.

But Bryn had believed him then. She still believed it now, despite the fact that his instructions had been laced with lies. Even at the point of death, he'd never admitted to her that he was a supernatural. He'd intimated that the Asetian Guard was a rival mob, and Bryn had let him hold fast to the pretense because the urgency in his tone had told her it wasn't the time for heart-to-hearts and hidden truths.

She'd made the call and done exactly as he'd said, never mentioning his name or her association with him, only begging for help with her missing daughter and invoking the name of Aset. It had worked. Roxy Tam had helped them, and then she, too, had grown paranoid and wary, telling Bryn to trust no one but *her.*

Bryn wished she didn't have to rely on any of them. She wished that she and Dana could just disappear in the crowd.

But wishes weren't worth a damn, and relying on strangers was a far better option than asking for help from her own kind. The price for that help would be unacceptably high.

"Just Roxy," Bryn repeated.

Dana made a soft, hiccupping sob and nodded. The sound broke Bryn's heart.

The pain of holding her life force in two was

growing stronger, deeper. Bryn nearly doubled over as it ripped through her in a crashing wave. The trick was to ride the pain, let it do what it would and not fight it. Easy in principle, not so much so in practice.

All around her, the feeling of supernatural energy grew and swelled. Closer. They were closer, now. She couldn't tell who—or exactly what—they were. Her supernatural skills weren't that adept. She only knew that they were not human, and that made them dangerous.

"We need to move," she whispered, panic gnawing at her, mixing with the pain, each feeding off the other.

Dana's fingers tightened convulsively on hers, but she nodded, brave and calm as a six-year-old should never have to be.

"Now." Holding tight to Dana's hand, Bryn sprinted, and like a trouper, Dana ran in her wake. They ducked between trees, hugging the darkest part of the woods.

The pain grew worse as Bryn forced her soul to splinter even further. It was a blade in her belly, a saw cutting through her limbs, but she forced the bubble of protection to mold around them.

Stronger, closer, the electricity sparking in the air stalked them.

With a cry, Dana stumbled.

Bryn scooped her up and ran with her child cradled tightly against her chest, her breathing labored, her heart pounding like a piston.

To her left she could see a light through the trees, and the glint of cars in the parking lot that backed onto the cut-through.

Almost there. She just needed to make it to the hill, just make it to the bottom and through the fence to the body shop parking lot. The car was in the northeast corner, next to the rear exit. Her arms tightened around Dana, who clung to her like a little monkey, fingers twisted in the cloth of Bryn's sweatshirt.

She could make it. She had to make it.

If her pursuers were demons, the ring of salt she'd buried to surround the parking lot would slow them down once she invoked it with her blood. Problem was, if they weren't demons, the salt wouldn't do a bit of good.

She hit the hill at a dead run, the grass slippery beneath her feet. With a cry she went down hard, twisting to keep Dana from being hurt, taking the force of the fall on her shoulder and hip. Pain layered on pain. She almost lost her focus, almost lost her hold on her soul. Almost sent it bursting into the night, then slamming back into her body.

Frantic, Bryn tried to push upright, but her daughter's weight and the slick grass hampered her. Giving up on that plan, she pushed off with her heels, sliding and scrabbling down the damp, grassy hill on her rump.

Between the bruising fall and the agony of holding herself in two jagged bits, her entire body was one long scream of pain. She couldn't hold it. Couldn't—

Panting, she let go, her soul pulsing outward, then surging back like an elastic, hitting her with a sharp snap.

Their protection was gone. She needed to move.

Again, she tried to rise and made it halfway. Then she stumbled and rolled, stopping only when her side slammed into a pair of biker-booted feet.

In that second, she knew she'd been putting the blame on the wrong shoulders. They weren't after Dana because she was Lokan's daughter, but because she was Bryn's.

The Underworld

DOZENS DEEP, THE SNAKES FORMED a writhing, heaving mass that surrounded the first gate, pouring down its sides. The hissing sound was all around them now, echoing off the cavern walls, making the guides in the prow and stern of the boat shift nervously.

The one in front turned his head and looked at Lokan over his shoulder. His eyes were the pure white of quartz, smooth as marbles. "We must go back."

"Not an option." Because for him, going back meant a place worse than this. "We must go on," Lokan urged, and when the man only stared at him, Lokan wrested the oar from his grasp, got down on one knee and dipped the paddle himself. This was the first gate. The first step to finding his way to the Topworld.

Excitement danced through his veins, mixed with a heavy dose of apprehension. He had no problem with reptiles, but these were special. Serpents were both sacred and reviled, the two sides of a coin. There were both snake-gods and snake-demons in the Underworld, and Lokan had no question as to where these fell.

A serpent as thick as his arm dropped from the top of the gate and sank into the river. There was a wild thrashing beneath the surface, and a far larger serpent surged upward, mouth open.

It swallowed the smaller snake whole.

Muttering words and incantations beneath his breath, the oarsman at the stern began to paddle backward, to set the boat in motion away from the snakes that were clinging to the stone and slithering down the sides of the gate.

"Hold steady," Lokan ordered, his tone even and calm. "Panic will not aid us in this."

"You must speak, or we must go back."

"Speak? Right. You want me to say a name. What name?"

They were almost directly under the mass of serpents now. It writhed and swelled above them and on either side. Only a few moments more and the very tip of the curved reed prow would enter the obsidian darkness of the gate.

One snake fell, then another. And finally, a third that slammed against the bow of the boat and hung there, scales glistening in the dim light. Its body was as thick as Lokan's thigh.

"You must do it now," cried the man behind Lokan.

"What?" Lokan flashed a glance over his shoulder as he leaned forward and used the tip of the paddle to try and pry the serpent from the bow. The second oarsman scuttled backward, his breathing labored, his body covered in a sheen of sweat.

"Prove you are the pure one, the magical one, the one who deserves to pass. Else all is lost."

Lokan was doubtful that he was either pure or deserving.

"Speak the secret name. You must say it," the man behind him insisted, his tone tense and afraid.

Both oarsmen had stopped paddling now, and the boat only hung there, almost entering the gate. But there was no current to move it forward.

Serpents began to drop like rain, each one larger than the last.

"I'd say it if I knew it," Lokan answered, flipping another snake out of the boat with the tip of his oar. "Why doesn't one of you say it? Isn't it your job to guide me through?" He looked back and forth between them. The man before him was huddled in a ball, keening and sobbing, of no use at all. The man behind him only stared at him with eyes white and opaque, his expression stark.

"We are not guides. We are only rowers." He flung

up his arm and cringed as a massive snake fell toward him.

Only rowers. Fuck. Lokan flipped the oar and used it like a bat to hit the serpent. "Might have told me that up front."

Unease slithered through him. The confidence he'd had before Sutekh had murdered him was just a memory. He'd dared the gate only because he'd thought his guides could get him through. But they couldn't. And he couldn't.

And that didn't leave any of them in a very good place.

The snake he'd batted away hit the water with a splash. A shadow moved beneath them. With incredible speed the larger serpent surged up and broke the surface, its head fully a third the size of the boat. It unhinged its jaws and swallowed the other snake whole.

Now there were two bulges along the length of its body, where each of the digesting remains of its prey lodged.

The scene was too familiar for comfort. Just like the serpent, Sutekh unhinged his jaw when he swallowed souls whole.

For Sutekh's prey that meant annihilation, no chance for rebirth, a true end.

Lokan wasn't fond of the possibility that that fate would be his if he ended up as a meal for a snake.

He would never see Dana or his brothers again.

Or Bryn.

The fact that he'd included her name on the list surprised him. But now wasn't the time to wonder why.

Again, a shadow moved beneath the water's dark surface, lifting the prow of the boat, then letting it fall, sending a geyser of water to splash the gate and the mass of serpents that coiled and twisted all around them.

Lokan grabbed hold of the side, steadying himself until the boat rocked into balance once more.

Another snake fell into the boat, slithering toward him, venom-tipped fangs bared. He tried to flip it out with the edge of the oar. It evaded and lunged for him, missing by a hair. He dove for it, caught it with one hand around the base of its head—a head so massive he wouldn't be able to fully circle it with two hands—and the other midway along its body, barely evading the length of its fangs. By the time he wrestled it out of the boat, he was drenched with sweat and breathing hard.

He shot a glance at the man in the stern. No help there. The guy was frozen in place, his skin chalk pale, his white eyes staring at the river.

A name. He needed a damned name to make it through the damned gate.

"Osiris," he roared, and again, louder, "Osiris." That was a name. But given the lack of response, it was the wrong one.

The serpents were filling the opening, their bodies

a surging, twisting barrier. There was barely enough room left. In a moment, the hole would be too small.

What the hell would happen if the boat didn't make it through? Would this be his new purgatory? Would he float on this section of river, trapped in one place until time ended?

The possibility chilled him. Been there. Done that. A repeat performance didn't appeal.

Air and water rushed against his skin as the serpent surged from the water and snatched the front oarsman from his place. The man's scream echoed and amplified in the stone cavern. Blood, hot and thick, sprayed Lokan's face and arms and chest.

And then there was silence.

There you go. *That* would happen if they didn't make it through.

"Back," he snarled at his remaining companion, grabbing the oar and dipping it in the water.

He didn't need to give the order twice. As he paddled backward with strong, sure strokes, he could hear the oarsman behind him doing the same.

Lokan didn't know a fuckload about the Twelve Gates, but it appeared that in addition to a pure spirit and the magical knowledge to get through, he needed a serpent's name—at least for this gate.

The only serpent's name that came to mind was one he didn't think would do the trick. But he tried it anyway. "Apophis," he snarled, and when nothing happened, he tried a different version of the same name, despite the strangled cry of horror that came from behind him. "Apep."

Nice try. No cigar.

The snakes grew even more agitated at his words, and the water beneath the boat turned turbulent and wild.

"Do not say it," the man behind him begged. "If you say his name, you will call him, and all will be lost."

Call Apophis. Not a nice plan. If Sutekh was the Underworld überlord of chaos and evil, Apophis was one step beyond that on the scale of very bad deities; in fact, Apophis warranted a scale of his own. At least Sutekh had reasons for the things he did, no matter how dark and vile those reasons might be. And his actions created a balance of power in the Underworld.

But Apophis had no logic or motive. He was evil, the deification of darkness. He knew no reason. He had neither friends nor allies. He sought only the destruction of all, the return to that which had spawned him: chaos. Utter and complete chaos.

Where Sutekh thrived on chaos, enjoyed it, fostered it for pleasure, Apophis knew no pleasure. He knew only driving need.

Putting his back into it, Lokan thrust the paddle forward through the water, trying to reverse the course of the boat. Without the name, they wouldn't pass the gate. That much was clear. The snakes had multiplied, and they almost completely obscured the opening now. No more gate. Just snakes. Thick, undulating snakes with scales that glinted greenish-black in the dim light and fangs that dripped venom.

The boat rocked and swayed, keeling almost fully onto its side. Lokan flung his arms out, fighting for balance.

He lost, landing hard on his knees, his fists closing on the bundled reeds that formed the edge of the vessel.

The man behind him screamed, a short, high sound that died an abrupt death. Gripping the edge of the boat, Lokan turned at the waist in time to see the man's legs disappear down the enormous serpent's throat. His torso was left behind, his white eyes staring up at the cavernous ceiling.

There was a rough bump against the hull, then another. The boat went over and Lokan was in the river, so cold he felt as if he'd been dipped in liquid nitrogen.

It made him think of another icy river, a train and a day when he'd been so certain he could never die. He remembered wondering how hard he'd fight to stay alive.

Turned out that he hadn't fought at all, not with his daughter's life on the line. The night Sutekh and his cult of followers had come for him, he'd let them kill him so Dana could be safe.

But he would fight today. With all he was, he would fight even though he had a hard time dredging up the will to believe he might win. Because he needed to get back to Dana, he needed to keep her safe. He needed to warn his brothers.

Something brushed his leg, a smooth, endless glide. The snake coiled its body around his and dragged him down.

He struggled and fought, the coils growing ever tighter.

Rage ignited in his belly, a dark ember. The snake was trying to rob him of his vengeance. Drawing on stores of power he hadn't even imagined he possessed, he thrashed and pushed against the ever tightening coils, freeing one hand, then the other, gouging at the serpent's flesh with clawed fingers.

For an instant, he thought he had won.

And then the water closed over his head, and he swore he could see Bryn, her dark hair floating out around her, her arms outstretched toward him.

CHAPTER FIVE

...magnify the great god above the little god
among the gods who are in the Duat, to place
the blessed dead upon their thrones, and the
damned in the place to which they have been
condemned in the judgment, and to destroy
their bodies by an evil death.

—The Egyptian Book of Gates

Detroit, Michigan
Present day

HEART SLAMMING AGAINST HER ribs, Bryn sprawled on
the grass at the foot of the hill. She rolled and came
up on all fours, tucking Dana underneath her body,
ready to scratch, bite, kick...do whatever it took to
protect her child. Dana would not be taken from her.

She looked up, past thick-soled, black biker boots
and faded jeans, to a scuffed black leather jacket,
silver snaps glinting in the moonlight. Her breath
stalled in her chest. She knew what she'd see even
before she reached the hard, handsome face.

"Jack," she whispered, her gaze locking on his.

Light blue eyes rimmed in navy looked back at her.

"Been a while, Brynja." His voice, so familiar it hurt, brought back a slew of memories. Some good. Others…not so much.

Refusing to lie on the ground with him standing over her, she pushed to her feet, drawing Dana up with her. She needed to get away. She needed to get Dana away. Her thoughts spiraled through plan after plan, and she discarded each one, moving to the next.

"What are you doing here?" she rasped.

He flicked a glance at Dana, who edged even closer and locked both arms around Bryn's thigh.

Stupid, stupid question. Jack was here for her. Worse, he was here for her daughter, too.

"You need to come with me." Not a request. No surprise there. It never was. As far as Jack was concerned, his way was the only way. He told people what to do and expected that they'd do it. He never asked.

He wasn't in the habit of offering even the illusion of free will.

"I must decline your lovely invitation." She stroked one hand along Dana's hair, keeping the other looped around her daughter's shoulder. Instinct screamed for her to run, to hide. But if she gave in to that urge, Jack would catch them and take them. She needed to use her head, her logic, as Lokan had taught her. If she let panic reign, they were lost.

Reaching deep, she summoned the last of the power she'd almost exhausted getting herself and Dana this far. She just needed to figure out an effective way to use it. That trick she'd employed, splitting her soul to hide them in plain sight, wouldn't work a second time. Jack would be expecting that now. Besides, her reserves were so depleted she doubted she could pull it off, anyway.

Her power sparked along her limbs, a ghostly light here in the dark shadows of the trees.

Jack's brows rose a fraction of an inch. "I don't recall you having that skill in your bag of tricks."

She hadn't. She had been nowhere near this strong the last time she'd seen him.

"I'm different," she said, her tone even despite the razor-sharp anxiety that bit at her and tied her stomach in knots. She was, but not different enough. Not powerful enough. Her one consolation was that he had no way to know that. Even if he suspected, he had no proof. Jack wasn't the type to take chances on a maybe.

"Pax." *Peace.* He held both hands out, palms forward. "We'll talk first, Bryn. Just talk."

"You expect me to trust you?"

His head jerked back, as though the words held the power of a slap. "I give you my word that if you want to leave after you hear all I have to say, I'll let you."

His word. Out of all of them, Jack was the one who stuck to the letter of any agreement he made. The trick was to make certain the agreement had no loopholes.

He was a master. She was no match for him. She never had been.

The thought was an ugly, twisted sapling sprouting in her heart. She forced it back into the dark crevice that had spawned it. Dana needed her to be strong, and so she would be. She'd leave the baggage of the past rotting in the Dumpster where she'd thrown it seven years ago when she'd left Jack and the others behind.

"Let's reword that." She forced herself to stay calm, to keep her tone even, to betray none of her desperation. Dana reached for her hand, small fingers tightening around hers, and she gave a light, reassuring squeeze. "Here's the deal, Jack. Once you're done talking, Dana and I will be free to leave and you'll do nothing to hamper me."

She drew a measured breath, then amended, "*Us*. You will do nothing to hamper us. You will not follow or send anyone else to follow. You, and all those in association with you, will not hunt me. You will not hunt my daughter. Ever."

Jack nodded slowly, his expression utterly blank, his eyes shrewd.

But a nod wasn't enough for Bryn. "Say it. Repeat the terms and give me your word."

"I talk. You listen. You want to go after that, I'll let you—" he dipped his chin toward Dana, and his expression softened for an instant "—and her with you. I won't come after you."

Bryn wasn't about to be lulled by that softening.

"And you won't send anyone else, or let anyone else come after me—*us*. Now or in the future."

One side of his mouth quirked. "So not only do I have to agree to not come after you or send anyone else, but you want me to stop anyone who tries to hunt you."

"That about sums it up, Jack."

"Not sure you're in a position to make those demands."

Bryn refused to give anything away. She only squeezed Dana's hand lightly once more, offering silent encouragement, and said, "But you can't be sure that I'm *not* in a position to make those demands."

Again, she sent a flicker of power dancing along her skin, visible to any with the skill to look. And Jack definitely had that skill. He couldn't know how shallow the well of that power was, though, so he had to be wondering. She hoped.

"Where'd you learn to twist a deal so well?" he asked.

"From someone with a political mind." From Lokan. He had been a master of negotiation, and after the first time he'd found out that a car salesman had swindled her, he'd made sure to teach her how to watch her own back. How to pinch her nails into the skin between her thumb and forefinger, creating enough sting to remind herself not to talk just to fill the silence. To appear strong even if she felt like a marshmallow on the inside. He'd done it for Dana's sake, he'd said. But a tiny part of her had whispered that maybe it was for her sake, too. That maybe he'd cared, just a little.

Then she'd squashed that part, because caring about Lokan Krayl, or imagining that he cared about her in any capacity other than as his daughter's mother, was a dangerous and stupid path to take. She could trust no one but herself. Care for no one but her daughter. That was just the way it had to be. Lokan was a supernatural, and that meant he was the enemy. They had an uneasy truce only because of their daughter.

Except, over time, the truce had become easy.

She lifted her chin and met Jack's gaze. "Do we have a deal, Jack?"

She didn't know why he'd agree to it. He was the one with the winning hand. She could only hope that he didn't know that. Or if he did, that there was enough of a shadow of a doubt to give him pause.

He scraped his palm along his stubbled jaw. "Can't promise I'll never try to look you up again. I'll let you go—both of you—if that's what you want after you hear me out. And I won't follow. But if I decide to look for you in the future, all bets are off. It'll be on you to make sure I can't find you."

Not a perfect deal, but better than she'd expected. "Your word on that?"

Jack dragged his fingers back through his dark hair. The gesture seemed off. For a second she thought it was because she was used to seeing his hair buzzed short, not straight and long enough that the ends brushed his collar. Then she realized it was because that small gesture gave him away. He was concerned about something.

What could be big enough, bad enough, to make Jack concerned?

A shiver chased up her spine.

"If it's the only way to get you to listen," he said, "then, yeah. My word."

The band that had felt as if it was crushing her chest eased. She took her first free breath since she'd sensed a supernatural outside her house.

Bryn wanted to glance at Dana. She wanted to tell her not to be afraid. That everything would be fine. But she didn't want to direct Jack's attention back to her daughter, not even for a second.

Instead, she gave Dana's hand another reassuring squeeze as she held his gaze and said, "So talk."

LOKAN TIPPED HIS HEAD BACK—*slowly,* because any sudden movement might make him lose his balance or throw up—and studied the pyramid that loomed above him. Dizziness grabbed him and spun him like a top. The world tilted at odd angles.

And maybe he was seeing things, because that pyramid…

"What the fuck?" he muttered, and his hand shot out to rest against the smooth, cool wall of glass. He forced himself to stay perfectly still, to focus on each breath until he felt reasonably certain that he wasn't going to fall on his ass. Then he tried to get his head around the questions that buzzed in his muzzy thoughts like a bunch of hornets.

Last he remembered he'd been about to drown. Or be eaten by a serpent whose head was the size of a minivan. He had no clue if either of those options could kill him because he wasn't precisely alive at the moment, what with Sutekh hacking him to bits and sending his soul to what amounted to purgatory.

He stared straight up and tried to focus on what was in front of him. The dim cavern and the boat and the snakes were gone. In their place was the slanted wall of a massive, shiny, black pyramid that danced and swam before his eyes.

Damn, he was pathetic. A shadow of himself. Dirty, starving. Racked by pain so deep and constant he had trouble remembering a time when he hadn't hurt. Some fucking all-powerful demigod he was. More like a mewling kitten.

He took a deep breath, filling his lungs until they protested the stretch.

Right here, the pity party stopped. Confidence was a state of mind, and if he lost hold of his, he'd never be able to get back to Dana. So even if he wasn't feeling it, he'd better damn well find a way to pretend.

Tipping his head a little more, he studied the details of the pyramid. Lights ran up the seams where the black glass faces met, bright against the night sky. At the very tip was a glaring spotlight pointed straight up into space.

This was not the Underworld or a null zone.

It was the Luxor. In fucking Vegas.

He laughed, slinging one arm across his belly to hold in the ache, to hold himself together, because he felt if he let go he'd fracture into a thousand pieces that would spiral off into the ether.

Here he'd thought he was trapped in purgatory, and instead he'd ended up in Vegas.

There was a message here. He was sure of it. But he figured that deciphering it could wait.

One second he'd been in an icy river, the next, he was Topworld. Only a fool looked in a gift horse's mouth, so while the questions of *why* and *how* might beg for answers, now wasn't the time to look for them. He was here, and he needed to make the best of it.

He'd been trying to find a way back to reality for… He had no idea how long it had been. Time passed differently in the Underworld so he had no way to measure the weeks or months. Or years.

Dana.

His daughter was human and all-too-mortal.

He may well have missed her entire life. She could be grown by now. Or dead and buried, her soul gone somewhere he could never reach. That had happened to his brother, Alastor. When he'd first come to Sutekh's realm, he hadn't understood the discrepancies in the way time moved, and by the time he'd gone back to the world of man, his entire human family had been gone.

Lokan didn't want to face the possibility that the same thing had happened to him. Or that Dana's soul might well have gone to Sutekh.

He needed to get to his daughter. He needed to make certain she was safe. He needed to warn his brothers.

And he needed to see Bryn.

As soon as that last thought formed, he tried to thrust it aside.

He wasn't going to think about her at all. She was his daughter's mother. That was it. He'd be wise to remember that. Adding her to his list of concerns would only fragment his concentration.

Except he remembered that he'd thought of her in his purgatory. He'd seen her again and again in the fevered images he'd manufactured. He'd seen her at the bloodred river. He'd seen her again when he'd relived the day he'd taken Dana to the park. He couldn't explain why she'd haunted his thoughts, why he'd felt as if she'd actually been *there,* close enough to touch.

And at the moment, it really didn't matter.

He glanced around, looking for some clue as to what year it was. A line of people stretched along the red carpet, held back by a velvet rope guarded by a burly, dark-suited bouncer wearing wraparound shades. At night.

The women in the line were wearing barely there scraps that looked pretty much like the barely there scraps they'd worn before Lokan had…died. So either the fashions hadn't changed much since he'd been gone, or he hadn't been gone very long.

He didn't dare open a portal to carry him where he wanted to go. He had no idea how he'd ended up here in the shadow of the Luxor, and he didn't want to risk getting trapped in the place between Topworld and Underworld once more. Besides, he felt so drained he doubted he had it in him to grab the energy that surged between the Topworld and the Underworld and combine them to create a fracture between the realms.

Noise slammed him: a car horn, the blare of music, the roar of human voices, raised in conversation. Laughter. He jerked at the onslaught. Only then did he realize that he hadn't been aware of the sounds until that exact second. The cacophony of the Topworld. It was as if a bubble of silence had burst, letting a deafening wave crash down on him.

So he really was here. He really had escaped. His pulse amped up a notch, sending blood rushing through his veins.

He pushed off the wall of the pyramid and strode away. He made it six steps before he was yanked back as though a giant hand had pulled on his collar or a rope tethered him in place. Frustration surged, but he tamped it down and tried again in the opposite direction. Same results.

He wasn't going anywhere.

But he didn't have time to ponder that. To his left, a door opened and the sleek glass facade of the pyramid disgorged a second bouncer, dressed as a twin to the one guarding the velvet-roped line. He crossed his arms over his chest and said, "Boss wants to see you."

Lokan crossed his arms over his own chest and asked softly, "Which boss would that be?"

As far as he was concerned, there was only one: Sutekh. His father. His murderer.

The bouncer just stood there, head turned to fix his gaze about three feet to the left of where Lokan stood.

That was odd.

Seconds ticked past. Then the bouncer reached back, opened the door and jerked his head in a "get a move on" motion.

He held the door long enough to allow someone to walk through. Then he followed, as though someone *had* walked through.

Something wasn't right. The bouncer hadn't looked at him. Hadn't spoken directly to him or answered his question. Almost as if Lokan wasn't even there.

Lokan watched the door swing shut, unease uncoiling in his gut.

Damn it to fucking hell.

He spun and stared at the black glass of the pyramid. The lights of Vegas danced there in sparkling reflection, and he could see the reflected line of club-goers snaking along behind him.

But he couldn't see himself.

For all intents and purposes, he *wasn't* there.

Panic knotted his gut as the possibility struck him that he wasn't actually in Vegas, but rather still trapped in a world of his own imagination. Everything he'd experienced there had been only ghostly shadows of memories he'd conjured. Nothing had been real.

Was he trapped in purgatory still?

Had he only imagined that his body and soul had reunited, that his Ka, Ba, Sheut, Ren and Ib had all connected and made him whole once more? Had that, too, been only a creation of his fevered, desperate mind?

Maybe he hadn't escaped the null zone after all.

The fear that clawed at him was ugly and so powerful it almost knocked him to his knees. He didn't trust anything, least of all himself.

In his pre-Sutekh mortal life—the one where he had been a human boy with human parents and an all-too-human brother who'd drowned in a gray and murky lake—he had known fear as any mortal did. It was part of human existence.

Then he'd discovered the truth of who he was: Sutekh's son. After that, fear had no longer been a consideration.

Until the day he'd found out he had a daughter. Then he'd been afraid for her, for what might happen to her if rival Underworld lords found out about her.

His murder had added a whole new layer to that

fear. Because his killer wasn't a rival deity, but his own father.

And that fact still caused him pain.

He despised his own weakness, both emotional and physical.

But he could make himself strong. He could use his mind even if his body failed him. He needed to think. Logic. Rationality. He could combat the doubts that assailed him and determine the truth of his situation.

Again, the sound of a woman's drunken laughter carried above the general din, grounding him. He turned, followed the laughter to its source. There was noise all around him, as there never had been in the null zone.

He *was* Topworld.

The door opened once more, and a man stepped through. Tall, dark-haired, dark-eyed, he looked vaguely familiar. Lokan tried but couldn't place him. A human? He didn't think so, despite the fact that he could detect no supernatural energy signature. As a soul reaper, Lokan could camouflage his, so it stood to reason that others could do the same.

Turning his head, the man looked directly at Lokan. *Saw* him.

"My apologies for Graham's behavior," he said, his tone conversational. "I told him to explain that he couldn't see you and to request that you follow him inside. I was very clear in my instructions. But you know how it is. Send a Topworld grunt to do a simple task…" He shrugged. "The moron actually thought you were tagging after him like a tail."

Lokan took a moment to process the fact that someone Topworld could see him, speak with him. Then he asked, "Who are you, and how did I get here?"

"Remiss of me. Boone Falconer. I'd offer a hand, but you wouldn't be able to grasp it. We're not actually on the same plane at the moment."

Not on the same plane. "So I'm not physically in Vegas?"

"You are and you aren't. Think of it as a sort of dimensional box, a defined fracture between realms."

Like the portals Lokan and his brothers summoned to move between Topworld and Underworld. But this was a box rather than a tunnel, which explained why he couldn't go more than a few feet in any direction.

"So we have the *who* out of the way. Let's work on a few more simple answers. Why bring me here? And how did you manage it?"

Boone smiled, a brief flash of white teeth. That smile reminded Lokan of his brother Mal. A pirate's smile. The kind Mal flashed when he was about to rob someone blind. And enjoy it.

CHAPTER SIX

*Let radiance arise from that which hath
devoured me, and which hath slain men and
is filled with the slaughter...*
                                        —The Egyptian Book of Gates

*The Underworld,
The Territory of Sutekh*

ALASTOR KRAYL WAS HAVING A spot of trouble with
his temper. His mate, Naphré Kurata, had been taken
by the Matriarchs of the Asetian Guard, ostensibly
for her own protection. But he wasn't buying that.
Given that he was a soul reaper, enemy of Aset's
kind, that left Naphré in danger while Alastor was
here in Sutekh's realm, forced to attend the Underworld and face his father. Who also happened to be
his brother's murderer. Bloody fucking hell.

He strode along the sandstone gallery that led to
his father's greeting chamber, malice and rage and
worry burning in his gut. He needed to find a way to
tether those emotions before he entered his father's
presence. Sutekh fed on anger and chaos, and Alastor had no interest in stoking his hunger.

He shoved open the doors and crossed the vast greeting chamber to a second set of doors that stood open at the far end. There, he paused and took a slow breath. He needed to master his demons, his rage and pain.

Stepping through the doors, he saw the garden with new clarity, not as an oasis of palm trees surrounding a tranquil pond, but as a representation of all Sutekh coveted. For six thousand years, Sutekh had been bound by the cease-fire agreement that saw all the powerful Underworld deities locked in their own realms. He had created a garden with trees and water and even had fish brought in from the river Nile. But he couldn't replicate the sun. He couldn't walk the Earth. And so he'd killed Lokan and tried to take over his body, to use it to circumvent the ancient agreement.

Alastor hated this garden now. And he hated his father with a deep and malevolent revulsion. But he—and his brothers—were still bound to Sutekh, still subject to his will, still forced to attend when he demanded it.

And he'd demanded Alastor's presence.

"My son," Sutekh said, offering a greeting before Alastor did. That in itself was unusual. A peace offering? Did Sutekh really believe it would do anything to soothe the abhorrence in Alastor's heart?

Rage clogged his throat, and he thought that was a good thing, because if he spoke right then, he couldn't vouch for what would come out.

Sutekh rose from the boulder he'd been sitting on and turned. He had the ability to take on any appearance at will; Alastor had never seen his true face. Today, Sutekh had chosen to wear Lokan's face—*Lokan's.* His hair was honey-gold, his form tall and leanly muscled. But the eyes were wrong. Lokan's were light blue with a hint of gray. Sutekh's were flat black and soulless, without emotion or depth. Still, it was a horror to stare at his brother's face, his *murdered* brother's face, being worn by his murderer.

Alastor's anger ramped up a notch, and in that second he craved the power to annihilate his father.

"Yes," Sutekh said, meeting his gaze, "feed me. Sate my hunger."

And all became clear. Sutekh had chosen this guise on purpose to draw Alastor's hate and pain to the surface, to feed off it because Alastor had come empty-handed, without a darksoul for his father to consume.

So it was on him to leash his emotions, on him to deny his father the meal he craved. He thought of Naphré, his love, his mate. He thought of her ability to betray nothing of her inner turmoil, to present only a calm and cool facade. He held on to that as he wrestled his own emotions back to the hidden, dark swamp they usually inhabited.

Sutekh's eyes narrowed. Alastor could feel him reaching for the chaos and pain and anger. And he denied him. He refused him entry. He only crossed his arms over his chest and held everything he felt in check, and said, "You called?"

"You are angry." The air around Sutekh shimmered and danced, and then Alastor wasn't looking at Lokan anymore. He was looking at straight dark hair, an athletic build and a smile that showed a dimple in each cheek. A smile that was chilling. "An improvement?" Sutekh asked with Naphré's voice.

Alastor felt as if a band tightened around his chest and another around his skull. He couldn't breathe. Couldn't think. And then it hit him. Sutekh had never met Naphré, never seen her, so the only place he could be pulling this image from was Alastor's own mind.

"How's a little tit for tat?" he asked as he cleared his mind of everything save one thought—the image that Kemetic art represented as his father's true form: a creature with a doglike head, the snout of an anteater and a forked tail. Again, the air shimmered and danced, and there it was, the creature Sutekh had never shown him. Was it accurate? Didn't matter. It wasn't Naphré or Lokan, and that was enough for him.

"You are cunning," Sutekh said, and Alastor wasn't certain if it was a compliment or a criticism. Didn't matter. He cared nothing for his father's opinion now. "Perhaps I will train you as my right hand now that your brother is gone. You may have an aptitude."

Alastor let the comment pass. It was bait, a lure for his rage, and he wasn't going to feed the beast.

"You are unafraid."

"Is that what you want? My fear?"

"Your loyalty."

"You had that. You had all our loyalty. Until you bloody well killed our brother." Why? He barely managed to bite back the question. But he wasn't going to give Sutekh the satisfaction of hearing him ask. As if he trusted his father to tell him the truth.

But Sutekh surprised him, offering information for free. Or was it? With Sutekh, nothing was ever free.

"The prophesy."

"Right. That's apparent. You killed Lokan to steal his body and walk the Earth once more."

"You see only the obvious," Sutekh said and, with a languid motion, beckoned a servant forward. The woman carried a tray, and Sutekh helped himself to a honeyed sweet, then waved her away. As she turned, Alastor saw her face; her eyes and mouth were sewn shut. Sutekh's newly implemented way of ensuring that no servant could betray him.

Sutekh had only started doing that after his second-in-command, Gahiji, had been killed. He'd claimed that there must have been a traitor in their midst, and that was how Gahiji's killer had gotten in. But as Alastor stared at the servant's maimed face, he realized that the killer was Sutekh, that there was no traitor, and this brutality had no underlying purpose other than to hide any possible disclosure of Sutekh's guilt.

Not that Alastor minded brutality. It came with the territory. Hard to be a soul reaper and gracefully tear out hearts and darksouls. But that was different. Those souls were dipped in fetid slime.

This was different.

Sickened, he looked away.

"What should I see other than my brother's eviscerated and dismembered corpse, with you wearing a sign that says 'guilty as charged'?"

"Guilt is relative."

"Are you claiming that you didn't kill Lokan?" He couldn't keep the disbelief from his tone.

"No."

"And knowing that, Dae and Mal and I are still supposed to serve you. We're supposed to remain in the ranks and feed you darksouls and trust that you won't hack one of us to pieces next?"

"The choice is yours. You may leave."

"And by *leave,* you mean be consumed and annihilated."

"Yes."

"Not much of a choice."

"The option is that you find another deity willing to accept you in their ranks."

Right. As if that was a bloody option. No one would trust Sutekh's sons in their midst. He couldn't blame them. Were he an Underworld power broker, he wouldn't trust Sutekh's sons, either.

Then his father surprised him as he said softly, "It was necessary to sacrifice Lokan, to lose one of my sons. That only makes my remaining progeny all the more—" He paused, and an odd expression crossed his features, as though he were searching for a word so foreign and unfamiliar that he was having great difficulty finding it. "All the more precious to me."

"Precious?" Alastor asked incredulously. "You want me to believe that I…we…are highly valued? Much loved? By you?"

Sutekh flicked his forked tail and assumed a different form, this one a young man wrapped in royal cloth with a narrow beard and kohl around his eyes. "I grow disinterested in this dialogue. I summoned you to address your exact question. Lokan was the one, the pure one, the magical one. He alone of all of you could act as a vessel."

Something in the way Sutekh said "all of you" jumped out like a neon flare. Alastor's thoughts ran through options and possibilities, and then he asked, "Why? Why Lokan?"

"He had a level of power that you lack. He did the impossible. He created a child, and thereby showed me that he possessed the power of life. That power would sustain me in the world of Man."

Alastor stared at him. *The power of life. He alone of all of you.* "So Dae and Mal and I don't make the cut."

"You do not."

Alastor had an uneasy feeling in his gut.

"I offer you a gift, Alastor. And to your brothers, as well. You may return to the Topworld and hunt your mates."

"So you can see if one of us creates a child? If one of us has the power of life?"

"You do not. Not you or Dagan or Malthus."

Alastor's gut churned because he knew where this was going and what Sutekh was thinking.

Sutekh inclined his head, a languid nod. "And so you have my permission to retrieve your mates—" his distaste dripped from the word like hot wax "—and utilize their unique skills to assist me in finding that which I seek, that which I had but was taken from me by Roxy Tam of the Asetian Guard. A vessel that is not yet ripe."

A vessel. Having failed with Lokan's body, Sutekh was looking for another option.

Detroit, Michigan

"MOMMY?" DANA LOOKED UP AT Bryn, eyes wide, face pale, her arms tightening even more around Bryn's thigh. "I want to go home."

Home. Where was that? The house they'd just left? Or the two before that? Or the one in Oklahoma City that they had lived in from the time Dana was born?

Bryn smiled at her daughter, feeling as if her face was going to crack.

"I need to finish talking to Jack, and then

we'll go." Go where? She had no clue. There was nowhere safe.

"Jack," Dana repeated the name and nodded as though she understood. A bit of the tension left her small frame. Maybe by naming him, Bryn had made him seem less frightening.

"That'd be me. Hello, pumpkin," Jack said gently.

Bryn's heart twisted. She didn't want him talking to Dana. Too late. She didn't want him to even know about her. Too late, again. Not that he'd hurt her. He wouldn't.

In fact, he'd protect her. And his definition of protection was locking her away in a glass cage like a priceless treasure with no autonomy, no life, no hopes or dreams.

Bryn ought to know. She'd been in that cage. That was the reason she'd hunted down Lokan Krayl all those years ago, the reason she'd gotten pregnant. So she could escape that cage.

But everything had changed with her pregnancy and Dana's birth. *She'd* changed.

"State your business, Jack." She kept it short and to the point, burying the part of her that was inclined to keep talking, to babble endlessly to fill the silence. Jack would chew that girl up and spit her out. So Bryn needed to be the woman who could bite back to keep her daughter safe.

Jack hooked his thumb in the belt loop of his jeans. "Took a bit of effort to find you."

Typical Jack. He'd tell her his business when he was good and ready, and not a second before.

"A bit? You always were the master of understatement." It had taken him seven years of effort. She drew a slow breath, forcing herself to stay calm though her pulse pounded so hard she could hear the blood rushing in her ears. "Well, that was definitely a worthwhile chat. We're leaving now. Don't come after us."

"Bryn, please—" Jack caught her upper arm, his grip gentle but firm "—just hear me out." She hadn't heard him move, but she hadn't really expected that he'd simply let her walk away.

It was the "please" that made her stop. She didn't think she'd ever heard Jack use that word before. At least, not when he was speaking to her.

The moon glinted off the rows of silver hoops he wore in each ear.

"You want me to hear you out? Then say what you need to say."

His brows rose, and then he gave a short nod. "You can't run anymore, Brynja baby—"

"Don't call me that." Was that her voice, so calm and low and full of authority? The last time she'd seen Jack, she'd been a rambling fool.

His lips drew taut, and the skin around his eyes tightened. "You don't realize how deep the pile of—" he glanced at Dana "—how deep it is, what you've gone and stepped in."

Bryn gave a hard laugh. "Oh, I think I do realize." She figured she knew more than he did, but she wasn't about to tell him that. It'd be like dangling raw meat in front of a hungry beast. Then she looked around, just in case the threat was bigger than Jack. He had found them. That meant others could, too. "Are you alone?"

"Yeah. We figured I had the best chance to get you to listen. That you hate me the least."

"I don't—" She didn't hate any of them. But they were a threat to her. They had been back then, and they still were now. More importantly, they were a threat to Dana. They would want to use her the way they had used Bryn until she'd escaped.

As though he read her thoughts, Jack shook his head. "We're the least of your worries right now." He sent a speaking glance at the top of Dana's head, and in it Bryn read the words he didn't say. They were the least of Dana's worries, too.

"She displays no traits," Bryn said, making it clear that Dana could be of no use to him.

Jack shrugged. "Kids often don't. Sometimes it comes later." He watched Dana for a moment, an indecipherable expression flitting across his features. "She afraid of all strangers, or just me?"

The question told Bryn a great deal: Jack didn't know that Dana had been kidnapped by the Cult of Setnakht and rescued by the Asetian Guard. If he did, he wouldn't have asked that. She didn't offer that information. The less he knew, the better.

Dana sidled closer, her arms snaking around Bryn's thigh once more.

Jack opened his mouth, closed it, then frowned and finally shot a glance at Bryn. She tensed for a second until she realized what that look meant. He was asking permission to speak to her daughter.

"When did you ever ask my permission for anything?" she murmured.

"I'm asking now."

At her nod, he hunkered down until he was eye level with Dana.

"Hey, pumpkin, what's that in your ear?" he asked.

Dana shot him a sidelong glance. "Nothing," she whispered.

"Naw…it's something." He reached out very slowly, and only when Dana didn't flinch away did he touch her ear and pull out a coin.

Dana turned her head and watched him, unsmiling.

"And what's in this ear?"

"Nothing." She wasn't whispering now.

He pulled a second quarter from her other ear.

Seconds ticked past, then Dana sighed, put one hand on her hip and kept the other looped tightly around Bryn's thigh. "Mommy showed me that trick. I know how it works."

"Do you, now?" Jack asked, his expression solemn. "I taught your mother that trick."

Dana glanced at Bryn, then took a coin from Jack. "Lean closer," she ordered.

When he obliged, she reached up and, with a flourish, pulled the coin from his ear. "See?"

Jack gave a low laugh, and after a second's delay, Dana laughed with him. Bryn froze, memories slapping her hard. Because she remembered what it had been like before Lokan died, when Dana would laugh like that all the time.

And because once upon a time, before she'd understood that he was her enemy, her jailor, Bryn had laughed at Jack's tricks, too.

"I...brought something," Jack said. "For her."

Bryn offered a stiff nod. Whatever faults and flaws marred Jack's nature, any gift he'd brought would be harmless.

At her nod of agreement, he said, "Got a present for you, pumpkin."

"Pumpkins are round and orange, and if you keep them too long after Halloween, they smell," Dana said solemnly. "I am a girl."

Jack blinked. His brows rose. "You want the present?"

"Yes, please."

He pulled a small, wrapped package out of his jacket pocket.

The sight of it slammed Bryn like a fist in her gut.

He came bearing gifts wrapped in pink paper with white cats—Dana's favorites. That meant he'd been out there for who knew how long, watching her.

Watching Dana. And Bryn hadn't sensed a damned thing.

"How long have you been here?" she asked, her voice low and tense.

"Just tonight," he said. "Before that, I hired a guy. P.I. A human. That's why you didn't sense me. You would have, if I'd come close enough."

Those were a lot more words than Jack usually strung together at one time. Which meant he was making a needle-sharp, stiletto point: Bryn could sense supernaturals. She'd know if one got close enough to be a threat. *So what?* Clearly, all anyone needed to do was hire a human to watch her, and she wouldn't be able to keep Dana safe.

Why hadn't she thought of that? Was she ever going to think like one of them? And if she didn't, how was she to protect her daughter?

Dana was staring up at her with a wary expression, making no move to take the small package from Jack's hand.

"It's okay, baby," Bryn said. "Why don't you unwrap it and we'll see what's inside?"

"Right now?" Dana glanced around. "Here?" Her mixed emotions were evident in her tone. She was clearly eager to find out what was in the package. But the fear and urgency of the preceding events— their headlong flight into the night—had left her edgy and afraid.

Bryn pressed her lips together, hating that her

daughter always had to be ready to run. But the alternative was far worse.

"Go ahead and open it, Dana. Jack always brings great presents." It was the truth. The presents weren't the problem. It was the strings attached to them that would weave themselves into a cage.

Dana tore the paper and handed it to Bryn, who folded it and tucked it away in her pocket. Dana pulled off the lid of the small box and gasped.

"Flopsy," she whispered.

Inside was an old and ratty stuffed toy, a white cat. Well-worn. Well-loved. One they'd been forced to leave behind with all their other belongings the night Roxy had called and told them to run.

Jack must have been to that house. Had he watched them there, as well?

The one-shouldered shrug he offered answered that question. He had. Or rather, he'd hired someone to watch them, knowing that Bryn would sense his presence if he did it himself.

How long had he known exactly where she was? Where Dana was? And why hadn't he made himself known or demanded what Bryn knew he wanted, a walker to guide souls to the Underworld to curry favor with powerful deities?

"Look, Mommy." Dana pulled the small stuffed toy out of the box and hugged it close. "It's Flopsy. She found me."

"She did find you."

Dana smiled shyly at Jack. "Thank you," she said.

"Welcome." He grinned, a full, open un-Jack smile that transformed his face and made him look far less intimidating.

"Is there somewhere we can talk?" Jack asked as he straightened from the crouched position he'd been holding as he spoke to Dana.

"Just up here." Bryn led the way up the path until it opened to the small park behind the elementary school. "You can go on the swing if you like, Dana," she said.

"Okay." Humming to Flopsy, Dana wandered a few feet away and sat, unmoving on the swing.

Jack was quiet for a couple of minutes, just watching her, then he asked, "Should we push her or something?"

"She gets queasy," Bryn said. "She just likes to sit on it. She doesn't actually like to swing." She didn't add that before her father was murdered, Dana loved to swing. She'd laugh and scream for her daddy to push her higher.

"Hmm."

In the silence that followed, they could hear Dana lecturing the cat about getting lost. Bryn stifled the urge to call her back, to physically hold on to her. She had to force herself to acknowledge that Dana was only a few feet away. That she was safe. And that the small bit of distance gave her enough privacy for a quick conversation with Jack.

"Talk," she said.

"You do need to come with me, Bryn," he said,

then turned his head to stare down the path that they had just taken.

Bryn followed his gaze, the fine hairs at her nape prickling. Was something else out there?

"The answer is no." She shifted a step closer to Dana as Jack turned fully to face the path. "I'm not going to be your gilded prisoner or your pawn. And my daughter is not going to be payment for my freedom. Besides, she's human."

"That might change. She's young yet. At that age, you were human, too."

Two teenagers wandered into the light as they left the path, the tip of a cigarette, or perhaps a joint, glowing in the darkness. At the sight of Jack they stopped short and changed direction, cutting across the field behind the school.

"I'm still human," Bryn said. But she wasn't. No matter how hard she pretended, she wasn't human, not fully. "I won't let you take her." She met his gaze. "I won't, Jack."

"You—" Jack cut himself off and changed tack, his gaze still on the darkened path, his posture alert. "This isn't about that. It's about Lokan Krayl."

"Shh." Lokan's name coming from Jack's lips gave her a shock. Bryn shot a glance at Dana. Her head was down as she talked quietly to the cat in her lap. "What about him?"

"He was a soul reaper."

"I know." She'd figured it out. Not at first. At first, she'd thought Lokan Krayl was a psychic or a lesser demon or maybe a Djin. But over time, there had been clues, and she'd realized what he was.

"There's more."

She blinked, startled that Jack didn't just come out and say it. He was a blunt kind of guy. The fact that he was holding back made her edgy. "Okay." She drew the word out, her thoughts spinning. Then she waited for Jack to finish.

"They're hunting—" His gaze shot to Dana, telling her exactly who was being hunted. A buzzing started in her ears, like a swarm of bees.

"Who's after us?" she asked.

His gaze locked on hers, and she saw a whole world of concern there.

"Sutekh's soul reapers."

Her breath stopped, fear knotting her chest. In that second, she understood what was big enough and bad enough to make Jack nervous.

Sutekh. Lord of Chaos, Lord of the Desert, Mighty One of Twofold Strength. He was a god known for cruelty and blind rage, the most powerful of the Underworld deities. He was Lord of Evil, and he was hunting her daughter.

"Why?" The word came out choked and strained. Why would Sutekh want Dana? Because Lokan had been a soul reaper? So what? Sutekh had an army of them. "Why?" she asked again.

"He was Sutekh's son."

Dead silence. Then she laughed, the sound dead and hollow. Jack was wrong.

Lokan couldn't be Sutekh's son.

Lokan was dead. Murdered. It was almost unthinkable that someone had dared to kill a soul reaper. But…Sutekh's son?

"Lokan Krayl was Sutekh's youngest son." Jack shot another look at Dana. "Which makes her his granddaughter."

"No," she whispered again, shaking her head. Nausea churned in her gut.

"I ever lie to you, Bryn?"

She shook her head, unable to choke out a single word.

"I'm not lying to you now."

Lokan had dropped hints that he was the son of someone very dangerous. He'd pretended he was some crime lord's kid. She'd let him. Because calling him on it, telling him she knew he wasn't human, would have given away her own secrets, and that, she wasn't willing to do.

Now she understood that there was a grain of truth woven through the lies.

And that changed everything.

She backed up a step, wanting to run and hide and cry, and there was nowhere to run. Nowhere to hide.

Sutekh.

"There's more…" Jack reached for her, appeared to think better of it and dropped his hand. The expression on his face was not one she'd ever seen there before. Compassion. Empathy. Sadness. And that made her all the more afraid, though she couldn't say why.

Then he spoke, and she knew exactly why.

"Bryn," Jack said, his voice low, "it was Sutekh that killed him."

Her gaze shot to her daughter. Lokan's daughter. Who was now being hunted by Lokan's killer.

CHAPTER SEVEN

*None shutteth the door against you, and the
damned do not enter in after you.*
— The Egyptian Book of Gates

*Zugspitze Mountain,
Germany*

DAGAN KRAYL KNEW WHAT IT WAS like to struggle and
fight, to ache for freedom. His mate, Roxy Tam,
knew it, too. She'd been a prisoner the first time he
saw her, bound and gagged in the basement of an
abandoned warehouse in Chicago, all guts and grit
as she worked at escaping.

Now, she was a prisoner once more, only this time
it wasn't some twisted bastard bent on rape and murder who had her. It was her own kind, the Asetian
Guard, the elite force she had given a decade of her
life to.

His enemies.

Dagan was here to get her back, and he hadn't
come alone.

His brother Mal stood beside him at the edge of a
barren, rocky precipice. Dagan shifted his gaze from

the mountain directly in front of them and looked down, way down. The distance made the trees below him so small they resembled twigs. Good thing he had no problem with heights. And Mal, well, Mal loved them. Lean out just a little and they'd both fall. Dagan held his place, but Mal rocked his weight forward, skirting as close to the razor's edge as he could.

"See anything of interest?" Calliope Kane asked from behind them, her voice cool and even, smooth as water flowing over rock. She was here for a shit-load of reasons, some of which Dagan knew, some he figured were buried so deep that Calliope might not even be able to find them.

She'd been Roxy's mentor in the Asetian Guard. She was Roxy's friend. And now she was Mal's mate. Dagan had saved her life once when what he'd believed to be rogue soul reapers had tried to kill both her and Roxy. Now he knew they hadn't been rogue; they'd been acting on his father's orders, hunting for Lokan's daughter and covering up the fact that Sutekh had killed Lokan, his own son.

Dagan and his brothers still hadn't been able to process that.

"I don't see a damn thing," Mal said. "If there's a castle here, it's playing hide-and-seek."

A blast of icy air touched his skin, and Dagan glanced over his shoulder as Alastor stepped through a swirling mass of smoke and darkness to join them.

"You find anything on the kid?" Dagan asked once the portal closed.

They'd been searching for Dana since the meeting of allies had ended, fearful that their father would find her first. Lokan had kept her existence a secret, even from his brothers, and they knew he'd done it to protect her.

But now Lokan was gone, and the job of protection fell to them. Problem was, they needed to find her before they could figure out a way to keep her safe.

So far, they hadn't turned up a damn thing.

"She may as well have vanished into thin air," Alastor said. "And I have to be careful about how I put the word out and where I look because I don't want to draw attention to her. We can't risk someone else finding her first and tipping off Da—" He cut himself off, clearly still getting used to referring to Sutekh as something other than Dad. He leaned against a large boulder, one hand in the pocket of his impeccably tailored slacks. "The only good bit of news in the whole sodding mess is that our father hasn't found her, either."

"And you know this how?" Dagan asked.

"Spoke to Kai. He told me that much. He's sympathetic, but his hands are tied."

Kai Warin was their father's new second-in-command. His hands *were* tied. If he went against Sutekh, he would be annihilated. The only edge he had was that he was mated to the daughter of Asmodeus, the demon of lust. While that wouldn't necessarily save him if he chose to cross Sutekh, it might at least buy him a little time because, in the Underworld, political alliances were key, and offing your ally's son-in-law wasn't good politics.

"So Kai knows about Dana?" Mal asked, and Dagan knew why there was strain in his tone. Kai might somehow betray her existence to his mate, Amber, who in turn might betray the information to her father.

"He knows the old man is looking for her," Dagan said.

"But he doesn't know why." Alastor finished the thought.

"So you, uh, spoke to Sutekh?" Mal asked.

"Unfortunately, yes. He actually played the 'my sons mean something to me' card."

Mal snorted. "Like any of us could believe that now."

There was an uncomfortable silence because all of them had believed it before. They'd believed that a creature incapable of anything but self-service had harbored some form of affection for them.

"Any news here?" Alastor asked, his eyes shadowed, his mouth grim.

"We're still looking," Mal replied.

"One would think that a fortress with a multitude of guards would be hard to miss. To my recollection, castles are rather large."

"Fuck off."

Alastor quirked a brow at his brother, then glanced at Calliope. "Are you certain this is the place?"

"I am."

"Then where the bloody hell is it?" Alastor snapped, his British accent more pronounced than usual. He liked to be in control, and ever since Naphré had gone missing, he must have been feeling that control slipping through his fingers. Dagan understood that; he was feeling a little out of control himself.

Mal spun and glared at Alastor, obviously pissed at the tone his brother took when speaking to Calliope. But before either of them could explode, Calliope stepped between them and held out her arms to either side, palms out.

"Remember why we are here," she said, a thread of steel bracing the serenity of her tone.

"Bloody hell," Alastor muttered and glanced at Dagan, his expression stark. "Roxy was one of them. That might protect her. But Naphré—" He broke off, and his jaw tensed. "Naphré denied any connection to them. They won't have kind feelings for her."

They being the Asetian Guard—the elite forces of the goddess Aset—and the Matriarchs—the powerful entities who ruled the Guard.

"Calm must prevail," Calliope said. "Aset stated they were taken for their own protection."

Dagan wasn't buying into that. Not without solid proof.

"For three hundred years, Aset and the Asetian

Guard have been my enemies," he rasped. "For thousands of years they've been my father's enemies. Now, they have my mate, and my brother's mate. I have a hard time putting faith in Aset's claims."

He clenched his jaw, refusing to say any more, refusing to set free the worries that ate at him like maggots on rotting meat. He didn't like the feeling. Emotion wasn't his thing.

Calliope's gaze slid to Mal, and he shrugged. "Aset did say that Roxy and Naphré would be returned when the meeting of allies was over," he said. "It's more than over. No more meeting. No more allies. Just an Underworld on the verge of war with almost everyone looking for a piece of Sutekh. And by extension, us."

"I believe Aset's exact words were that they would be returned to us when this is over. She never specified what she meant by 'this,'" Calliope pointed out, all cool, irritating logic.

Dagan couldn't fault her for that. A cool head was better than churning emotion. Emotion meant mistakes, miscalculations, especially for a soul reaper who wasn't used to feeling a damned thing other than pissed off. But between Lokan's murder and his relationship with Roxy, he seemed to be in a constant state of emotional upheaval. He wasn't liking that much.

"I—"

Mal cut him off. "The meeting of allies might be over," he said, "but we don't have Lokan back. We don't know when or if he'll be returned to us." His voice lowered. "And we've yet to deal with the fact that our father is our brother's killer." He looked at each of them in turn. "We need to work together, not turn on each other like bickering children."

They all froze and silence fell. Because the "bickering children" remark was one Lokan had used. He'd always been the politician, the most reasonable among them. And more than once, he'd been the peacemaker between brothers, as well.

"You think his body found his soul?" Mal asked, voicing aloud the question they'd all been thinking since they'd forced the dismembered remains of their brother through a dimensional rift at the meeting of allies. None of them had dared to ask it aloud until now.

They'd had all the parts of the prophesy in place: The blood of Aset. The blood of Sutekh. The union of the two was supposed to allow the god to pass the Twelve Gates and walk the Earth once more. But they'd foiled Sutekh in his plan. They'd stopped him from using the body he had stolen from Lokan. They'd stolen it back and sent the fourteen parts to meet his soul, so that, though not a god, Lokan would be the one to walk the Earth.

But he hadn't come back to them.

From the second they'd found out that Lokan had been murdered, they'd wanted him back and they'd wanted vengeance, raw and bloody. And how the fuck were they supposed to get that when the killer was their fucking father?

The silence lengthened.

"Not talking about that now," Dagan said, his tone terse.

"We need to at some point," Mal said.

"But not now." Alastor's tone brooked no argument. "One step at a time. Right now, we bloody well focus on Roxy and Naphré. We get them back. Then we look for answers. With Roxy's help, we find Dana Carr. We keep her the hell away from Sutekh."

"And us." All eyes turned to Dagan when he said that. "We keep contact with Dana to a minimum. Given that Lokan never even mentioned her existence, that's obviously what he wanted."

"But things have changed," Mal argued.

Dagan held up his hand, palm forward, and as he did it, the gesture made him think of Roxy. He dropped his hand. To cover his unease, he pulled a lollipop from his pocket, tucked the cellophane wrapper away and popped the candy in his mouth.

"We'll argue that when we find her," he said. "For now, we need to focus on the task at hand."

"Rather than storming the bastion and stealing Roxy and Naphré away, we should request an audience with the Matriarchs." Now all eyes turned to Calliope. She was their best bet for intel. She was—had been—a high-ranking officer among the Asetian Guard. Moreover, she had the gift of prescience, fleeting views of what the future likely held. That was the reason she'd been able to tell them the general location of where they needed to look. She'd seen this mountain and the forest below. So, out of all of them, she had the best idea of what to expect and inside knowledge about those they were trying to find. "They know a great deal. They may know where the child is. I suspect they have answers to questions we haven't even thought of yet."

"You think? They've been wrong before." Dagan barely managed to keep the snarl out of his tone, but this wasn't Calliope's doing and the last thing he needed was to piss off his brother by biting off his mate's head. "Weren't they the ones who said the traitor who killed Lokan was one of Sutekh's sons?"

Calliope glanced at Mal and quirked a brow.

"Yeah, I did mention that to him," Mal said.

She looked at Dagan once more. "Actually, no. That erroneous conclusion was mine. They said only that the true traitor was higher in the ranks than Gahiji. My reply was that there was no one higher in the ranks save Sutekh's sons. They did not clarify further, so I made the assumption. It never dawned on me that Sutekh himself was the killer."

"Yeah. Never dawned on us, either." Which meant he couldn't hold her assumption against her.

Silence hung in the air. The wind whistled down the mountain.

"I have a suggestion," Calliope said. "What if we don't knock at the front door, but rather go directly to the chamber of the Matriarchs?"

"We'd have to find it first," Mal pointed out.

She inclined her head. "We would."

"Do they know we're here?" Dagan asked.

"Likely, they do. They are powerful." She shot him an arch look. "And quite possibly vindictive."

"Aset and Izanami were complicit in kidnapping Roxy and Naphré," Mal pointed out. "Do you think Izanami would allow harm to come to the child of her bloodline?"

"No," Calliope said. "But they will have no qualms about harming me. They see me as a traitor." She paused. "I *am* a traitor."

"Why?" Alastor asked, stepping forward. "Because you took a soul reaper to mate? By that logic, they'll see Roxy and Naphré as traitors, as well. You're not exactly putting my mind at ease."

"On the off chance you're right," Mal said, not waiting for her to answer Alastor, "you're staying behind. I'm not risking your safety or your freedom."

One dark brow lifted a fraction of an inch. "It isn't your call."

It wasn't. And Dagan figured Mal had to hate that.

He knew how his brother felt. They'd all fallen for equally stubborn women who weren't inclined to let the men in their lives call the shots. Which made for some interesting dynamics when each of those men had the intense urge to protect their mates.

"We'll have trouble getting inside," Calliope continued. "There are technological barriers to block entry, as well as spells and magics. The Matriarchs are adept, their skill immeasurable."

"I gained entry to their secure facility before,"

Mal pointed out. He'd managed to penetrate their mountaintop fortress in Bugaboo Provincial Park. He had opened a portal directly to the room where Calliope was being detained, and he'd gotten her out the same way. "The wards they set weren't effective against dimensional portals."

"Now that they're aware of it, they may have fixed that loophole." Calliope's tone was wry. "But…"

"But what?" Alastor asked when her voice trailed away.

"But what if they haven't fixed it? That is the crux of my plan." She looked at each of the three brothers in turn. "To open a portal, you need to know precisely where you're going, correct?"

"Correct," Dagan said. "We need to have been there before, or we need a specific address, a picture of the precise location…something that gives us a clear fix."

"How did you manage to get inside the fortress last time, then?" Alastor asked, turning to Mal.

"Shared dream. It gave me a location and I opened a portal."

No one asked what he was talking about. Dagan had spent years dreaming about Roxy. Despite the fact that, as a rule, soul reapers didn't dream, shared dreams had happened to each of them after their mates had sampled their blood. Daughters of Aset were pranic feeders. They sipped the life force of others in order to feed their power. And feeding from another supernatural meant they formed a psychic bond.

"I don't see how that'll help this time, mate," Alastor said. "Calliope already said they'll have wised up to that possibility, so we're no farther along."

But Dagan could almost see the wheels turning as Calliope spun a plan.

"Care to share, pretty girl?" Mal asked.

"The security measures and the stairs to the Matriarchs' lair will be almost exactly as they were in the compound in Bugaboo."

"How do you know?" Dagan asked.

"Because the layout is identical in each of their strongholds throughout the world. It is based on ancient Egyptian numerology. Seven flights of seven wooden stairs. Then seven flights of seven stone stairs, growing narrower with each step down. I'd be able to touch the walls on either side with my shoulders."

"Why so tight?" Dagan asked.

"So only one person can go through at a time, with little maneuvering room in the event they need to defend themselves."

"Nice." Dagan strode forward, seeing the possibilities. "Any spells or magic associated with the number seven?"

"Spells or magic, no. Symbolism, yes. Seven is the symbol of effectiveness, completeness. Perfection. But there are spells and magics closer to the Matriarchs' greeting chamber.

"I've been to the chamber twice before. I know what it looks like. Perhaps there will be some differences here, but as I mentioned, there will be elements that are exactly the same. If I describe them in minute detail, will that be enough for you to create a portal?"

Dagan ran a hand along his jaw. "Could be." He shot a glance at Mal, who shrugged and said, "It might work."

"What's the worst-case scenario?" Calliope asked.

"We summon a portal and end up at one of their other identical fortresses," Alastor answered. "Or we end up nowhere."

Calliope arched a brow. "That doesn't sound particularly terrible."

"He means *nowhere,* Calli," Mal said. "As in we end up anywhere or nowhere. A null zone. In an Underworld territory we have no business entering. In outer-fucking-space. Anywhere."

"That could be terrible," she conceded.

"Anyone have a better plan?" Alastor asked. When no one replied, he offered a tight smile. "Then Calliope's plan it is, mates."

Mal grinned. "I've always had a hankering to visit outer space."

Las Vegas, Nevada

"Join me." Boone hauled open the door and swept his arm before him.

"I'm not sure exactly what sort of party you're inviting me to," Lokan said, "but I'm not one for surprises."

Boone laughed. "You're going to make this difficult, aren't you? Here's the thing. I have food you can eat. A shower you can use." He made a show of looking Lokan up and down. "And a change of clothes. Unless you prefer the skirt and sparkly collar."

Lokan didn't need to glance down to know that he was wearing the items he'd been given in the cavern—a strip of linen around his waist, a jeweled necklace—and nothing else. So, yeah, clothes would be nice. The food and shower even nicer. But he wasn't the type to grab for the dangling carrot.

"And I should trust you because...?"

"Because you have nothing to lose." Boone shrugged. "What will I do? Kill you? You're already dead, my friend."

He was. Dead and, for all intents and purposes, buried. He couldn't seem to find a way to go Top-world, and he couldn't find a gate that would open to the Underworld. Even though he was standing here in the shadow of the Luxor's pyramid, he wasn't free to move about at will. Despite the return of his body, he might as well still be stuck in the null zone, except instead of being an entity without form, he was now a walking corpse. Nice.

Again Boone swept his arm before him in invitation. "After you." When Lokan made no move, Boone glanced around. "I'll be more comfortable having a conversation in a secure location."

"Secure." Lokan mulled that over for a second. "For my protection, or yours?"

"Both." One side of Boone's mouth quirked when Lokan pinned him with a hard look. "All right. More mine than yours," he admitted. "There are few who could actually bend dimensions to get to you." He let the door swing shut and crossed to Lokan with sure strides, then chopped the side of his hand against Lokan's torso. It passed through like it was cutting air. And Lokan didn't feel a damned thing.

"There's nothing here that can hurt you, Lokan Krayl, because there's nothing here that can touch you—" he returned to the door and yanked it open "—so you may as well be clean and fed while we talk."

True, and true. But he couldn't find it in him to trust so easily. Beyond that door might well be a trap.

"You don't recognize me, do you?" Boone asked.

Lokan shook his head, wondering if he'd ripped out the heart and darksoul of some friend or relation. Was this about vengeance? If it was, what was the point of using an undoubtedly enormous amount of resources to get him here from purgatory just to kill him and send him back?

"I'm not at my sharpest, given my recent history," Lokan said, studying the other man carefully. Dark Hair. Dark eyes. Features that were saved from being pretty by a strong jaw shadowed with dark stubble. There *was* something familiar about him. "Care to explain?"

"You make a habit of saving humans?"

"No. You make a habit of saving supernaturals?"

"No." Boone lowered his head and stared at the ground. "But I decided to make an exception for you, soul reaper."

He lifted his head once more, and his gaze collided with Lokan's, blue eyes shining unnaturally bright.

Blue. Except a minute ago they'd been brown.

Just like…

Lokan shook his head. "I knew that day would come back to bite me in the ass."

CHAPTER EIGHT

May you grant power in the sky, might on earth and vindication in the god's domain, a journeying downstream as a living soul, and a journeying upstream as a heron, to go in and out without hindrance at all the gates of the Duat.

—The Egyptian Book of the Dead

The Bridge at Spanish River
January 21, 1910

LOKAN WAS EXPECTING DEATH, AND death was what he got. Except he was supposed to be the one doing the killing, not some random twist of fortune that robbed him of his prize.

The wind howled down from the north, bitter and uncompromising, buffeting him where he stood. Below him, the metal husk of a railway car punched a jagged hole through the smooth, frozen face of the Spanish River.

Half a railway car, actually. The other half clung to the iron bridge, engulfed in flames, belching smoke into the gray, midafternoon sky.

Only moments past, he'd been standing to one side of the track, waiting for the train, and then in a blaze of screeching metal and sparks and screams, the second-class car had spun sideways, hit the bridge and split in two. Half had gone over the side and into the river. The first-class coach had followed, punching through ice that was a foot thick before sinking deep. The dining car was pulled along and stood on end now with the tables submerged and the galley poking up through the ice.

Still hoping to nab his prize, Lokan vaulted the side of the bridge and skidded down the embankment, only to stop when he realized the futility of his efforts. There was no way to catch his prey alone now, and he wasn't about to do a harvest in front of an audience.

Damn and blast, this was supposed to have been an easy grab. Wait for the train. Hop aboard. Catch Karl Gilbert Bell alone and harvest his heart and darksoul. Because that's what soul reapers did. It wasn't as though the bastard didn't deserve to die. For years, he'd been using his employment with the railway as a means to travel about the continent and butcher innocent women. Which made him Lokan's perfect target, a soul that stank of filth and malice.

It was Karl's turn to know abject terror. To bleed. To die.

Karl's name was inscribed in the book of records that Sutekh, the most powerful Underworld lord, kept on a pedestal in the center of his greeting chamber.

Sutekh had chosen Karl's name from the multitude because his darksoul was black as pitch, dipped in slime, a perfect morsel to feed Sutekh's voracious appetite.

And being Sutekh's son would not save Lokan from his wrath if he returned empty-handed—which was looking like a possibility. At this moment, Karl was either being incinerated in the burning car on the bridge or lying at the bottom of the river. And soul reapers didn't usually harvest the dead. Too complicated. The darksoul might already be pledged to another Underworld deity, and stealing it could only stir up trouble.

Which meant that Lokan's plan was a bust.

He should leave.

There were other darksouls he could claim and carry to his father in the Underworld. New York City always had a lovely array, as did London, Paris and Berlin.

But something held him here. As the howling wind snared his overcoat and sent it flapping like a crow's wings, the river below him rippled, and a man's head broke the surface. Gasping, the fellow struggled to pull himself out of the water and onto the ice.

Lokan watched him, feeling nothing. It wasn't in his soul reaper nature—or his mandate—to offer assistance to a dying mortal. It had been almost two hundred years since his father had sent for Lokan, yanking him from the human life that was all he had ever known. He had spent those two hundred years doing Sutekh's bidding, tearing out still-beating hearts and ripping darksouls free of their mortal shell. These he carried to Sutekh, meals of pure power.

But Lokan was no mere soul reaper; he was a prince among his kind, second only to Sutekh.

He had forsaken his humanity long ago.

Finally, the man pulled himself up and lay trembling and shivering with his torso flat on the ice and his legs trailing in the water.

The shriek of twisting metal and the belch of breaking glass rent the air, and Lokan spun to see the Pullman car that perched on the embankment above him inch lower. With a long, keening cry it tore free of its precarious perch, then slid along the snow in a rush, gouging runnels in the earth as it went.

Twisted with terror and desperation, the faces in the windows passed in a blur.

The train hit the ice, skidding and spinning and finally slamming against the portion of the dining car that protruded through the frozen face of the river. Then it sank into the blackness, the screams of those trapped inside snatched by the howling wind.

Lokan turned away to see that the lone man had pulled himself fully out of the water now. Shivering uncontrollably, he tried to rise, one hand extended toward the giant hole that had swallowed the Pullman car. Then his legs gave way and he collapsed in a broken heap.

Lokan watched as he maneuvered himself to lie flat and offered his hand to another human who flopped and thrashed at the broken edge of the ice. The man in the water clutched something against his chest, hampering his efforts to drag himself out of the water.

"Damn," Lokan muttered as he saw what that something was.

A child.

And there, uncurling inside him, was a part of himself he had thought eradicated long ago. He took a step forward, then froze, appalled by the uncharacteristic urge to lend a hand. He had no business holding on to the tattered remnants of kindness or compassion. But that child—

For an instant, Lokan only stood there, taking in the carnage, trying to convince himself that he felt nothing.

Then he was moving, running, heading down, down toward the river, with no idea what he meant to do. And no idea why he meant to do it.

He pulled off his overcoat as he strode across the ice with perfect balance, moving with inhuman speed. Reaching down, he clamped his fingers around the wrist of the man's free hand and hauled him effortlessly from the water.

"Get your coat and shirt off, man. Quickly now. And the boy's," he ordered. No sense saving them from drowning only to let them freeze to death. The child was chalk pale, eyes closed, lips tinged blue. But he was breathing. Barely.

For the briefest instant, Lokan saw a different sodden, pale child, not dark and thin, but plump, with sandy hair and freckles on his nose. He saw a small boat and a lake and a sky leaden with cloud; he'd never quite gotten over his aversion for boats. He blinked and the memory disappeared, buried beneath two hundred years of other memories. Better memories.

The man's fingers were clumsy, the cold temperature and the wet fabric impeding his every attempt as he fumbled with the buttons of the child's shirt. Impatient, Lokan fisted the cloth and tore it in two, then helped peel it away. With quick efficiency, he did the same for the man, thrust the child into his arms and wrapped the two of them in the warm, dry overcoat. He could do nothing about their wet trousers.

He stripped off his suit coat and offered it to the other man, the one who had been first out of the water. An afterthought. He cared nothing about the lives of the adults. Only the child.

"Get closer together," he ordered. "You'll be warmer that way."

Both men looked up at him before scooting closer. Only in that second did he realize that he had allowed these humans to see his face. While not strictly forbidden, it was frowned upon for soul reapers to reveal themselves. He gave a mental shrug. The horse had already left the barn. No sense worrying about closing the door.

He had no idea why he helped them, no explanation as to why he was now standing here in shirt-sleeves in the bite of the January wind. Not that the cold could harm him, but it was damned uncomfortable.

His gaze slid back to the pale, still child.

Premonition skittered up his spine. He should leave. Go. Right now. He had the strangest idea that what he did here today would haunt him at some point in the future.

A foolish and impossible thought.

The lives of these mortals were no more than a beat of his eternal heart. They would age, then die, and Lokan would still be exactly as he was. No mortal could influence his existence. No mortal could harm him. He was a soul reaper, son of Sutekh. He might bleed and suffer and know pain, but he would heal. He would always heal.

And he would never die.

Despite the clothing Lokan had given them, all three were shaking uncontrollably. The child moaned. His eyelids fluttered. Then he jerked upright, struggling against the weight of the coat that wrapped him. His gaze skittered to the black water framed by blue-white ice, and he tried to surge from the arms of the man who held him.

"M-m-m-my b-b-b-b-brothers." The words were

garbled and indistinct. But Lokan understood them and the emotions behind them.

For a split second, his gaze collided with the child's. Blue eyes, icy pale irises rimmed in indigo ink, bright, as though lit from behind. There was desperation and fear in those eyes. And guilt.

Lokan knew all about the guilt. He had lived while his brother had died. The brother of his childhood. The older brother who had played with him and teased him and guided him. The brother he had failed.

Only years later, after Sutekh had sent for him and he learned that he was a supernatural creature, a soul reaper fostered out to be raised by a human family, did Lokan understand that Richard might have been the brother of his heart, but not of his blood. Only then had he learned that he *did* have brothers of his blood, three of them, soul reapers all. Dagan. Alastor. Malthus.

Gaining three brothers he had never known hadn't lessened the pain of Richard's loss. But that loss made his living brothers all the more precious, bound him to them as surely as if he had spent his formative years growing up with them. He would kill for them. Sacrifice for them. Bleed for them. They would do the same for him.

As he watched this child struggle against the arms that confined him, struggle to get back in the frigid water and search for his siblings, he knew the thoughts and anguish running through his mind.

Damn it all to hell. He didn't want to feel any sort of kinship with a human, least of all a human child.

But he did.

"I'll find them."

The child turned his head, and for a second there was only the two of them in a place far different than where they were now. The wind and the noise, the smoke, the screams, all disappeared.

"Promise." A child's voice with a man's resolve.

"Yeah." A promise he would keep. But he never promised that he would find them alive.

The wind returned with a vengeance, bitter and wild.

With a snarl, Lokan turned and dove into the black water. Powerful strokes took him ever deeper. The cold reached inside him all the way to his bones. He didn't see how the mortals in that train could possibly survive this. Their fragile forms could not withstand the water's glacial temperature.

Though it was only midafternoon, the darkness beneath the ice was thick and oily. There were bodies inside the first railway car he passed, floating in their murky graves. And then he realized that there were some still alive. They clung to the hat hooks, holding their heads above water in the small bubble of air that had floated up to the top of the car.

A woman. A man. Two little girls.

But no sign of the brothers the child had spoken of.

Lokan turned away, intending to leave them to their fate.

Damn and blast. *This* was why he avoided children. They made him weak. The adults he would turn his back on with ease, but the girls...

He spun back and punched through the glass, ignoring the pain as shards sliced his skin and left him bleeding. The water rushed in, stealing the last of the air. They swam toward him and he toward them. He grabbed the woman and tried to push her toward the window, but she resisted, her attention on the girls.

Catching hold of the smaller girl, Lokan thrust her into the man's arms. The man shot an agonized look at the woman, then swam toward the surface, leaving her behind.

Lokan grabbed the second girl, and the woman, holding their collars, one in each hand. He wrestled them through the window. Then he swam for the surface, towing them both.

His clothing and shoes and the leather pouch slung across his shoulder dragged against his movements, and he imagined the humans were hampered even more. But a mortal's will to live was a powerful thing. He remembered that in some hazy part of his mind. He wondered how hard *he* would fight in the face of death, and then he let the question slip away because it was not one he would ever be called upon to answer.

He thrust the girl and the woman through the hole and onto the ice, and he saw that there were others there now. Rescuers with blankets and helping hands.

They took the child from him and whisked her away. They grabbed the mother and wrapped her in a blanket. They offered hands to help him from the murky water.

The two men he had given his coat and overcoat to were nowhere to be seen. But the boy he had saved earlier still sat on the ice at the edge of the hole, wrapped in Lokan's overcoat, ignoring the hands and words that urged him to rise. He stared at Lokan with huge, frightened eyes. Waiting for Lokan to bring his brothers to safety. Waiting for them to come up alive.

As Lokan had waited at the edge of a lake so long ago.

For all his vast supernatural power, in this moment he felt inadequate. His particular abilities were suited to killing humans, not saving them.

He dove once more, searching the murky depths. His chest ached. His lungs screamed. But unlike humans, he couldn't die from lack of air; he would only feel discomfort. Pain.

And then he saw them. Two small forms near the edge of the ruptured second-class car, thin and dark-haired like their brother. Their eyes were open, bright blue in the dim light. But they were dead. They had to be dead. They'd been in the water so long.

A wash of self-loathing hit him, memories and emotions from two hundred years in the past. He'd thought that time had dimmed all that. He'd thought he'd forgiven himself. Guess he'd been wrong.

Maybe that was what motivated him here. Atonement.

He grabbed both boys by their collars and swam for the surface, then flung them up, out of the water onto the frozen face of the river. There was a commotion. Rescuers ran toward them. The boy on the ice, the one wrapped in Lokan's overcoat, turned his head and met Lokan's gaze.

Blue. Lokan could swear the kid's eyes had been blue.

But they were brown now, so dark they looked black.

Lokan pulled himself from the river, water sheeting off him and puddling on the ice. He meant to say something. What? All the things people had said to him when Richard drowned never helped worth a damn.

People milled about. Those who had escaped the carnage were either sodden and shivering or blackened with soot from the fire. Those who had come to help worked with quiet efficiency.

He would leave these brothers to their kind. There was nothing more he could do. He took souls, he didn't restore them.

Turning, he strode away toward the bridge and the remains of the train cars. One still burned. Another lay on its side on the embankment. His steps were jerky and quick; fury drove him. Anger at himself. He had no explanation for what he'd just done.

But anger was a wasteful emotion, eating up energy and distorting thoughts. He must remain emotionless, as his father had taught him. He must see every angle and exploit it. Where was the angle here? There had to be a way to turn the events of the day to his advantage.

A moan drew his attention, and he realized there was someone at the base of the bridge behind a large mound of snow. He moved behind it, and his mood improved dramatically.

"Hello, Karl," he said with a grin. Blood flowered crimson on the snow, and a pole protruded through Karl's abdomen. Lokan glanced up at the bridge, then down. "Looks like you took a bit of a tumble."

Karl moaned and turned his head toward Lokan. Pain and fear etched his features. He gestured feebly at the pole that held him pinned like a bug.

"Let me just take care of that for you," Lokan said, bending low over Karl's supine form until their faces were close together and the smell of blood was strong and copper sweet.

Hope sprang to life in Karl's eyes.

Tensing his fingers until they curved like claws, Lokan thrust his hand through Karl's chest. There was a sharp sound as ribs snapped and a suction squish as the chest cavity opened, both drowned out by the cacophony of the accident scene. Karl's mouth opened in a soundless scream, the breath stolen from his lungs.

The hope in his eyes died.

Then the life in his eyes died as Lokan ripped out his heart. Blood sprayed in an arc, splattering the snow and Lokan's pant leg.

"Lucky my trousers are black," he murmured as he tucked the heart into the leather pouch that was slung across his shoulder. Then he shoved his hand back in the gaping hole and coaxed the darksoul to him. "Come to papa, sweetheart."

The darksoul wound up his fingers and around his wrist, like oily smoke, dark and fetid. The chill of it was masked by the frigid temperature and Lokan's cold, wet skin. Up his arm it snaked, writhing and twisting, rising then receding, as though it couldn't make up its mind if it wanted to be taken.

Not that it had a choice.

Free of Karl's body now, the darksoul dipped and swayed and finally rose to a point above Lokan's shoulder as he tethered it with a band of fire. There it hung, an amorphous black balloon, jerking to and fro with each gust of wind.

Lokan drew a slow breath. Despite the mind-numbing cold, he felt better now, more grounded, more even. He had come to kill and harvest, and that was exactly what he had done, despite his little uncharacteristic detour.

He would forget the aberration that had led him to dive into an icy river and snatch a handful of mortals from death. He would forget the glint of humanity that had peeked through the layers of tarnish on his soul.

He was a soul reaper, his father's willing minion, a creature of darkness and death. And he liked it that way.

Knowing that the humans who found Karl's remains would use the accident to explain away the carnage, Lokan turned, ready to leave.

He nearly stumbled over the boy, who stood an arm's length away, watching him.

The child looked directly at the darksoul that by all rights he—a human—should not be able to see. Then his gaze met Lokan's, his eyes blue and bright once more.

And the whisper of premonition Lokan had felt earlier became a roar.

CHAPTER NINE

*Truth is yours, live ye on your food. Ye your-
selves are truth.*

—The Egyptian Book of Gates

*Las Vegas, Nevada
Present day*

LOKAN FELT A MILLION MILES away from his cocky
younger self. *He was the son of Sutekh. And he could
never die.* Right.

His gaze slid to Boone.

"The train… You lived."

"I did. My brothers, as well. Thanks to you." He
paused. "Been a while, Lokan Krayl."

"Had a feeling that saving you would come back
to bite me in the ass. Looks like I was right." A
sardonic smile tugged at his lips. He'd saved three
kids. Who were now three adults. Three *supernatural* adults. That one act just might bite him in the ass
hard enough to make him bleed. "I'm guessing you
didn't bring me here to chat about old times. What
is it you want from me?"

Boone spread his hands, palms up. "You have a suspicious nature."

"It's a natural by-product of betrayal. Once you've been stabbed in the back, you tend to look askance at anyone with a knife."

"A rather harsh and candid assessment. I had heard you were a smooth talker, a man of patience and eloquence. A politician. Did I hear wrong?"

That observation drew Lokan up short. He mentally replayed his conversation with Boone and realized the way he'd handled it was far different than he would have in the past. He'd changed. Not in a good way. He was being rash, letting anger and frustration lead his actions and words. He forced himself to remain quiet, to wait for Boone's next move.

"You think that I want something other than the repayment of the lives I owe you?" Boone asked. "We might not be mortal now, but as children we were. My brothers and I might have died that day if not for you."

Lokan didn't doubt the truth of that statement. As a child, he'd been mortal, too. His supernatural abilities hadn't kicked in until he was an adult. Same deal with his three brothers. But he still wasn't about to trust Boone Falconer.

"I always wondered why you helped me," Boone said softly.

"Then you understand why I'm wondering the same thing about you now. Yeah, I think you want something from me. I don't know any supernatural that does something without an eye on personal gain."

"What did you gain when you saved my brothers?"

"Let's not talk about me," Lokan said. "Let's talk about you. I'm not buying the whole payment of a debt act. So why did you bring me here, Boone?"

"I'd be happy to fill you in. Inside."

Why the hell not? At this point, he didn't have a ton of other options.

Lokan followed Boone along a hallway into a luxurious room done in dark colors and dim lights, a club within a club. There were three bartenders behind a gleaming bar and a number of patrons in rich leather booths. Boone kept going and Lokan followed down yet another hallway that cut off the main room. At the far end were metal doors covered in padded leather, and as they slid open, Lokan expected to see the inside of an elevator. Instead, he saw a second set of metal doors. Boone spoke his own name and leaned in for a retinal scan. The second set of doors slid open without a sound.

Lokan stopped walking. He could feel power and magic shimmering in the steel.

"What?" Boone asked with a glance over his shoulder. "I thought we already addressed your paranoia."

"Paranoid's my middle name." Lokan offered a tight smile. "I'm guessing that since the lock is attuned to your voice and retina on the way in, the same holds true on the way out."

"And?"

"How do I know I can get out when I want?"

For a second, Boone only frowned at him. Then he gave a short laugh. "You think this is some sort of prison? That once inside, you won't be able to get out?"

Lokan crossed his arms over his chest. "The thought did cross my mind."

"I was opening it for *me,*" Boone said, "not for you. You can enter and exit at will. These doors are no barrier to you. Open. Closed. You're playing by different rules at the moment, my friend."

"I tried walking away outside. I couldn't get more than a few feet."

Boone slanted him a glance through his lashes. "You're bound to the pyramid. Inside, you can move freely. Outside, you have a range of ten feet." Then he walked through the doors, which slid shut behind him, leaving Lokan alone.

Expecting to feel something cool and smooth, Lokan rested his fingers against the door. He felt nothing. He applied a little pressure, and his fingers passed right through until they were buried knuckle deep.

"No barrier." He huffed a sharp exhalation. "Like I'm a fucking ghost." The fact didn't exactly thrill him.

But what thrilled him even less was staying where he was with no solid plan for escape. At the moment, it looked as if Boone Falconer was his only option.

So he walked through the doors and found Boone waiting for him, seated beside a glass dining table that boasted a feast.

The smells were so potent—roast meat and spices, mushrooms sautéed in butter—they hit him with the force of a train and almost knocked him to his knees. Everything in him howled to leap forward and fall on the spread like a ravening beast.

"What's the price?" he asked, his voice sounding as if it belonged to someone else, terse and tense and angry. Desperate. Or maybe he just imagined those layers in his words because that was the way he felt. It embarrassed him, that desperation.

"You already paid the price," Boone said and met his gaze, guileless and open. "My life and the lives of my brothers. I owe you. This is payback."

Lokan nodded. He believed Boone but not fully. There was something else, something just beneath the surface. He had so many damned questions, the most important of which was about Dana. He ached to ask about his daughter, to find out if Boone had heard any mention of her. But he dared not alert him to her existence. And he doubted that there was any reason for a Vegas supernatural to have heard about a human girl in Oklahoma City.

"Sit, please," Boone said with a gesture at the table. As he moved his hand, it passed right through the bottle of wine.

Which told Lokan the food was in his dimension,

not Boone's. That only made the power of his hunger swell. But he held his place, wary still.

"You're bending dimensions. How?" Soul reapers could do it, but only to create portals that allowed them to travel between two points. What Boone was doing far surpassed Lokan's skill. Lokan narrowed his eyes. "What are you?"

"At the moment? Your host. Please, eat before it grows cold. Unless you'd prefer to shower first?"

Lokan hesitated a moment longer, then shrugged. Every moment he spent interrogating Boone was a moment that kept him from finding a way back to his daughter. So he slid into the unoccupied seat and piled his plate until it could hold no more. He almost attacked the meal, almost began shoveling food into his mouth like a barbarian. But that was not who he was. He was smarter than that, more careful. To put on such a display before a man who claimed to be an ally but might well be an enemy was foolishness. Why give him any more proof of weakness?

Instead, he forced himself to snap the pristine white serviette free of the neat folds, then lay it across his lap. He lifted the silver knife and fork and cut a moderate-size bit of beef. Slowly he raised it to his lips, his hand trembling a little. Then he put the food in his mouth and fought back a groan of relief.

He took his time, savoring each mouthful, while Boone chatted of small, inconsequential things.

The score of a baseball game. A pitcher's injured shoulder.

Lokan could feel himself healing, his emaciated body rapidly restoring itself as he ate. He worked his way through his meal, then loaded a second helping on his plate. But before he could begin on that, a wave of dizziness swept him, and his belly cramped as though a knife had settled clean and deep just below his breastbone.

His gaze snapped to Boone. Poison? He should have sensed it. He pushed halfway to his feet, the room spinning, his gut churning.

Boone held up his hands, palms forward. "There's nothing in the food, Lokan. It's just your stomach fighting against the unfamiliar."

The unfamiliar being food of any kind.

He knew Boone was right, but it didn't lessen his discomfort as sweat beaded on his forehead, and he felt as if he was going to toss every bite he'd just taken in.

And then he realized this was exactly why Boone had held off talking about anything important.

"You knew what the food would do to me."

"Been in your shoes a time or two. First time I jumped dimensions, I got caught for three weeks. Not pretty. I don't possess your healing capacity."

"You don't heal?" A tidbit to store away in case Boone proved to be an enemy in the end.

"I do. More slowly than you."

The dizziness began to pass, and the knot in his gut loosened.

"Damn, you look the worse for wear," Boone offered.

"Been a rough day."

"Day? I'd say it's been a rough few months."

Months. Was that how long he'd been dead? "And you know this because…?"

"Because word on the street travels. One of Sutekh's sons was murdered. He was tattooed and skinned, his skin sent to his father in a black plastic frame to prove his death."

"Got all up close and personal with the skinning," Lokan said, "but the black plastic frame's news to me." Why would Sutekh send a kill trophy to himself?

"Word on the street also had it that Sutekh's right-hand man was involved in the murder. What was his name?" Boone snapped his fingers, then pointed his index finger at Lokan, inviting an answer to the question.

"Gahiji," Lokan supplied. He remembered every detail of his murder in a series of clean, clear snapshots. He remembered every dark emotion as the layers were peeled away right along with his skin, and the depth of betrayal revealed. He leaned back in his chair, feigning boredom. "You're rehashing old news. Been there. Lived and died it."

"Sorry. Don't mean to bore you. How about I share something new then? Gahiji's lost his head."

Lokan squelched the urge to sit forward and betray his surprise. "My brothers' handiwork?" He wondered if they had suffered Sutekh's wrath for that.

"Not according to rumor. At this point, the finger of responsibility seems to be directed at your father."

Again, Lokan masked his surprise. That actually made sense. A little thing like loyalty and millennia of faithful service wouldn't stop Sutekh from killing his right-hand man. Hell, it hadn't stopped him from killing his own son. But Sutekh was the one who had ordered Gahiji to kidnap Dana and use her as leverage to make Lokan complicit in his own death. Why kill Gahiji for doing what he'd been told to do?

In answer to Lokan's unspoken questions, Boone shrugged. "It appears that Sutekh killed Gahiji to defray suspicion, make it appear that he had been acting on his own. Then he made a public production of blaming everyone else for your death."

"Ah." That explained the tattooed skin in the frame. A smokescreen to hide Sutekh's culpability until he was ready for it to be revealed. Maybe even a tool to get the other Underworld gods and demigods pointing fingers at each other and betraying alliances. Typical of Sutekh. He was very good at setting things up so he created mayhem without taking the blame.

"Not feeling chatty today?" Boone asked. "I'd have thought you'd be starved for conversation."

He was, but he said, "You'd have thought wrong.

I talk when I have something to say." And right now, he was more interested in listening. "You know some fascinating things, and you seem inclined to share. Far be it from me to turn off a free-flowing tap."

Boone stared at him for a long moment, his expression familiar, but not. Lokan felt as though he had seen that look before, not when Boone had been a child, but more recently. He just couldn't think where.

"Your father called a meeting of allies and revealed your—" Boone lifted his upturned palm "—remains before the crowd."

"He unveil anything else?" *Anyone* else? Dana. Every cell in his body hummed with anxiety as he waited for Boone's reply.

Shadows moved in Boone's eyes. "Anything in particular you're thinking of?"

He knew something. Lokan was sure of it, but he didn't dare prod. One mention of Dana, and the whole of the Underworld could find out about her.

Lokan offered a one-shouldered shrug. "Just trying to get an accurate picture. So what was with the big reveal?"

"Apparently, he planned to inhabit your corporeal form and wanted an audience when he demonstrated his supremacy."

"Inhabit my corporeal form. A nice term for body snatching." Lokan didn't know why that shocked him. His father had killed him. There had to have been a reason for that. Stealing his body was as good a one as any. "My brothers know what he did? They stopped him?"

"Yes."

Though he'd asked the question, he hadn't actually expected that answer. Even combined, his brothers' power was no match for their father's. "And somehow sent my body back to me. How?"

"The blood of Aset. The blood of Sutekh. And the God will pass the Twelve Gates and walk the Earth once more."

The words meant nothing to him, yet Lokan thought they ought to. "Is that a riddle?"

Boone's gaze was intent. "A prophesy."

"That doesn't explain how they got my body to me." He waited for Boone to offer an explanation, and when all he did was shrug, Lokan continued. "But it does tell me why Sutekh wanted it. He was going to fulfill that prophesy, break the six-thousand-year-old agreement that saw him confined in the Underworld, use my body to go Topworld."

"That would be my guess."

"But every other god and demigod would still be bound to the Underworld. His power would be immeasurable."

"A prize worth killing his son for," Boone said softly.

A reason for having a son in the first place. The realization slammed into him, stealing his breath. All along, he and his brothers had thought Sutekh sired them so they could be his emissaries Topworld

or to other Underworld territories. But maybe that
hadn't been it at all. Maybe he'd created four sons
knowing all along that he was only waiting for the
moment when he could steal one of their bodies.

How long had he planned this? And why Lokan?
Why use him over the others?

He didn't bother asking the questions aloud.
Boone wouldn't have answers. There was only one
place to find them: Sutekh.

"That part about the Twelve Gates," Lokan
mused. "I can't see Osiris letting Sutekh take a stroll
through his Territory, and the magical binding of the
cease-fire agreement prevents it." Lokan tried to read
Boone's expression.

"But you're not bound by the same rules," Boone
pointed out, then he gestured to the dishes Lokan
hadn't yet sampled. "Please, help yourself."

"So you're saying what?" Lokan asked suspi-
ciously as he loaded his plate yet again. The cramps
he'd experienced earlier were gone, and he was rav-
enous once more. "That you know a way out?"

"You already have that. The Twelve Gates."

"Been there, thanks. Didn't go so great. Almost
got eaten by a snake." He took a bite of chicken in
apricot sauce, chewing slowly, savoring every subtle
flavor. "You got an alternative?"

"No." Boone smiled, but there was something off
in his expression. Something regretful, even…sad.
"But I do have a guide who can lead you through."

"A guide…" Lokan's words trailed off as it hit

him. That smile, the way the shadows hit Boone's eyes. Familiar, but not.

The sense of recognition he felt left him thinking he was completely losing his mind.

BRYN SAT BESIDE THE HOTEL ROOM bed and watched her daughter sleep. Dana's arms were flung wide, her head turned to one side. Flopsy was tucked against her cheek.

A bright stripe fell across the carpet as the door behind her opened. Then the door closed and the light disappeared, leaving her and Dana in darkness once more. But they weren't alone. He didn't make a sound, but she knew Jack was standing behind her, watching her watch Dana.

"I'm sorry," he said.

She believed him. She was sorry, too, more sorry than she could ever say. But she'd listened to all he had to say, and she knew he was right. She had no choice but to go. For so long, she'd run and hidden, used her talents only when she absolutely had to in order to keep Dana safe, used them to hide from Jack and anyone else who might be hunting her.

But her talents weren't enough anymore. Not with Sutekh doing the hunting.

Funny that the safest place for Dana now was in the care of the exact people who Bryn had spent seven years hiding from. And the only way to keep her safe was for Bryn to leave her with them.

Turning her head, she looked at Jack over her shoulder.

"You'll keep her safe. You won't force her to become what I was. You won't let the others force her to do anything she doesn't want to do. You'll make certain she has a choice and that she isn't coerced."

Jack offered a shallow nod.

This time, she didn't ask for the words. She didn't have to. She could read his heartbreak and regret in every tense line of his body, and she could read the sincerity in his eyes.

"You knew where I was all along, didn't you?"

"Yeah, we did."

She huffed a short laugh, devoid of humor. "Why didn't you tell me? Why did you let me go on thinking I'd escaped?"

For a long time, he said nothing. And when he did speak, his voice was soft. "Because you did escape, Brynja baby. When you ran, we finally got it. We held on too tight. We chased you away. We lost you." He paused. "And we regretted that more than I can say."

Tears pricked her lids, and she blinked against them, unwilling to let them fall. If she started crying, she'd never stop.

"The best we could hope for was that you'd come back when you were ready," Jack finished. With a nod, she turned back to her daughter, her heart twisting in a knot. She had this final night to watch her sleep.

CHAPTER TEN

*Come then, O thou traveler, who dost journey
in Amentet.*

— The Egyptian Book of Gates

The Underworld

LOKAN WOKE TO DARKNESS AND A raging hard-on.

He'd dreamed about Bryn, which made no sense because soul reapers didn't dream. The fevered imaginings he'd had in the null zone didn't count. They weren't dreams, they were more like…memories.

Maybe that explained it. He hadn't been dreaming of Bryn; he'd been *remembering* her, remembering the incredible sexual connection he'd had with her that night in Miami.

He'd spent months hunting for her, on and off. He'd searched, then told himself to forget about her, then searched a little more. There were no bank records, no car ownership, no credit cards. He had to wonder how she managed to exist in a world that was so focused on records. It turned out that finding her had been a hell of a lot harder than he'd imagined.

It had been a cookie that led him to her. He'd stopped at a coffee shop in Cincinnati, and he'd spotted a pile of cookies under a glass dome. One bite, and he'd known who'd baked them. Which was ridiculous. But he hadn't been able to shake the certainty. So he'd staked out the place until the next delivery was made. Then he'd followed the trail to the source, the baker who shipped to a bunch of coffee shops. Tracking her down hadn't been easy. It was as if she didn't want to be found, by anyone.

And when he *had* found her, it hadn't just been her anymore.

HE STOOD ON THE SIDEWALK, across the street and three houses up. Bryn was sitting there, looking down, her face veiled by the shiny, dark curtain of her hair. At first he thought she had no clue he was there. But after a moment, she lifted her head and her eyes met his, and he knew then that she'd been aware of him all along.

And that his presence here terrified her.

He had a second's disorientation. What the hell had he ever done to make her afraid?

Then he noticed exactly what it was that she'd been looking down at. A gray-and-white baby stroller.

His heart kicked up a notch.

Her eyes widened. A jolt of understanding arrowed deep and rocked him to the core. And he knew.

That baby was his. Bryn had given birth to his child.

Impossible.

Soul reapers couldn't reproduce. He couldn't reproduce.

But he had.

She watched him as he crossed the street and walked closer, her expression flat and unreadable.

"Boy or girl?" That gruff question was all he could manage.

She hesitated, shoulders tense. He was sure she wasn't going to answer. Then she did. "Girl." Her voice was low, the word torn out of her.

A girl. He stared at her, words beyond him. He was the father of a baby girl. It took everything he had not to rush forward and lift the child from the stroller, to hold her in his arms and keep her safe.

The calm he forced into his next words was the opposite of the storm of emotion that roiled inside him. But he'd been trained to keep his emotions under control, regardless of circumstances. In this moment, he was glad for the endless hours he'd spent in his father's shadow, because he had a feeling that if he presented a face that was anything but calm, Bryn would bolt.

"Why didn't you tell me?"

"I never wanted you to know."

Her words pierced him with a sharp, unexpected pain. Never know his child? His own child. His mortal daughter would have lived, grown old, died, and he would never have known.

In that second, he thought he hated Bryn Carr.

*And if the look on her face was any indication, she
was feeling pretty much the same about him.*

*She didn't even try to claim that she'd had no way
to get in touch with him. And if she had, he would
have known it for a lie. He'd left contact information at the hotel where they'd spent the night, hoping she'd come back and make inquiries. Not really
believing she would. And not really knowing why he
even wanted her to.*

*"I don't expect anything from you." Her voice
was high, the words rushed. Her hands clenched,
white-knuckled on the handle of the stroller.*

*"I have a right to know her." He mastered his
shock, his anger, forced his tone to be reasonable,
even cajoling. "She's mine."*

*She sucked in a sharp breath, her head jerking
back as though she'd been struck.*

*"No." Her voice was soft. She met his gaze, her
eyes hard, her jaw set. Despite her panic and fear,
she was resolute. In that second, she didn't look like
the soft, warm, eager woman who'd spent a night in
his bed. She looked tough and determined. "She is
owned by no one. Not ever. She is going to grow up
to be her own person. She is going to grow up loved
and free. She will be strong and she will make her
own choices."*

*Her tone challenged him to argue. But he couldn't.
Wouldn't. Because everything she said was what he
wanted for his daughter. Their daughter.*

"Yeah," he said, and meant it. "She will."

Bryn's chest expanded as she took a deep breath. She stared at him for a moment longer, her expression sad and wary and suspicious, as though she was trying to see right into his head, to judge the truth of his words.

He thought she would continue to deny him, and he silently spun a thousand arguments and pleas as the seconds passed. She wanted to send him away; that was abundantly clear. But something—maybe the sincerity that had colored his words—made her change her mind. She turned the stroller so he had a clear view of the baby sleeping inside, her arms flung wide, her tiny lips moving in a sucking motion.

Then his daughter opened her eyes—her denim-blue eyes—and looked straight at him.

His heart shattered into a million pieces, then reformed with her image at its core.

"You can visit," Bryn whispered, the words laced with resentment and pain. And still, a hint of fear. For some reason, that hurt. Ridiculous. He was a soul reaper, a creature of death and destruction. She should *be afraid of him.*

But he didn't wanted her to be.

"On a schedule," she continued. "You can come and see her on certain days. With me supervising. And you can't hold her yet. Not till I'm sure you know how to support her head. Or change her diaper. Well, maybe after a while. But first, you need to watch me and see how I do it. And she needs to sleep a lot. You can't wake her up. And—"

"There's the Bryn I first met. I wondered where she'd gone."

She stared at him, two faint vertical lines between her brows. He wanted to reach out and smooth them away, to tell her she had nothing to fear from him. That he would never let any harm come to either of them. Her lips parted. For a second, he thought they could talk, she could explain why she hadn't contacted him, they could figure out whatever it was that made her afraid.

Then she lowered her gaze, and her shoulders tensed once more.

"The Bryn you first met is gone. She made too many mistakes. This Bryn has to be smarter. She has someone else to think about now." She lifted her eyes to his once more, and her emotions were shuttered. "You can see her on a schedule," she repeated.

He could argue, but the politician his father had trained him to be stepped to the fore. Form a plan. Watch. Evaluate. Revise. Instead, Lokan offered a short nod and said, "Fine."

LOKAN GRABBED THE MEMORY AND held it close. Every recollection that returned to him had immeasurable value.

That had been the beginning of their truce. They'd been polite and pleasant to each other for almost seven years. Hell, he would even go so far as to say they'd come close to being friends. But he never saw the sexy, free, unfettered Bryn he'd met that first night again. She was walled up behind a barricade so thick and high that he had no hope of breaking through.

Oh, she'd chatted with him easily enough. They'd even gone on outings together, taking Dana to the movies or the zoo. There had been a time or two over the years when he'd caught her unawares, and for a fleeting instant he'd thought he wanted to kiss her, and he'd thought she might want him to. But those moments always passed. And Bryn never let him scratch even a millimeter below the surface of her shell. She made it clear that the only thing uniting them was Dana.

His baby.

His little girl. He would do anything to keep her safe. He *had* done anything to keep her safe.

He'd died for her.

Now, he needed to live for her. He needed to get back to her because his death had bought her a brief instant in time, and nothing more. He'd agreed to let his father murder him in exchange for a blood oath that Dana would not be harmed.

But he wasn't about to trust Sutekh's blood oath.

The first step on the road to getting back Topworld was finding the guide Boone had promised him.

He glanced around, but the darkness was thick and opaque. His soul reaper vision meant he could see in the dark as well as he did in the light, so the fact that he was blind made him edgy. He strained to see some hint of light, and when nothing appeared, he stopped trying, cleared his thoughts, changed his focus and his breathing. He forced himself to be calm, to be patient, to look inward rather than out.

He'd learned a great deal about patience while he'd been trapped in the null zone. He'd learned that all the patience he'd thought he'd gained by sitting at his father's right hand and negotiating with other deities on his father's behalf had been an illusion.

Gradually, the darkness faded, black to gray, and finally, a sepia-toned brown that colored his surroundings. There were mountains in the distance and stretching before them, a flat, open terrain of sand, sand and more sand.

The Luxor wasn't there. No surprise. The air felt different. He knew he wasn't Topworld—or even confined to a dimensional box that bordered Topworld—anymore.

Turning his head, he saw a falcon on a billowing cloth, amber eyes alert and wary, brown feathers ruffling in the wind.

"Gotta ask—" even though he was fairly certain he already knew the answer "—you wouldn't happen to be the guide…"

With a cry, the bird took flight, soaring to the sky.

"Guess that'd be a 'no.'"

And then there was no sky, no mountains, no sand. He was alone in a place that was gray on gray, rock and stone, and he was lying on his back on a cold slab, his arms crossed over his chest. Like a corpse.

He pushed to a sitting position and took a quick inventory. He was clean. He was dressed in the plain black khakis and black T-shirt that had been left for him in the bathroom where he'd showered. He couldn't begin to calculate the expenditure of power that had allowed Boone to shift an entire bathroom, complete with toiletries, clean clothes and towels into a dimensional box.

That only made him all the more suspicious of Boone's reasons. Payback was one thing, but the guy had pushed the bar so high it was hovering in the stratosphere. There was something else going on here.

A current pulsed in the air, and Lokan had the feeling he was about to find out what.

He reached for the crackle of electricity that fizzed and bubbled, and he tried to decipher which direction it was coming from. He felt the energy on his skin and in his bones, sparking through the cells of his tissues.

Someone was definitely here. But he couldn't say where, exactly. And the signature wasn't one he recognized. Whatever supernatural shared this space with him, it wasn't one he'd encountered before.

He rose, turned, but saw nothing except gray rock and shadows.

Then he did see something. Dark on dark. A shadow in the far corner that shifted slightly to the left.

If it was the guide he'd been promised, there was

no reason for subterfuge. And if his hidden companion wasn't the guide, then he was a potential threat.

Lokan forced himself to sit back down on the stone slab and wait. He'd let his opponent show his hand rather than tip his own.

Again, the current of air shifted, the sensation so faint he might have missed it if he wasn't so attuned to it. Whoever was out there was edging closer.

The silence was deafening.

Closer. Just a bit closer.

He surged to his feet.

One hand found his opponent's throat, the other closed on a wrist. His pulse pounded and blood rushed loud in his ears. The urge to thrust his hand through muscle and bone, to close his fingers around a still-beating heart, was nearly overwhelming. There was a cauldron of anger and resentment and hate inside him, bubbling and hissing. A kill strike would pacify his personal demons, at least for a little while.

The far more rational choice of subdue and question was only a faint glimmer at the edge of his thoughts. He reached for that option, forced himself to take that path.

With a jerk and a twist, he spun his captive to face away from him, arm wrenched high into the shoulder blade. There was a sharp inhale, followed by a feminine cry.

And then it hit him. The form was small and

curved, with a sweet, round ass that was pressed against his groin.

A fragrance teased his senses.

Vanilla.

"No fucking way. No *fucking* way." He let go, jumped back, his breath coming in harsh rasps, his thoughts spinning.

He stood there, panting, every rational thought screaming that this was impossible.

"Lokan," she whispered as she turned and lifted her gaze to his, rubbing the wrist he'd just released.

"You're—" *You're not really here.* That's what he was going to say. Except, she *was* here. Gut instinct screamed that she was.

"Bryn," he rasped, an ugly knot twisting in his chest. Fear swamped him, naked and barbed and poisonous. If Bryn was here— "Where's Dana? Did he get her? Is she—"

She laid her hand on his forearm, her touch electric. It brought home to him the fact that no one had touched him in a very long while.

"Tell me." The command almost choked him.

"She's fine. She's safe." Just hearing those words made the knot ease, even though logic screamed that she was wrong. "She—"

"What?"

"She misses you," Bryn said, and Lokan felt as if she'd shoved her hand in his chest and laid bare his heart. The words were both an agony and a gift.

"Where is she?" he managed, his voice strained

and tight. "Tell me he didn't get her. Tell me Sutekh doesn't have her."

Bryn hesitated, and he felt as if he'd been injected with liquid nitrogen, the blood freezing in his veins.

"Bryn—"

"She's with my brothers."

Her brothers. It took him a second, and then he remembered a conversation they'd once had, the night he first met her. She'd said she had three brothers. But in the seven years since, she'd never mentioned them again, not once. And neither had Dana. Which made him think Dana had never met her uncles on her mother's side, just as she'd never met her uncles on her father's side. Lokan hadn't dared let anyone know about her.

But why hadn't Bryn brought her brothers into her daughter's life?

"And Dana was okay with that? Being left with strangers?"

He'd hit the mark. A flicker of surprise gave her away. But she rallied quickly and said, "She took to Jack right off. He brought Flopsy back to her and she just lit up like fireworks, all bright and sparkly." She swallowed, and her expression darkened. "I didn't have a choice, Lokan. I wouldn't have left her if there had been a choice."

"There's always a choice." He shook his head, feeling as if his brain was chugging at half speed. "They won't be able to keep her safe."

Her expression hardened. "They'll do their

damnedest. And they'll do a better job than anyone else I could think of."

"The number I gave you. The Daughters of Aset—"

"Helped me get Dana back when she was taken by the cult of Setnakht." She was so tense, she was shaking. "It's done, Lokan. Dana is with my brothers. There's no sense hashing out other options now because I can't go back and change it. And the truth is, I wouldn't. I believe my brothers are our daughter's safest bet."

He felt as if he was looking at a stranger. She sounded hard and cold and certain. She didn't sound like Bryn and—

He frowned, trying to get his head around everything she'd said and the fact that she was here at all. "Bryn, what the fuck are you doing here?"

Her brows shot up. Okay, not the words he should have chosen, but they were out there now, and they got the job done.

"I'll explain. I promise. We'll have lots of time to talk on the way," she said.

"The way to where?"

"I have questions for you, too. But not now. Now, we need to go."

"Dana—"

"Is safe. I swear it. You need to trust me on this."

"She's safe? Bryn, you have no idea what might be after her." Sutekh. A god so vile he would skin and dismember his own son. The fact that Dana was his granddaughter wouldn't protect her. And it was Lokan's fault that Bryn didn't know any of that because he'd chosen not to tell her, not to prepare her. "There is nowhere safe."

"There is. At least temporarily. Until you can get back." She reached out, but just before her fingers connected with his arm, she curled them into a fist and dropped her hand. "Are you…okay?"

And that almost made him laugh. Chatty Bryn, and the best she could come up with was that?

"Yeah," he said and just let himself look at her.

The sight of her was a balm to the wounds deep inside him, and he had no idea why he felt that way. He looked at her, and he saw a plate of cookies and a glass of cold milk. He heard his daughter's laughter. He felt warmth and a room filled with…love. The thought made him uncomfortable. Or maybe he was just picking up the vibe of her discomfort. She looked wary, uneasy, as she glanced around, her gaze sharp as she took in their surroundings. The way she did it made him think she was looking for something in particular, and that she was damned nervous about being here.

"I thought you were dead," she said, looking everywhere but at him. There was a hitch in her voice that reached into his chest and twisted a tight knot.

I was dead. In some ways, I still am. But I'm going to find a way to undo that.

Her gaze returned to his, her eyes shimmering with unshed tears. He had the urge to rub his thumb along her lower lashes, to catch those tears and taste them.

"You crying for me?" he asked, startled by the possibility.

"I'm not crying." The tip of her tongue darted out to wet her lips.

He didn't think, then. He only acted.

Curling his fingers around the back of her neck, he pulled her against him. She didn't resist. Instead, she leaned into him and breathed deep.

"You smell like you," she whispered. "I mean, the soap smells different than the one you always use. But underneath, you smell like you."

"Like key lime pie?" he asked, his voice rough and low.

She shook her head. "Like you."

The sound of her voice and her skin warm under his fingers made him think things he had no business thinking.

But he'd lived what felt like an eternity in the null zone, feeling nothing but his own pain. And now here was Bryn in his arms, not just in his memories. He could feel her skin against his palm, and her body pressed to his, soft and warm.

He could smell the scent of her skin, hear the faint rasp of her breathing, a little shallow, a little fast. If he leaned in just a bit he'd be able to taste her. Proof of life. Proof she was real.

Proof that he really wasn't alone anymore.

"Fuck." The word tore from him as his thoughts and emotions collided.

Then he lowered his head and his mouth found hers.

CHAPTER ELEVEN

*I make to go back the Bark of the Duat which
beareth my forms, and verily I travel into the
hidden habitation to perform the plans which
are carried out therein.*
                            —The Egyptian Book of Gates

BRYN FROZE, TAKEN UNAWARES AS Lokan dragged her
tighter against him and kissed her. Hard. Hungry.
He kissed her as if she was the fount of life and he
was near death.

And for an endless second, she let him. It felt so
good, his mouth on hers, his heart pounding beneath
her palm where it rested against his chest.

His heart.

Alive.

He was alive. He had body and substance, and he
was here and she'd thought he was gone forever.

His lips were firm and warm, and she let herself
drown in the kiss, knowing she shouldn't, knowing she should pull away. When he was the one who
dragged his mouth from hers, she choked back the
urge to grab hold and pull him back.

"I'm sorry," he whispered, his voice ragged.

"Sorry for kissing me?"

He didn't answer. Maybe he was sorry for dying. For leaving Dana with only Bryn for protection. For lying about so many things.

He'd lied to her about who and what he was for seven years. He'd told her he was human. Of course, she'd known he was a supernatural, and eventually, she'd figured out he was a soul reaper. But she'd never suspected that he was Sutekh's son.

His lies had put Dana in danger. She should hate him for that alone. But if she did, she'd have to hate herself, as well. Because her lies were no better.

"Lokan," she whispered, not even sure what she wanted to say. She tipped her head back to look at him, and with a groan, he kissed her again, and she tasted an edge of desperation mixed with his power and need. It was unlike any kiss they'd ever shared— not the heated melding of the first night they'd met, or the kiss of a friend he'd occasionally bestowed on her cheek during the years he'd spent time with her and Dana.

She wanted to bury her hands in his hair and open herself to him and just stay like this while his kiss fed the parched edges of her soul.

She let him kiss her because he'd been gone, dead, and she'd been forced to face the part of herself that had mourned him.

So she pressed her palms to his chest and felt the drum of his heart while his mouth moved on hers, stirring lust in her blood and emotions in her heart. She almost let herself drown in the taste of him, the feel of his hard body, the fact that he was here and she was real and he was touching her as he'd touched her once, that long ago night.

Almost.

But not quite.

Because if she let herself feel those emotions, all would be lost. If she opened to him even a little, she would shatter; she would break. But if she held herself apart, this would be easier. At the end, when she had to let him go, it would be easier.

She told herself that, though she knew it was one more lie that she layered on the many.

She'd made so many mistakes. This wasn't going to be another.

After a moment, he drew his lips away and rested his forehead against hers, his breathing ragged. Her own panting breaths were the sole outward indication of the storm his kiss had churned in her soul.

Then he lifted his head and stared down at her, blue-gray eyes so like their daughter's.

His hair was longer than she was used to, falling in ragged spun-gold layers. Tiny lines that hadn't been there before etched the corners of his eyes. In the seven years she'd known him, he'd never changed, never aged. And he still didn't look any older, just…harder. Honed. Almost gaunt.

Without thinking, she lifted her hand and dragged the backs of her knuckles along his cheekbone. Their gazes met, held, and the air left her in a soft huff as she dropped her hand and looked away.

"Boone said you looked like hell," she said, using the harsh words as a shield.

"Boone," Lokan echoed. "You're the guide." He shook his head and released an incredulous laugh. "You're a supernatural and I had no fucking clue."

He didn't sound happy about that. She couldn't blame him.

"I am."

"I thought Boone reminded me of someone. Then I thought I was crazy."

"You weren't."

"He's your…"

"Eldest brother."

Lokan stared at her, his expression unreadable. She couldn't imagine what he was thinking.

"Dana's with him?"

"And Jack and Cahn."

"Your other brothers."

She nodded.

"And how the hell are they going to keep her safe?"

"The same way they brought you to Vegas. They've pooled their power to create a dimensional box for her. Nothing can get in or out."

He was silent for a long moment. "That's a cage, Bryn."

Didn't she know it. It had been her cage for most of her life.

"It's the only place Sutekh can't get to her," she said. "She'll be safe there until you get back."

Lokan gave a dark laugh. "And when I get back? What then?"

"Then you take over. You keep her safe."

"Like I kept myself safe?" His tone was ugly, filled with self-derision. She was stunned to hear it. He didn't sound like Lokan, not the Lokan she knew.

"The sacrifice you made was for her," Bryn said. "Boone told me."

"Yeah? Boone seems to be well-versed in a lot of things. What else did he say?"

"That you were willing to die so Dana could live. That you traded your life for your father's blood oath that he wouldn't harm her."

He closed his hands on her upper arms. "My father's blood oath isn't worth shit." His gaze dipped, and he stared at his hands, then he dropped them as though touching her burned hotter than any fire.

"It was worth enough that Roxy Tam had the chance to rescue Dana," she said. "It was worth enough that our daughter came back to me whole and healthy."

"Because Sutekh didn't have use for her. Not yet. Don't fool yourself, Bryn. The second he believes that Dana can be of benefit to him, he'll take her. He'll use her. He'll kill her. It won't matter worth a damn that she's his granddaughter."

She knew that. It was the reason for every decision she'd made since Jack started talking that night in the park. Leaving Dana with her brothers had been the hardest thing she'd ever done. "Just like it didn't matter a damn that you were his son."

Lokan nodded, then frowned. "Who's Roxy Tam?"

"Asetian Guard. She's the one they sent when I called the number you gave me."

"So they did help you. I hoped they would. It was all I could come up with under the circumstances." He offered a shadowed smile, one that hinted at what he had suffered that night.

The molecules in the air around them hummed and vibrated. Anxiety kicked up a notch, leaving her chest tight and her nerves raw. There was no more time.

"We need to go." She forced herself to step away from him.

He closed his hand around her upper arm again, not tight enough to hurt, just enough to hold her in place. "Bryn—"

"No, we—" She froze, her attention snared by the wall directly behind him. The rock appeared to be melting, its form surging forward even as it pulled back, like an oozing slug. She dipped her head in that direction, and when he glanced back at it, she said, "We need to go. I need you to trust me."

"Trust you?" He raised a brow. "I'm afraid my well of trust's just about dry."

Because he'd been betrayed by his father? Or because he knew she'd been lying to him all along? They were questions that would have to wait.

He followed her gaze to where the wall was morphing and transforming into a convoluted and twisted shape. "I'm not following you blindly. I can't. You need to give me something, Bryn. Anything."

She understood that. He was the one who had always been in control, the one who could stay calm under even the most intense pressure. She couldn't imagine what it had been like to be betrayed by all sides, to be murdered by his father, to lose all semblance of control.

"Where we are right now? It's a temporary gateway that Boone and Jack created, a doorway to where we need to get to," she said. "They needed a neutral place where I could find you. They can only hold it so long, and Boone's already running on empty because it cost him a great deal to get you to Vegas so he could have a conversation with you. On top of that, they're focused on keeping Dana safe. This place—" she gestured at the walls "—doesn't exist. It isn't even a dimensional box. It's just a doorway fashioned by thought and will, and it's coming apart. If we don't leave before it does, we'll come apart right along with it."

"That's a bit more than 'something,'" he said, one side of his mouth lifting in a wry twist.

She couldn't help but smile because he'd listened to her with that way he had, making her feel as if every word she spoke mattered. No one else had ever listened to her like that.

Reaching down, he grabbed a black backpack that

she assumed Boone had given him, and slung it over his shoulder. Then he caught her hand. "Follow me."

"No," she said. "You follow me. It's why I'm here."

She half expected him to argue. He was the leader, she the follower. Only once before had she stood up to him, the day she'd told him he could see Dana only on her terms. She'd never stood up to him again. Maybe because she'd exhausted her store of bravery that once. Or maybe because he'd never put her in a position where she'd felt threatened. When it came to Dana, he was always perfectly reasonable, and all their interactions revolved around their daughter.

But right now, she needed to lead. She needed to get them out of here.

A roaring sounded all around them, and the walls of the cave undulated. Their reunion was over.

"It's imploding." Bryn tugged hard on Lokan's hand. She turned and ran, feet pounding, heart hammering. Lokan kept pace beside her, his fingers holding tight to hers.

The walls pulsed, threatening to close in any second. The roaring grew so loud that the noise sent her hair whipping into her face and plastered her clothes against her body. The rock beneath their feet twisted and writhed like a living thing, making every step precarious.

Bryn shot a glance over her shoulder. Behind them, the cave closed in on itself. The rock rolled and curled, eating the ground seconds after their feet left the spot.

She refused to let fear overcome her, and she focused on each step, on the strike of her sole against the rock ahead of her rather than the void forming behind her.

As though he sensed her emotions, Lokan's grip on her hand tightened.

The roaring grew so loud, her eardrums felt as if they would burst. Cold clawed at her back. Ice formed on her skin, her lashes, and each labored breath puffed white.

Lokan was ahead of her now, dragging her along, his grip on her hand so tight she felt as if her bones might snap.

With the void surging at her heels, the rock beneath her feet gave a mighty heave, like a horse bucking against the weight of its rider. Her equilibrium tilted. Her stride broke, and her foot slid away into the icy darkness that chased them.

With a cry, she fell back. Her hand tore free of Lokan's grasp. She flung her arms wide, hands clawing at…nothing.

There was nothing to grab.

She was falling, falling, with only her terror and regret to cling to.

Zugspitze Mountain, Germany

DAGAN ARRIVED FIRST. HE stepped from the portal, leaving the bone-numbing chill behind, and turned to see Alastor come through and then Mal, with his arms wrapped firmly around Calliope. As the smoky, dark hole closed behind them, Calliope stepped away from Mal and went into sentry mode, doing a quick perimeter check.

They were on a landing that was at both the top and bottom of a flight of seven wooden stairs. Calliope gestured for the others to stay put, then she moved up the stairs, her back to the wall, and checked the next level up. Dagan leashed his annoyance; doing nothing while she took point grated like sandpaper, but this was her turf, and letting her evaluate the risks was the smartest option.

She moved like a wraith, soundless, blending with the shadows. He had to admire that.

She gestured to show the all-clear, and as her gaze settled on Mal, her expression softened just a little. The sight of that made Dagan's chest feel as if a weight was pressing on it. Her expression reminded him of the way Roxy looked at him. And he missed that. Missed her.

He'd spent his whole life without her, without knowing that he even had it in him to care about anyone the way he cared about her. Now she was gone and he wanted her back.

It was as simple and as complicated as that.

And he knew Alastor felt the same way. He and his brothers had a connection, not exactly a psychic link, but an ability to feel each others' pain and to sense when one was in trouble. So he could feel what Alastor was going through, and he knew Mal and

Alastor could feel his own turmoil. It wasn't something he was comfortable sharing, but there was no way around it, so he didn't waste energy wishing it were different.

Calliope gestured for them to follow her down the stairs, but Mal caught her arm and asked, "They know we're here?"

He was referring to the Matriarchs.

"Without a doubt," Calliope replied. "You—" her gaze slid from Mal to Alastor to Dagan and back "—can dampen your energy signatures. But I am a member of the Guard. They'll have picked up my vibe while I was still out on the mountain."

She jerked her head toward the stairs and started down with Mal at her back.

Dagan exchanged a look with Alastor. They'd argued that Calliope should be left behind and only the three brothers go in to rescue Roxy and Naphré. But Mal had agreed with Calliope that she had the inside track, and that made her their most valuable tool in this negotiation.

No arguing with fact.

So they were here, and she was here, and there was zero doubt in Dagan's mind that the Matriarchs knew it. The question was what would they do about it?

Alastor followed Mal down, and Dagan brought up the rear.

"You find it odd that there isn't a soul about?" Alastor murmured. "You'd think they'd put up at least a token protest to our incursion."

"Unless our incursion is exactly what they want."

Alastor's eyes narrowed. "Do you think she's leading us into a trap?"

"Leading us? No." A part of him wanted to suspect Calliope, but he'd come to know her a little, first through Roxy, then through Mal, and he knew that, though her loyalties were stretched between her lover and the Guard she'd blood-sworn her life to, she wouldn't betray Mal. She'd already proven that when she joined her blood with theirs and helped them to send Lokan's body to him in a null zone. What she'd done had to have gone against every instinct she had as a member of the Guard. But she'd done it for Mal.

"That doesn't mean there's no trap," he continued. "I just think that when it's sprung, she'll be stuck on the inside, with us."

"Well, that's encouraging."

They moved on in silence, the walls narrowing until Dagan had to twist a little to the side to fit his shoulders through. At the bottom, they bunched in single file. Sitting ducks.

Ahead of them was a steel door with a biometric scanner. Only problem was, the door was open.

"They're expecting us," Calliope said. "And they're inviting us in."

"Inviting us to tea or to slaughter?" Alastor's tone was crisp.

"Could be either one," she replied. "This door has a self-destruct mechanism. At least, that was the design at the compound in B.C."

"So you're saying that the second we walk through we might get blown to hell."

"I am."

"Roxy's here," Dagan said. "I can feel it." His gaze snapped to Alastor, who gave a sharp nod. Naphré was here, as well.

Shouldering past his brothers and Calliope, he forced each of them to press tight against the wall to create enough room for him to pass. Calliope cocked one dark brow a fraction of an inch but made no comment. He didn't hesitate, just stepped through into the hallway beyond the open door.

"Stop," Calliope ordered as he was about to continue along the narrow corridor to a second door. "Not another step or you'll make a mess of things."

Dagan hesitated. They'd brought Calliope along for exactly this reason, to warn them about pitfalls. But he couldn't see the risk here, and he wanted to move on. If anyone was going to get iced, it'd be him. He was the eldest. It was his job to keep the others safe, though they'd each argue that it was theirs. He already lived with the guilt of having failed Lokan. He wasn't about to let either of his other brothers down.

"For fuck's sake," Mal snarled and lunged forward to grab Dagan's forearm. "We brought her along because she knows things we don't, Dae. Stop being an asshole."

Dagan almost shook his brother off. Then he got his temper under control, gave a short nod and shifted to grasp Mal's forearm in return. "Asshole's my middle name."

"Don't I know it." Mal offered his pirate's smile, but it was a little strained around the edges.

Calliope and Alastor joined them, crowding them all together in what just might amount to their cremation chamber. But going back empty-handed wasn't an option, and this was the only way forward.

The door slid shut behind them, followed almost immediately by a faint click.

"And that was..." Mal prodded.

"The auto-destruct."

"Thought so." He stepped closer to Calliope, his chest resting against her back, as though he'd form a living shield between her and the blast, should it come. Which was exactly what Dagan would do if Roxy were here, what he planned to do the second he got her back by his side: stand between her and any threat.

But he had to admit a flicker of amusement when Calliope did exactly what Roxy would do: she gave Mal a look that dripped exasperation.

"We waiting for something special?" Dagan asked.

Calliope glanced at him. "Yes." And after a second she added, "This."

He felt it then, the first stirring of magic, damp tendrils that licked at his skin. They felt...off. Not quite dark magic and not quite light. A mixture of the two. Calliope watched him, her cat eyes green and cool. If the sensation of being tasted and touched bothered her, she wasn't letting on. He figured she'd been through this before; she'd said as much when she described what they'd face on their way to see the Matriarchs.

"Let's go," she said a moment later as the cloying touch of the spells receded. Then she headed along the hallway, taking the lead once more.

"No question about it now," Alastor murmured. "They know we're here."

"Can't wait to see what they have planned," Mal said with a grin.

"You're enjoying this." Calliope didn't sound surprised. Mal liked anything that gave him an adrenaline high. Walking into the lair of the enemy and facing security measures both technologic and supernatural definitely qualified.

"Did you notice these?" Alastor asked, jerking his chin toward the renderings on the stone walls, depictions of the Twelve Gates of Osiris.

"Yeah."

"Coincidence?" Mal asked.

"Doubt it," Dagan replied.

"The prophesy spoke of the blood of Aset, the blood of Sutekh and the Twelve Gates," Alastor said. "The Matriarchs could have chosen any delightful pictures to adorn their walls. But they chose these. Gotta wonder why."

They moved on with Dagan in the lead and came to a second steel door, this one open, as well. This time, no one hesitated. They stepped through in quick succession.

And slammed into a wall of glass.

Dagan spun. Too late. The door behind them was already shut. Mal snarled and threw himself against the metal.

They'd walked into a trap, right where their enemies wanted them.

And Calliope wasn't in there with them.

CHAPTER TWELVE

*This great god cometh to this gateway, and
entereth in through it, and the gods who are
therein acclaim him.*

—The Egyptian Book of Gates

The Underworld

LOKAN GRABBED THE FRONT OF Bryn's shirt and hauled
her up against him as he leaped back to avoid the
oozing darkness lapping at his toes. He spun, set her
on her feet, pausing only long enough to make certain she had her balance and snarled, "Run."

He was done with pretending to let her lead. He'd
lost everything. Even his life. He wasn't about to lose
her, too.

He clamped his fingers around her wrist and
dragged her along, feet pounding gray stone that
evaporated behind them, leaving nothing but endless void in their wake.

The path forked dead ahead.

"Which way?" He was already veering to the left.

"Right," Bryn ordered.

He couldn't afford to hesitate or question.

She was the guide Boone had sent him.

So he'd fucking well let her guide. But not lead.

He changed direction and they ran on. Was the stone beneath his feet more solid? He concentrated on each heel strike and decided that, yeah, it was. And the roaring behind them had dropped a decibel or two. He shot a look over his shoulder. The void had slowed, no longer eating the ground at their heels.

A moment later, when he checked again, it had slowed even more.

They rounded a corner, and the terrain changed. It seemed vaguely familiar—a corridor formed by massive stone blocks.

"Stop." Bryn tugged her arm, and when he didn't immediately free her, tugged harder, her breath coming in harsh rasps, her skin sheened with sweat. She dropped forward at the waist, resting her palms on her thighs as she hung her head and tried to catch her breath.

"We need to keep moving, Bryn."

She shook her head. "It's okay." She took another gasping breath. "It won't follow."

A look over his shoulder confirmed her assertion. The tunnel disappeared around the bend, and there was no sign of the void that had eaten everything behind them.

"Guess you were right about not going left," he said.

She turned her head and looked at him through the long, dark strands of her hair. A sharp image of his daughter superimposed itself in his thoughts. Dana loved to toss her hair forward and look at him through the golden strands. *Peekaboo.* Little girl laughter. The sudden wave of longing to see her caught him unawares. It stole his breath and twisted him up inside with true, physical pain.

"Here, in this place, I'll always be right," Bryn said, drawing him back to the moment. "This is the one thing I never make a mistake at."

There was something in her tone that made him edgy. Bitterness? Maybe. But something else.

"Yeah, about that…care to define 'one thing'? You want to tell me what the hell is going on? I've known you for nearly seven years, and the whole time it never dawned on you to mention that you aren't human?"

There it was, lying naked and ugly right in front of him. He had to wonder what the hell else she'd been lying to him about. He had to wonder about the ramifications of Bryn being whatever the hell she was. What did that mean for Dana?

But who the fuck was he to point fingers? He was a soul reaper, son of Sutekh. He had no idea what that meant for Dana's future, either.

Bryn pushed up to a standing position and looked at him dead-on, her eyes dark and flashing. If he reached out and touched her, would that fire singe him? He thought it might be interesting to find out. Bryn in a temper wasn't something he'd seen often. Ever. He'd never seen this in her. She was always just even-tempered, chatty Bryn. His safe place. The one place he didn't have to be "on," the one place he could just relax and *be*.

Damn, where had that thought come from?

He grappled with it, wrestled it away. It was on the tip of his tongue to tell her he'd missed her. Thought of her. Images of her had haunted him. He reached for her, but just as he was about to touch her, her wall snapped back in place. It was as though she'd taken a step away from him, even though she hadn't moved an inch.

Whatever he'd thought he wanted to say slithered back to the hole it had crawled out of. Better that way.

"I've known you for nearly seven years," she echoed, "and the whole time it never dawned on you to mention that you're a soul reaper? And not just any soul reaper, but Sutekh's son."

They stared at each other, a chasm of deceit and hurt between them. Finally, Lokan shrugged. "It never came up." He hadn't meant to say that.

Bryn nodded, her expression shuttered. "Ditto."

But they were both lying. Again. It *had* come up. How many times had she given him the opening to tell her about who and what he was, and he'd lied to her, let her believe he was a crime lord's son? Which he was, in a convoluted, twisted way. Just not a human crime lord.

He'd given her the same opportunities. But all she'd ever told him was that she was estranged from her family.

Yeah, there was an abyss of deceit yawning between them. And he didn't want their daughter to fall in and drown in the morass.

Their daughter...

"Is Dana—" he made a loose gesture "—whatever you are?" He already knew Bryn wasn't a soul reaper. They were invariably male. Or a fire genie—Xaphan's concubines gave off a specific energy signature, and they looked anything but human. She wasn't one of Izanami's Shikome—from all that he'd seen, they had no true form other than a draping of living, writhing centipedes and spiders and maggots.

She wasn't part of the Asetian Guard. He'd seen Bryn naked, and he knew she didn't bear the mark of Aset anywhere on her skin. In his capacity as emissary for Sutekh, he'd visited the realms of many of the other Underworld deities. He figured he knew more about the different supernatural entities than most, and she wasn't anything he'd encountered before.

Bryn cut him a glance through her lashes. "Dana is human." A simple statement that conveniently avoided an explanation of what Bryn was.

"I was human, too, Bryn, until I grew up. And I'm guessing so were you. She's human now. What about in ten or twenty years?"

She dipped her head as though the stone at her feet held the wonders of the world. "I don't know."

"You don't know, or you don't want to say?" Lokan asked, not willing to let it go. He caught her arm. She lifted her head, and in her eyes he saw a world of hurt. Worry. Fear.

"I don't know," she said again. "I only know that right now, she's human. And that means she's in danger. She can be killed. By your father. Sutekh." She spat the name as if it was poison. It was. Sutekh was poison.

"That's why I'm here, Lokan. Because you need to go back." Her tone was low and hard, and she barely paused for breath before she continued. "You need to keep her safe. You're the only one who can. Anyone else can try, but eventually, they'll fail. If Sutekh wants her, he'll get her. Unless you stop him."

Lokan felt as if she'd knifed him in the heart. "You think I don't want to protect her? You think I didn't spend every lucid second I had thinking of her, missing her, missing—" *You.* He almost said it; he caught himself just in time.

He'd missed Bryn. When the hell had she come to mean something to him? She was his daughter's mother. That's how he thought of her. Wasn't it? He thought of her as smiling and warm, smelling of vanilla, chatting with him as she prepared Dana's dinner, asking him to stay more often than not. He'd grown somewhat fond of homemade mac and cheese.

She was just…there. And he hadn't realized until this second, with her standing in front of him, jaw set, eyes flashing, that he'd taken her for granted.

He'd expected her to be an amazing mother. He'd expected that they'd get along perfectly well, her raising their daughter, him popping by like an overgrown playmate to light up Dana's day. Oh, he'd done his share of soothing Dana when she was ill, holding her when she was feverish, taking her to the dentist for her first checkup. But he'd *chosen* to show up for those things. He'd never had a moment's doubt that Bryn would have taken care of everything if he didn't happen to come by that day. That she *did* take care of everything when he wasn't around.

She wasn't just warm, chatty Bryn, his comfort zone. She was capable Bryn, who dealt with anything that got thrown at her. Even this.

And he wanted to touch her. Kiss her. Stroke her hair back from her temples and kiss her there.

Her pupils dilated, leaving him wondering if she was thinking along the same lines.

"What?" she asked. "Why are you looking at me like that?"

"Like what?"

"Like you're seeing me for the first time."

Maybe he was.

Seconds ticked past. He couldn't stop himself. He brushed his knuckles along her temple. She held perfectly still, and then she closed her eyes. Her breath hitched.

He wanted to kiss her. He wanted to do more than that. He wanted to press her down beneath him and tug her jeans down her hips and push himself inside her. Because that would be proof that he'd survived.

But if he pretended that was the only reason, then

he was the worst sort of liar. The sort who lied to himself.

He leaned in.

She opened her eyes and spun away. "Come on," she said. "We need to move. The window of opportunity is closing, and if we miss our chance, we're stuck here." She sent him an arch look. "How would that work for you, Lokan Krayl? Stuck here for eternity with only me for company?"

She didn't wait for his answer, only walked off along the corridor.

The stuck here for eternity part, not so much. The Bryn for company part—*that* was oddly appealing.

"I'VE BEEN HERE BEFORE," Lokan said after they'd walked along the tunnel for some time.

"When?" Bryn asked, stepping to the left to avoid a massive platter of stuffed pigeons sitting on a bed of saffron rice. The food of the dead. Not something she planned to eat.

Not until she had to.

Lokan traced his fingertips along one of the massive stone blocks that formed the tunnel wall. "Right before I got in the—" his head jerked up and he stopped dead in his tracks "—boat."

He pinned her with an incredulous look. "You aren't saying *this* is the way out? Been there. Tried that. Almost ended up as lunch for a snake."

Ahead of them were dual lines of souls and beyond them, a boat of papyrus reeds. Bryn didn't see the problem.

"Didn't Boone tell you that he was sending a guide to take you through the Twelve Gates?"

"And the only way through the gates is by boat?"

"You have something against boats?" she asked, just as a recollection flitted through her thoughts. A sunny day. Lokan. Dana. A ferry ride. Lokan had stood by the rail staring at the water, and he'd refused to let go of Dana's hand the entire time.

She reached for him, hesitated, then put her hand on his arm. His skin was warm beneath her touch, his muscles solid and strong. She stared at the fine gold hairs on his forearm, not sure why touching him felt so good. Her gaze lifted to his. "What's wrong?"

"Wrong? I'm Sutekh's son. This is the antechamber to Osiris's Twelve Gates. There's a little issue of Sutekh killing Osiris and hacking him to bits." He paused, and Bryn wondered if he was thinking about how his father had done the same thing to him. Her chest tightened at the thought of what he had suffered. "I only got out of here last time because your brother managed to create some sort of dimensional rift. Seems to me that going back for a second go isn't my best plan."

"It's the only one we have. I thought Boone explained that. And he's dealt with things. Made a deal. Osiris will do nothing to hinder you."

Lokan wasn't fooled by her careful choice of

words. "He'll do nothing to hinder me, but he won't exactly help."

"No. But if you can find your way through the gates, he'll not stand in your way."

"And Boone knows this because he's a psychic?" There was an edge to Lokan's tone. He didn't trust Osiris. She didn't blame him. His own father had betrayed him. Why would he believe that his enemy wouldn't do worse? And by extension, why would he believe her secondhand assurances?

"I can guide you through the Twelve Gates, Lokan," she said softly, wanting to say more. Not daring to say more. If she told him the whole truth, he would never go along with it. She knew that. Just as she knew there was no other way. "It won't be like your first try because I'll be with you. You failed in your first attempt only because you lacked the words," she said. "You had no scroll or spells or magics."

"And you have those things, Bryn? Where are you hiding them?" Lokan looked her up and down, making his point.

Then he blinked. Looked her up and down again, slower, his gaze lingering for an instant on her breasts. That was new. As was the sizzle his perusal ignited. She'd known him for nearly seven years. She'd eaten meals with him, gone on walks with him, sat on the couch watching the latest little girl craze on TV with him—always with their daughter in between. Never once had he looked at her like this, not since the first night in Miami. Never once had she felt…heat.

What the frack was wrong with her that here of all places, and now of all times, she was thinking about Lokan Krayl like *that?*

"I don't have those things." She rolled her lips inward, swiped them with her tongue. "I *am* those things. I carry the knowledge inside me."

He folded his arms across his chest. "Bryn, talk. Make it clear and concise, because I'm done with going around in circles." His lips turned a dark smile. "Which is actually amusing, coming from me. I'm usually the one talking circles."

"As Sutekh's ambassador."

His brows lifted. "Yeah. Boone tell you that?"

"Yes."

The silence stretched, and Lokan just stood there, waiting.

She felt the rock and the hard place crushing her from either side. Tell him the truth about how this journey would end, and he would refuse to go on. Refuse to explain and he would…refuse to go on.

Lying wasn't an option. She didn't want to lie to him, not again. She'd spent so long watching every word she said to him, lying by omission if not by commission. But she didn't want that between them now. She didn't want his last memories of her to be tainted by untruth. There were still so many things she didn't dare tell him, not yet. But she could tell him parts, and those parts, she'd make sure were true.

"I don't know everything about the way this works." She chose her next words with care. "My brothers kept me in the dark for a long time. They used my skills without explaining the source."

His eyes narrowed, but she held up her hand and shook her head. She'd long ago gotten over her anger at her brothers. But she'd never quite gotten over her anger at herself. She'd been such a stupid, naive girl, thinking that getting pregnant would solve all her problems.

It hadn't. It had only compounded them.

She'd gotten pregnant with one goal in mind: escape. But during her pregnancy, something had changed. She couldn't pinpoint the exact second. It had been a subtle shift. So she'd started to make plans and set things in motion.

Certainty hadn't crystallized the second she'd held Dana in her arms, or even the first time she'd fed her. Funny, but it had been the first time she'd changed her daughter's diaper. She hadn't known much about babies then. She hadn't even known if the diaper was wet. And the second she got it off, Dana had peed all over her hands. Then she'd opened her eyes, her denim-blue eyes, and offered a lopsided baby smile.

And that's when Bryn had fallen in love with her child.

She'd planned to hand her daughter over and then run. Instead, she'd bundled her up and run *with* her, learning along the way how to hide, how to cover her tracks. How to ensure that her brothers didn't find her.

How ironic that her brothers had known how to find her all along and had chosen not to. Even more ironic that the safest place for Dana right now was with Boone and Jack and Cahn, after Bryn had done everything possible to keep them from ever knowing about her daughter or ever being able to find her.

Lokan was watching her, waiting, expecting her to explain things she didn't dare tell him. But, no, that wasn't quite true. They were things she didn't dare *not* tell him. He needed to know. For Dana's sake.

"I am a guide of souls. A psychopomp. Not in the Jungian sense. I mean I'm not a mediator between the conscious and unconscious. Though I suppose if you made a stretch you could argue there is some relevance to that because I can walk through dreams sometimes. Not all dreams, just—"

"Bryn," he said and lifted his brows. Just that. Her name. The way he said it, laced with affection and amusement and some other ingredient she couldn't quite place, sent a little shiver dancing across her skin.

She stared at him for a second and then realized that old habits died hard. She was talking to fill space, to mask her nervousness, which only served to accentuate it.

"Sometimes, I can walk in the dreams of others, but that isn't the most important thing. I am a walker. I can guide souls to the Underworld." And for once, she managed to keep it short and sweet. She didn't elaborate, didn't tell him that she could tear her soul from her body and go even a step beyond that. That she could tear herself in two. There was no reason to reveal all her secrets, and every reason not to.

"A walker," he mused. "A psychopomp."

Something in the way he said that made her ask, "You've heard of my kind?"

"Of walkers? No. Of psychopomps, yes. That's what Valkyries are, right? They guide the dead to Valhalla. And Shinigamis. So, a walker is something like that?"

She nodded.

"And your brother, Boone, he's…a walker?"

She shook her head. "No. Only females." And that was the reason she'd run all those years ago. Because she could do what Boone and Jack and Cahn couldn't. She had a skill they lacked, one so valuable that they'd locked her away in a figurative cage—and at times they deemed dangerous, in a literal cage— and taken her out only to use her particular skills. She'd been pampered and protected. And stifled. Owned. But those were also things she chose not to say, not right now when she needed Lokan to trust Boone's help.

Her role in her brothers' hierarchy was what she had run from. The life she'd known was not the one she wanted for her daughter. But the safest place for Dana right now was with Bryn's brothers. Until Lokan got free.

Lokan only stared at her, his gaze intent. She felt as if he was seeing things she didn't want him to see, reading the truth of her motivations that long ago night in Miami.

She couldn't bear for him to know that she'd gotten pregnant with the specific goal of offering up her daughter in her place. The truth of that was horrific.

"And Dana?" he asked.

She gasped, then realized he had no idea where her thoughts had strayed.

"I told you already. I don't know. I don't know if she'll be like me. I don't know what the union of soul reaper and walker will produce."

"Not just a soul reaper," he pointed out softly. "Sutekh's son."

She hated that truth, hated it with all she was. But she couldn't change it. She could only move forward. She could only do everything she could to make certain that Dana stayed safe. And that meant getting Lokan out of here. Back to the Topworld. Back to their daughter.

"Okay. Let's focus on what you do know." He sounded calm, rational, despite the fact that her revelations had to be tripping him out. "Just tell me how you're going to get us out of here without a map."

His word choice didn't escape her. He didn't ask how she thought she'd get them out, but rather how she *would* get them out. "You sound as though you believe I can do it."

"I do. I just want a rundown of the mechanics." He

paused. "In the seven years I've known you, Bryn, I've learned that you don't claim to do something unless you really can do it. Remember the train cake?"

She did. For her fourth birthday, Dana had wanted a cake in the shape of a train. Not just a train on the cake, or a flat train-shaped cake, but a 3-D train complete with engine and caboose and tracks. And Bryn had done it. She'd said she would and she did. She'd never thought it was a big deal. She was surprised Lokan even remembered it.

"It was a cake," she said, her voice flat. "I'd say this is a little more challenging than that."

"Challenging or not, my point is that you don't make claims without delivering." He smiled at her, white teeth, blue eyes, so handsome he took her breath. It took her a second to process his words. To understand that the glow warming her from the inside out wasn't just because of his smile but because he had faith in her, believed in her, without even knowing all she truly was capable of. Funny how much that meant.

"Tell me how you're going to get us out," he repeated.

"You mentioned Valkyries…I am of the line of the Valkyrie Kára."

"So you're a Valkyrie? You're going to fly me to Valhalla? How is that an improvement over where we are?"

She opened her mouth. Closed it. Everything in her rebelled at giving him the power that he would find in the knowledge of what she was. But she needed to tell him. He needed to know what Dana might become. There would be no way for him to protect her if he didn't know.

"I am also of the line of the grandniece of Izanami-no-mikoto, a shinigami," she said.

"Okay." He frowned. "So you're a shinigami and a Valkyrie?"

She'd been taught never to reveal the truth. She'd been indoctrinated with the need to keep it only between herself and her brothers.

And now she was going to trust Lokan Krayl, soul reaper, son of Sutekh, with her secret. She was going to trust the man who had lied to her since the moment he met her. Because he needed to know. He needed to know why every Underworld deity would be hunting Dana if she became what her mother was. He needed to know in order to properly protect their daughter.

Still, she couldn't make herself speak the words. So she dropped yet another hint. "And I'm descended from Pinga."

By his expression, she saw that it took him a second to place the name, and when he did, he said, "Inuit goddess who guides the newly dead." He was silent for a long moment, and his expression grew shuttered and cool. *Click.* She almost thought she could hear the pieces snap together in his mind.

His eyes narrowed. "Anyone else?"

Trust Lokan to home in on the key point.

"*Everyone* else," she said, meeting his gaze, knowing that her answer didn't surprise him now. "Name a spirit guide, and I can trace my heritage back to them. I'm a melting pot. I have a patchwork quilt of Underworld deities in my genetic pool."

"Spell it out, Bryn." But she didn't need to. He already knew.

She crossed her arms and rubbed her palms up and down along her upper arms until Lokan reached out and caught her wrists, stilling her movements. "I retain genetic memory. Name the Underworld Territory, and though I have never been there, I can navigate it. I am the map. I am the guide. I can take *any* soul *any*where."

Dead silence. His expression gave nothing away.

When he finally spoke, his voice was flat. "You're the fucking master key to the Underworld. You can open any gate, navigate any realm." He paused. "You can go anywhere, infiltrate any Underworld Territory. Without detection?"

She swallowed and nodded.

"So, without consequence."

There it was, out in the open. Everything she'd ever feared, the possibility of being found out and trapped, imprisoned, used for some Underworld deity's gain.

Lokan Krayl, son of Sutekh—the most vile and powerful of the Underworld gods—knew what she was.

He just didn't know that it was too late for him to exploit the knowledge.

She was bound to guide souls in. Not out. The price of passage was always a soul.

If she was going to lead him out through the Twelve Gates, payment would be due. A soul to balance the one she removed.

Hers.

Boone had gone to their father, who in turn had gone to Osiris and brokered the deal.

She would never be free.

She would be bound here, forced to greet the souls that came to the antechamber, forced to guide them through into Osiris's presence. The Twelve Gates were the entirety of her world now.

It was a choice she'd made. A choice she'd had to make.

For Dana's sake.

She would get Lokan out. She would send him to walk the Earth once more. Her daughter would be safe. Lokan was the only one who could make certain of that.

And he didn't even know it yet.

CHAPTER THIRTEEN

There is darkness on the road of the Duat.
——The Egyptian Book of Gates

BRYN INSISTED THAT THEY LEAVE the rowers behind and continue on alone, just the two of them. Lokan wasn't inclined to argue. The rowers who had accompanied him on his first attempt at the first gate hadn't been a hell of a lot of help. He had their annihilation on his conscience. As he saw it, it had been his responsibility to get them through, and he hadn't.

He and failure mixed like oil and water. And each new failure ate away at his already frayed confidence. He couldn't afford that, not if he was to get himself and Bryn back to the Topworld. Not if he was going to face his father in the Underworld. He needed to move past what had been done to him.

Easy as pie.

The river was exactly as it had been the first time he traveled its deceptive face: smooth as a mirror and stagnant. No current sped them on their way. They only moved if they paddled.

"Bryn, go back the way you got in," he said, trying to convince her to leave for the third time since they'd climbed in the boat. He didn't want her here. Especially now that he knew what he knew. "If any Underworld lord finds out what you are, that you're here within reach, he'll go after you."

"You're with me," she said.

"And you think I can keep you safe?"

She glanced back at him, her eyes fathomless and dark. "Yes."

Such faith. Too bad he didn't share it. Not anymore. Not since he'd been killed.

The knowledge of his limitations tore chunks out of his soul. For centuries, he'd been puffed up on power, certain that as a soul reaper, a son of Sutekh, nothing could touch him.

He'd been Sutekh's ambassador, and he'd been good at it. He'd managed to parley with even the most unreceptive of Sutekh's enemies. He'd figured he was invincible and any twinge of nerves he'd felt walking into an enemy's lair had been more of a high than a low.

He'd even managed to parley with Sutekh the night he'd taken Dana, with Lokan's life as ransom. He'd negotiated for his daughter's safety then. He needed to negotiate for her mother's safety now.

But she was a tough nut to crack.

"Just give me directions and a list of the names I'll need to pass each gate and I'll get through," he said. "I'll meet you in the Topworld. We'll take Dana to Disney World when I get back."

She dipped the oar, once, twice. Finally, she said, "I can't do that."

"Can't or won't?"

"Can't."

Frustration surged, but expressing it wouldn't win him the prize. "Why not?"

"For many reasons, the most important of which is that I won't know the way or the names until the path opens before me. That's the way it works." But something in her tone made him think that it was one reason, but not the most important one.

"So you don't know what's around the next bend? You don't know the name we need to speak to get through the gate?"

"Not yet, no."

Lokan considered that for a second and saw a definite benefit in that setup. "That actually protects you, doesn't it? If you're put in a position of being forced to take someone through an Underworld Territory, they have to keep you alive." He saw her shoulders tense as he spoke, and he wondered why a guarantee of her survival made her nervous. Maybe she was so used to keeping her secrets that it made her edgy to have them revealed. That, he understood. He felt odd having her know what he was after all these years of pretending to be something else. "You can't just give them the information to take themselves through. You have to be present and aware."

She said nothing. That didn't bode well.

"Bryn?"

"The gate's just ahead. I need to concentrate."

Her refusal to discuss it only made him wonder what the hell was going on. But she was right. The first gate was just ahead, the mass of snakes writhing and twisting up and down the walls, the water beneath them churning as the serpents of the deep rose toward the boat.

"Now'd be a good time to share that name," he said as he surged forward and used his oar to swat aside a small snake that fell from overhead. "I'm not liking the whole déjà vu thing."

The last time he'd come this way, his companions had been ingested by a serpent. The thought made him feel as if there was a 747 sitting on his chest. Because he couldn't let that happen to Bryn. Problem was, he hadn't been so good at taking care of anyone, including himself, since the night Sutekh had had him skinned and dismembered. What if he couldn't keep Bryn safe? What if—

No. Thinking that way was only feeding the monster, making the pressure tighten until he felt as if it would break him in half. So he thought about Bryn's kitchen, smelling like cookies, the sound of her voice washing over him as she talked about everything and nothing.

And the pressure eased.

He glanced at Bryn, but she wasn't talking now. She was still, too still. Lokan moved forward and crouched behind her. He grabbed her shoulder and turned her to face him. Red streaked her cheeks. She was crying tears of blood, her eyes staring up at him, unseeing. Marble blue. Except Bryn had brown eyes, so dark they were almost black.

"Fuck," he snarled throwing off a snake as it landed on his arm. He shook her. "Bryn!"

"Saa-Set." Her voice was tinny, echoing off the walls.

Lokan lifted his head and shouted the name. "Saa-Set."

The hissing crescendoed in a wave. The writhing mass swelled and surged toward them. Lokan rose, straddling Bryn's prone form, the paddle raised like a club as he shielded her from the snakes.

"Saa-Set," he cried, and still they advanced, a squirming, teeming mass. Something bumped the boat from below. Lokan had a feeling that the next hit wouldn't be just a bump.

Bryn stirred. "Together," she rasped. "We need to say it together."

"Now," Lokan cried, and their voices united, "Saa-Set."

And the snakes receded.

He stood over her, panting, his blood racing. He threw the oar into the bottom of the boat and crouched to gather her in his arms. She was limp, her head lolling back, and the fear that chased through him was cold as the north wind. Blood streaked her cheeks, and there were deep shadows beneath her eyes.

"A good argument for cooperation," he said, keeping his tone light, determined not to let her know that for an instant he'd doubted that they'd find a way through. He'd doubted himself.

He'd thought he'd fail again. Wasn't that a pretty truth, all wrapped up with a bow?

She made a dark little laugh. "You could say that."

"You okay?"

She ran her knuckles along her cheek. They came away smeared in blood. She stared at it for a long time, saying nothing. Then she raised her gaze to his. "That's new."

"Never happened before?"

She shook her head. She looked both tough and vulnerable, battered and brave.

The feel of her in his arms was so…right. His gaze dipped to her mouth. He wanted to kiss her, taste her. So he did. He lowered his head, his lips meeting hers, a kiss that meant so many things he couldn't even put names to them.

For a second, she kissed him back, her lips parting, welcoming, clinging to his. And then she pulled away.

Pressing her palms against his chest, she put up a barrier, as though she didn't want to open even the tiniest crack to let him get close. "We should go."

"Yeah." He exhaled a long breath. "Yeah, we should."

But he didn't want to stop holding her. He had the crazy thought that if he let her go, he was letting go of something precious, something he was going to lose.

"We should go," she said again, and wriggled away from him as she reached for her oar.

So he reached for his and got settled in back and got them moving, focusing on the task because focusing on his bizarre and unwelcome emotions was making him crazy.

The gate was a massive black rectangle framed in blue and gold. Dipping his oar, he paddled with hard, sure strokes until they passed beyond the gate. The water was like polished onyx, the walls of the tunnel gray and rough.

"They all going to be this easy?" he asked. They'd both come through intact without any significant parts missing, which meant it had been almost too easy. He didn't trust that. Whatever unique skills Bryn had, they were still in the Territory of Osiris, and Osiris didn't take kindly to trespassers.

He couldn't shake the feeling that whatever challenge they'd just faced was just the tip of the iceberg.

Bryn had indicated that she could move through unnoticed. But the same wasn't true for him. He was the son of Osiris's enemy, and if Osiris got his hands on him, he wasn't sure how that would turn out. Last time he'd faced the king of the dead, it had been as Sutekh's ambassador, with the protection of his father's name behind him. If he faced him now, it would be naked and alone. His confidence flickered like a flame in the wind.

Bryn looked back at him, her face chalk pale, her

eyes massive and dark. "Easy?" Her lips shaped a strained smile. "I doubt it."

He rummaged through the backpack Boone had prepared for him and pulled out a bag of lollipops. Not his favorite, but they were a sugar hit. He pulled out two and passed one to Bryn. "Sugar'll help," he said.

She swung her legs around so she was facing him, the two of them at opposite ends of the boat, and took the candy. "Why would Boone pack lollipops?" she asked, staring at him thoughtfully. "I know you have a sweet tooth, but it seems a bit of a frivolous thing for him to send."

"Sugar hit," Lokan replied. "It's basic physiology. Whatever humans eat ultimately gets converted to glucose as an energy source for their cells. My cell metabolism is half-god. That means I can't starve to death. But it also means I need more energy and more fuel."

"So you can't starve, but you can feel the pain of starvation."

"Yeah, that about sums it up." Her gaze held his, and he figured she was thinking about the months he'd been lost in the null zone. He didn't want her pity. He wanted her—

What? What exactly was it that he wanted from Bryn?

Not willing to answer that question, he said, "Candy's a quick delivery system."

She nodded but appeared remarkably unfazed by his explanation.

"How long have you known?" he asked.

"Known what?"

"That I'm not human."

Her gaze flicked away. Just for a second. But it was enough to tell him she was going to lie. Bryn was going to lie to him. Again. It hit him then. He'd been so thrown by seeing her here, so shocked, that he'd neglected to focus on the most important point. She'd been lying to him all along.

"Don't lie," he said, forcing aside the dark thoughts and emotions that swirled beneath the surface, focusing instead on the fact that since he'd done his share of lying as well, they were on an even playing field. The best he could hope for was truth from here on out. "Not this time. There are enough lies between us to pave the road to hell, don't you think?"

She sheared off a bit of the candy, and he could hear it crunching between her teeth.

"I've known since the second I saw you," she said. "Even before that. I went to that club because Jack used to go there and I knew that where Jack hung out, there would be other supernaturals. I was counting on the fact that at least one of them would be male. And there you were. I sensed you the second I walked in."

The events of the night they'd met played through his thoughts like a slide show. "So it could have been anyone. Any supernatural. It didn't have to be me."

She nodded, licking the lollipop, then popping it in her mouth and…sucking. He watched the movement of her tongue, her lips, and his thoughts slid to later that long-ago night, when she'd gone down on her knees in the shower and wrapped her lips around his cock.

Grabbing the backpack, he shoved the bag of suckers inside and took his time zipping the pouch. Because if he watched her suck on that candy for a second longer, he was going to be hard as stone. He was already halfway there.

"That's flattering." He paused, remembering how she'd commented on his looks and made it clear that being handsome wasn't a criterion. At the time, he hadn't paid any attention to that. Now, it was clear that he should have. "You want to tell me what the fuck is going on? You want to tell me what that night was about? You came looking for a supernatural to—"

She winced, and he felt a twinge of regret. He hadn't meant for it to sound like that.

"Your silver tongue seems to be a bit tarnished," she said. And licked that damn candy again before pushing it past her lips. He stared at her for a moment, until he realized she was watching him with a puzzled expression.

Hell, didn't she know what he was thinking?

The two tiny lines between her brows deepened, and he realized that, no, she had no clue. She was watching him, trying to figure it out. And he wasn't ready for her to know. He didn't want to give her that knowledge, the power of his wanting her.

"You wanted sex that night, and you wanted it with a supernatural," he amended, gentling his tone. "You want to tell me why?"

"No. I don't want to tell you why. Because I don't want to lie, and it isn't something I'll tell the truth about. Not right now. So let's leave it at the truth I'm prepared to tell, Lokan. Let's leave it at what I've explained and nothing more. No more lies. From either of us."

Then she turned away, shifting her legs to angle forward once more, giving him her back.

He had to hand it to her. Nice evasion. As good as any he could have come up with when he'd been glib and quick and not tied up in knots by a bunch of ridiculous emotions he had no business feeling.

"Not right now," he repeated. "Does that mean you'll tell me another time?"

She shot him a glance over her shoulder.

"Match point," he murmured.

She huffed a breath and turned forward with a shake of her head.

His little Miss Bryn had layers he'd never expected. And he had the urge to peel them all away before their boat ride was done.

"I WANT YOU TO GO BACK."

"You're repeating yourself." Bryn sighed. "We've talked about this, Lokan. I can't go back. I can only go forward. Think of me as your tour guide down a one-way street. The gates open to let us through, then lock up tight behind us. There is no going back."

Lokan leaned forward and caught her wrist, his fingers warm and strong, his grip solid but not painful.

"I don't believe that. If you go back, you can get out the way you came in. Get to Dana. Keep her safe."

She set her own oar across her thighs, taking her time, gathering her thoughts and her words because if she let them flow free they would carry all her fear and insecurity and desperation. For herself. For Lokan. But most of all for her daughter.

When she spoke, her tone was purposefully flat, and she stared straight ahead rather than looking back at him. "And even if I could find a way to do that, to go back, how would I keep Dana safe? How would I manage to outwit your father? My brothers are powerful, but they're no match for Sutekh. He'll find her. He'll take her. He'll do to her what he did to you." She swallowed, feeling sick even as she said it. Because she knew it was the truth. "I have no choice but to go forward with you, to guide you out. You're the only one who can keep her safe."

Behind her Lokan made a strangled sound. "I couldn't even keep myself safe."

She heard it in his voice, all the fear and pain and self-derision for mistakes made. She was no stranger to that herself. There wasn't a day that she didn't dedicate at least a moment or two to beating herself up for past mistakes. Maybe it was time to change that.

Now she did look at him, turning her head to find him close. Too close. His eyes were darker in this dim light, not the blue she was used to, but a shade closer to gray, like a storm cloud. They were so close she could see each individual lash and the fine lines etched beside his mouth by the experiences of his recent past.

"Maybe the only way for us to go forward is to truly let go of the past. Not forget it, but learn from it, use it to make the path ahead less rocky than the path behind."

His lips were drawn in a tight line as he sat back, dipped his paddle and picked up the pace.

Bryn held her paddle straight out toward the wall of the tunnel. The tip scraped rock.

"It's been getting narrower for a while," Lokan said.

She didn't ask what he meant by a while. Likely, he wouldn't be able to tell her. If her life depended on saying exactly how long they'd been down here, she wouldn't be able to. A year. Ten minutes. Each gate was supposed to represent one hour of the night, but measuring that hour on an Underworld clock was a complicated thing.

It broke her heart to miss even a moment of Dana's life. She couldn't begin to process the fact that she was going to miss *every* moment, that she was never going to see her daughter again. So she didn't. She thought only of the task, of getting Lokan through. And she focused on how and when she was going to tell him everything he needed to know.

"That pattern on the wall…" Lokan mused.

Thick, dark lines marked the rock on either side. She craned her head to see how far back they went. Not far. But they got thicker as the boat rounded a lazy curve.

"What about it?" She looked back at him, but he only shrugged.

"It smells in here," she said. "Like sulfur."

"Maybe there's a hot spring—Bryn!" Lokan surged forward and shoved hard on her shoulders. The boat rocked and swayed as she slid down into its belly, barely missing being impaled by a massive spike that protruded from the wall. The tip caught her and drew a deep gouge up along her shoulder.

The pain was bright and sharp, her blood a warm trickle down her arm.

Lokan arced back, but the tip of the spike grazed his shirt, dragging the hem free of his khakis and leaving a long tear in the material.

"You okay?" His gaze was locked on her bloody shoulder.

"A scratch," she said and hoped she was right. It wasn't the time to look.

"Stay down," Lokan ordered, as if she needed to be told.

Massive spikes protruded from the walls, puls-

ing in and out to constantly changing depths, forming a deadly maze between them and the gate that
shone dull gold before them. She tipped her head
back to get an upside-down view of Lokan moving
inhumanly fast as he dodged the thrust of the spikes,
retrieved his paddle and got them moving forward
again.

There was no fear in his expression, and no hesitation. His jaw was set, his eyes hard.

He looked like the demigod he was.

She wasn't used to seeing him this way.

Bryn didn't have Lokan's strength or speed, and
she didn't want to distract him. So she stayed quiet
and still in the bottom of the boat, waiting for the
moment when her role in this would begin.

The gate loomed before them, Lokan's strokes
bringing them closer and closer still. And then in
the shadowed corners on either side of the gate, she
saw movement and the reflection of light shimmering off…scales. Her breath hitched.

Serpents, far larger than the ones at the previous
gate. These could swallow a man whole. Frack, they
looked as if they could swallow a bus.

The smell of sulfur stung her nostrils.

Her gaze shot to the blackened walls. The pattern
wasn't drawn or painted, it was burned.

The serpents uncoiled, rising up.

Fear curdled in her stomach. "Lokan!"

"I see them. Looks like they're gearing up for
roasting dinner over the open fire, and we're the

main course." He paddled hard, dipping and swaying to avoid the thrust of the spikes. One grazed his scalp. Blood ran from the wound, dripping into his eyes and turning his sun-bright hair dark.

"Down," Bryn yelled, heart slamming against her ribs as a spike came straight for him. But he'd seen it—or maybe sensed it—before she had and was well clear of it as they passed.

Just ahead, the snakes appeared to grow and swell as they uncoiled and unhinged their jaws, forked tongues flickering, venomous fangs bared. The smell of sulfur grew stronger. With a roar, flames poured from their mouths, blackening the wall next to them. She could feel the heat on her skin, like a blast furnace.

Terror tugged at her as she groped for the name and the path they were supposed to take, but everything evaded her. There was only fog, and then there was an answer that couldn't be right.

Into the flames.

She wanted to tell Lokan to go back, the instinct for self-preservation screaming and railing against the certainty that they must go forward into the fire. It was too hot, too strong, the flames rolling up to the ceiling and dancing along the surface of the water.

Certainty won.

"Into the flames," she said, her voice not sounding like her own. She heard herself speaking, as though she was standing at the opposite end of a very long tunnel, the words flowing out without her will or intent. The same thing had happened when they went through the first gate, but this time it was stronger. Her cheeks felt wet, and she thought she must be crying blood tears again.

It took enormous will and energy to force herself to turn and look back, to meet Lokan's gaze. She saw him but didn't see him. His image was a distorted outline of gold and bronze, shimmering like the air above hot pavement, his features obscured.

The aura of his soul.

She'd seen them before when she'd guided the dead. But she'd never seen one quite like this, darkness and light blending to a color and texture that was both frightening and beautiful.

"Into the flames," she said again, sinking back to stare up at the gate that was so bright now she could hardly bear to look upon it. Then she saw what had been hidden from her sight before. Another serpent, cunning, aware, watching them approach as its massive form filled the opening to the third division of the Duat, the Underworld of Osiris, the king of the dead.

She was so weak, her limbs like jelly, her neck muscles flaccid. It took her an eternity to look back behind the boat, a sense of dread and premonition driving her. And then she saw what was behind them, the curved coil of another serpent as it dove beneath the surface of the water. Evil. Terrifying. Far worse than anything that lay ahead.

Apophis.

Her blood turned to ice in her veins.

Go forward and they would be incinerated. Go back, and they would face evil incarnate, worse even than Sutekh. There was no choice now. Perhaps there never had been. Not for her. Instinct drove her and guided her words, millennia of genetic memory speaking through her lips.

"Into the fire," she said, watching the bend and thrust of Lokan's body as he paddled hard. "The flames replenish. The flames ignite. And the god shall walk the Earth once more."

The smell of sulfur grew stronger, stinging her eyes, her nose, dancing across her tongue. She could taste it.

Then she realized he was paddling in reverse, away from the gate and the flames that erupted from the serpents' mouths.

He didn't trust her. In that second, she thought that maybe he didn't trust anyone. Not even himself.

"Into the fire," she said again, the voice coming from a part of herself that was running on instinct, not even in her full control. "Through the gate of Aqebi."

She wanted to beg for his trust, to tell him they must go on. She wanted to beg him to listen to her, to truly *hear* her, the way he always had in the past, but the words lodged in her throat. She could only say the name, over and over.

Again, the snakes opened their mouths, shooting fire that filled the small space and danced along the surface of the water. Blistering heat filled the cavern, and the spikes began to move faster, pulsating in and out.

Her will was not her own. Her strength leached away.

The boat continued back, inch by inch, the flames a wall of heat and red-orange glow before them. Apophis lurking behind.

No.

Listen to me.

Lokan, please.

Turning her head, she met his gaze. She willed him to see the truth in her eyes. There was no way but forward. No chance but the one she gave them.

She didn't know what he saw. Did she look like herself, or was she in that moment a stranger to him, her face marked by blood tears?

With the flames roaring around them, she held his gaze for what felt like forever.

She said the only thing she could. The one word her lips would form. "Aqebi."

Lokan's mouth tightened in a grim line. *Tick. Tick. Tick.* The seconds of their lives flowing like sand. And then he paddled hard for the gate.

"Now," he said as the serpents on either side rose up to bathe them in flame once more, and the god of the gate showed himself, massive and terrifying, his jaw open to receive them.

Annihilate them.

"Aqebi," they cried as the flames roared around and through them.

CHAPTER FOURTEEN

*Come thou unto us, O thou who sailest in thy
boat.*

—The Egyptian Book of Gates

Zugspitze Mountain, Germany

DAGAN SPUN AND TOOK IN THEIR prison. The metal door
was behind them. The rest was a cage of glass. He
tapped it experimentally.

"My guess would be bullet resistant with a strike
plate layer," Mal said, his voice vibrating with rage.
His mate had been taken. Dagan had no doubt that
the Matriarchs were hoping he and Alastor would
accuse Calliope of betrayal, of having lured them
into this trap. It was good strategy to weaken the
bond between himself and Mal and Alastor by sow-
ing seeds of mistrust. But he wasn't falling for it. He
was wise to their ways. So he said nothing.

"That would make it resistant to .50 caliber
armor-piercing rounds," Alastor said.

Mal hauled back and punched the glass full force.
The skin over his knuckles split, and blood dripped

from his hand, but the glass remained exactly as it had been. "Which means resistant to us."

Dagan nodded and looked for an alternative. The floor was stone. The ceiling more of the same glass. There was nothing else here. Except for him and his brothers and the power of their rage.

He reached for the energy that flowed between the Topworld and the Underworld. If he could just grab hold of those threads, he'd be able to combine them to create a fracture between the realms and open a portal. He could feel it flowing just beyond his reach. But the harder he tried to catch it, the more distant it grew.

Alastor shook his head, indicating that he was having no better luck opening a portal.

"Me neither," Mal said and turned a full circle, again looking for other options.

Curling his fingers, Alastor struck the metal door. The results weren't impressive. Not a mark. He drew back his hand and did it a second time and a third. His movements were methodical, controlled, betraying none of the turmoil that Dagan knew he had to be feeling.

"Wait," Dagan said, catching his brother's wrist.

Beyond the glass, lights came up, illuminating a vast and empty space. No, not empty. There was furniture: three chairs on a stone dais at the far end of the room. The sight was reminiscent of the gilded throne Sutekh used in his greeting chamber.

"Chairs fit for the gods," Alastor murmured.

Mal lifted a brow. "I wonder if they got a volume discount."

Energy surged in the space that confined them, the molecules vibrating frenetically. Dagan turned and stared at the far end of the room, the source of the surge. Someone was coming.

"Showtime," he said.

Alastor and Mal moved to flank him, and they watched as armed guards entered at the far end of the room, forming a phalanx around three women. The Matriarchs. Wine-red robes embroidered with black threads covered them from crown to toes. No part of them was visible. Even the sleeves extended past their fingertips.

But it wasn't the Matriarchs that held his attention. It was the woman ushered in in their wake.

With an inarticulate sound he surged forward, ready to throw himself against the glass. Alastor shot his arm straight out, a solid barrier that slammed against Dagan's chest even as Mal closed his fist on the back of his shirt.

"Easy," Alastor said, tension vibrating in those two short syllables.

Dagan was barely aware of them, his eyes on Roxy. She looked tired. Worried. Then her bronze-green eyes met his, fierce and unyielding. She paused, cocked her hip, her posture all sass and challenge despite the shadows beneath her eyes, and he knew it was her way of telling him she was fine.

Only as the pressure eased and he took a breath

did he realize that he'd stopped breathing the second she'd walked in, his chest tightening as if it was being crushed in a vise.

Just behind her was Naphré Kurata, Alastor's mate. She was cool and composed. Expressionless. Then she turned her head, and her eyes found Alastor's. Her lips curved in a barely there smile, and she said in a whisper that punctured the quiet, "You made it in time. Again. That's two for two."

Her words meant nothing to Dagan, but they obviously meant something to Alastor because some of the tension bled from him.

The Matriarchs froze in their tracks and turned as one. Certain that Naphré had breached some protocol by speaking, Dagan tensed, ready to leap on Alastor and hold him back. But to his surprise, the garbed figures only continued on their way, their movements spare and fluid, so graceful it appeared as though they floated above the ground. Maybe they did. Hard to tell with the robes flowing past their feet.

The Matriarchs seated themselves. The guards melted back. And no one said a fucking thing. The silence stretched. They were waiting for something, and Dagan bit back the caustic observation that he and his brothers outranked these women because that was not a good way to open a dialogue.

His little foray into the realm of Osiris, when he'd had to slice out his heart and put it on a scale to measure his worth, had taught him a thing or two about watching his words. Crossing his arms over his chest, he kept his expression neutral, and his brothers followed his lead.

The cowled figure on the left spoke first. "I am Amunet," she said and then gestured at each of the Matriarchs in turn as she spoke their names. "Beset. Hathor."

Dagan took his turn with the introductions, and the second he was done, Mal said one word. "Calliope."

The one called Beset jerked ever so slightly, enough to make Dagan think she was surprised.

She turned her head and nodded toward the shadows, and a moment later, Calliope entered, flanked by black-clad guards, double the number that were on Naphré and Roxy.

Mal swore under his breath and stepped forward, "She had no choice," he said. "I forced her to bring us. I threatened her. If anyone should be held accountable, it's me. I—"

"—am trying to defend what is indefensible," Beset cut him off. "A member of the Guard brought our enemies into our midst."

"The enemy of my enemy is my friend." Mal's words echoed through Dagan's thoughts, leaving him feeling disoriented, as though he were hearing them in his mind rather than with his ears and hearing them spoken in a different voice. Lokan's voice.

He glanced at Mal, then Alastor, but neither appeared to have felt anything. Either that, or they were far more adept at subterfuge than he.

Mal had eyes only for Calliope. "You okay, pretty girl?" A barely there nod was his only answer, but it appeared to be enough. He stepped forward until he was so close to the glass that his breath puffed against it as he spoke to the Matriarchs. "She couldn't have brought us if you didn't allow it," he said, his tone hard and certain. "You wanted us here, so rather than play at political games and waste time, tell us what you propose. And while you're at it, tell us how to get our brother back."

Their cowls obscured their faces, so Dagan had no idea why he thought it, but he'd swear the Matriarchs were amused rather than affronted.

Hathor turned to Calliope. "He is brash."

"I do not deny it," Calliope replied.

"But he will work with us?"

Work with them. Music to his ears.

Calliope met his eyes through the glass. "They all will. For the moment, enemies are allies, united by a common goal."

"What goal is that?" Dagan asked.

"I wish to formally state my disapproval once more," a woman said, stepping from the shadows behind the Matriarchs. She was tall and elegant, dark-skinned, dark-eyed, with high, curved cheekbones and full lips. Her hair was a tightly curled cap cut close to her head.

Hathor glanced at her. "Duly noted, Zalika."

Zalika. Calliope had mentioned that name. Calliope trusted her, valued her. And it appeared that the Matriarchs did, as well.

"And your arguments have merit," Hathor continued. "But this is the best solution. The collective before the individual. You will set aside your repugnance of the soul reapers and we will work with them for the greater good."

Dagan didn't look at his brothers, but he could feel the tension humming off them like electricity off a naked wire. How was it for the greater good to get Lokan back? He knew why he and Alastor and Mal would see it that way, but he couldn't see a single benefit to Aset or her Daughters.

Zalika's dark eyes slid to Dagan, then Alastor, and finally, Mal, assessing. Judging. They lingered on Mal the longest. Then she inclined her head and stepped back, and as she did, Calliope reached over and squeezed her forearm, a gesture of reassurance, a sign of friendship. Guess that explained that look. Zalika had been sending Mal a silent message, the kind that promised mayhem if he betrayed her friend.

Oddly, it made Dagan feel a bit of an affinity for her.

"Work with the soul reapers, huh?" Dagan asked, his gaze sliding to Roxy. He wanted out of this cage. He wanted her in his arms. He wanted to run his hands over every inch of her and make certain she was unharmed. The pain of almost losing her when Gahiji had tried to rip out her heart was still too fresh, too raw. He didn't like this situation, didn't like any situation that posed a threat to her. But she looked okay. Unharmed, if a little tired. It was only that that allowed him to keep his temper under control. "You might want to ask us how we feel about working together all tight and cozy. Better yet, tell us what exactly it is that we'll be working on."

Before the last word left his mouth, Beset was no longer across the room but directly in front of them with only the glass between them. This close, he could see the individual black threads that decorated her robe and the glint of the gold chain that hung around her neck.

He couldn't see her eyes, but he felt her regard for a long moment before she said, "You do not permit me to see your thoughts."

"No shit." He hadn't meant to say that. He needed to remember to be political. "I mean, yeah. No go. My thoughts are private."

"Roxy," Beset said, and Roxy strode closer. He watched her walk, noting her usual swagger, which told him that her legs were in working order—no sprains or breaks. He could see her arms and hands. They looked fine. No bruises or wrist marks from rope. Her apparent well-being offered him a measure of comfort.

She stood beside Beset now, and he drank in the sight of her.

"You have a link with him?" Beset asked.

"I do," Roxy said, referring to the psychic link

that had bound them ever since she had taken first blood from him.

"You will utilize the link to obtain answers for me."

"No." Roxy held Dagan's gaze. "No, I won't. I won't betray the Guard, but I can't betray him. I won't let you climb inside his mind through me."

"You would betray us to him?"

"No more than I would betray him to you."

Beset was quiet then, and he felt the intrusion as she pried at the edges of his thoughts, looking for a chink in his defenses. Fat fucking chance. He'd been putting up walls against Sutekh for centuries. Beset had nothing on the old man.

She was powerful, immensely so. But then, so was he.

"You aren't poking around in my head, so stop trying," he said to Beset. "You got a question, ask. I'll answer."

"Will you, soul reaper? And will your words be truth?"

"They will. With conditions. You free my mate and the mates of my brothers, you offer no threat and we're all good here. You meet the conditions, you get answers."

"And if I refuse?"

Dagan drew a slow breath. His hand shot out, through the glass, straight to Beset's throat. He closed his fingers only tight enough to hold her but not harm her, then he stepped through the glass and stood chest to chest with her outside the cage she'd made for him.

"Then you have a bit of a problem," he said.

The Underworld, The Twelve Gates of Osiris

THEY DRIFTED. LOKAN RUMMAGED through the pack, hauled out a bottle of water and crawled forward until he reached Bryn. Her face was streaked with blood. But there was no sign of the ravages of the fire. Her clothing wasn't burned. Her skin wasn't blistered. He glanced at his own hands and realized that neither were his.

Then he realized that he felt better, stronger. She'd said the flames replenished. She'd been right. He felt as though he'd eaten a pound of sugar or slept for twelve hours straight.

But even as he lifted her head to cradle it on his thighs, Bryn didn't stir. Worry surged. He set the bottle in the bottom of the boat and tore the hem off his shirt. He wet that with a bit of water from the bottle and stroked Bryn's cheeks, wiping away the blood, then did the same with the wound on her shoulder, the one she'd said was just a scratch. He wouldn't go that far, but it was shallow.

Her lids fluttered, and she opened her eyes to look back at him. Relief was sharp and sweet.

Sloe-eyed Bryn, so pretty, all warm and soft. His gaze dipped to her lips. She'd bitten the bottom one at some point in their ordeal. He could see the marks.

He wanted to kiss the spot. He wanted to kiss her. He leaned in just a little and knew both disappointment and frustration when she used her elbows to push herself away, then push herself to a sitting position. She didn't meet his gaze as she picked up the water bottle, unscrewed it and took a sip.

He should leave it alone. He should just pick up the paddle and get them moving. Everything about her posture and actions told him she didn't want to walk this path. Not with him.

But he couldn't leave it alone.

Gently, he laid his fingers on her jaw and turned her head until she was looking at him dead-on.

"I want to kiss you," he said. "I want to hold you so close that I feel your heart beat against mine."

She gasped, her lips parting, her eyes never leaving his.

He let his fingers trace down her neck until he felt her pulse beat against his fingertips. She tensed but didn't move away.

"I want to kiss you here—" he moved his fingers down to her collarbone, sliding them beneath the neckline of her shirt. Her breath hitched "—and here—" he tucked his fingers inside her collar and let the backs of his knuckles slide lower until they grazed the swell of her breast "—and here."

She closed her eyes and swallowed.

His fingers dipped lower, grazing the hard bud of her nipple. She exhaled in a rush but stayed perfectly still.

"And you're going to let me," he said.

Her eyes flew open, and the pain he saw there stunned him.

"Please, Lokan. Just—" She shook her head, her breathing rapid, and then she closed her fingers on his wrist and drew his hand away. "I'm sorry."

She reached for her paddle and moved as far from him as the boat allowed. He let her go. Pushing now wouldn't win him the prize. He'd bide his time. Study his prey. And when the opportunity was right, he'd convince Bryn to explain her mixed signals and angst.

They paddled for a time. Lokan thought it must have been hours, but it was hard to tell. Technically, he knew the Twelve Gates represented the twelve hours of the night, but the Underworld was a twisted place. Hours could translate into years or seconds, depending on what Territory one entered.

The river was smooth as glass and the current nonexistent. If they didn't paddle, they wouldn't move. So he put his back into it, figuring getting through faster was better than slower.

"Why don't you lie down?" he asked Bryn. Her shoulders were slumped, her posture screaming exhaustion. Lokan had demigod strength. But Bryn didn't. "Have a rest."

"I'd protest, except it's probably a good plan."

"Lie here." He dipped his chin toward his lap.

She met his gaze. "You need to paddle."

"I don't use my lap to paddle." The thought of her head in his lap…

The backpack lay between them at the center of the boat. She reached for it, dragged it over, used it as a pillow and stretched her legs out toward the prow.

"Chicken," he said softly.

"What gave it away? My feathers?" She shifted, looking for a comfortable position. Her eyes were closed, her hair fanning out from the elastic of her ponytail. He wanted to weave his fingers through the dark, straight strands, bury his face against her neck, breathe in her scent. And yeah, he admitted that whatever the hell he was feeling for Bryn, it had been there for a while. He just hadn't let himself see it.

The attraction wasn't one way. Neither was the emotion. But she was holding up a bright red stop sign, and he needed to figure out a way to get her to change it to green for go.

He kept the boat going, the walls of the cave never changing, just gray stone interrupted here and there by crevices and dark areas. He had the feeling that eyes watched them pass, but he didn't look too closely. No point. If a threat appeared, he'd deal with it.

Some time later, Bryn stirred. She pulled a bottle of water from the pack, took a sip, then passed it back to him. Then she split an energy bar in two and passed half back to him—the bigger half. He didn't miss that. Their eyes met, their fingers brushed.

She looked away.

He was all for companionable silence at times, but he was disappointed when she didn't start to talk. The Bryn he knew was a chatterbox. She rambled and strung ideas together in a way that didn't always make sense. But was always…cute.

Except this Bryn was different. It was as if by coming to the Underworld, she'd donned a different persona.

In the null zone, he'd been alone with only his own thoughts, his memories and the images he'd manufactured in his mind for company.

He'd been locked in silence.

He wanted to hear Bryn's voice, the easy chatter that was so much a part of who she was. Thinking back on the years they'd known each other, he realized how much he'd liked listening to her talk about anything and everything mishmashed together in a lump.

He chewed and swallowed a bite of the energy bar, then stared down at it, repulsed. "What flavor is this?"

She glanced at the wrapper before putting it in the backpack. "Chocolate marshmallow. Why?"

"Tastes like sawdust." He paused, a memory dancing through his thoughts. "Remember when you made those oatmeal cookies? The ones with the melted chocolate on top. And then you put a marshmallow on and grilled it golden brown?" He could almost taste it now.

She shot him a sidelong look over her shoulder. He couldn't read her expression, but he thought he saw the corner of her mouth lift in a smile.

"Make me some when we get back."

That was a mood killer. She hunched over her energy bar, shutting him down. He wanted to touch her. He wanted to make her tell him what the fuck was going on, why she was so skittish. He wanted to tell her he'd keep her safe, he'd get them both home, back to their daughter.

But he didn't want to lie. Who was he to tell her he'd get them home when she'd had to come here after him?

"What did you call those cookies again?" he asked, hoping to get her talking. He wanted the sound of her voice to wash through him, and he knew that she could talk endlessly about ingredients and recipes and kitchen gadgets.

Again, she glanced back at him. There were shadows in her eyes that he couldn't read.

"S'mores," she said.

Then she turned forward once more and lifted her paddle, leaving him to watch the curve of her back, the movement of her arms and shoulders, and to wonder why he felt as if something important had been taken from him.

CHAPTER FIFTEEN

That which belongeth to you, O ye sacred serpents who are in this lake, is to guard your flames and your fires so that ye may hurl them against enemies, and your burning heat against those whose mouths are evil.
— The Egyptian Book of Gates

THE RIVER WAS A DARK, glossy ribbon before them when Lokan opened his eyes. They'd taken turns sleeping, one grabbing some rest, the other keeping watch. He wouldn't say it had been ideal, but with the pack as a pillow, it hadn't been bad. Everything was relative. Compared to the null zone, it was pretty near perfect.

In the distance, he could see a massive gate, and through it flames that danced and writhed. After a moment, he realized they weren't merely flames, they were the souls of the damned, their movements a tortured dance of agony as they were consumed by fire.

"Lake of fire," he said. "Makes me wish I had Mal along for the ride. He has a bit of a thing going with a few of Xaphan's concubines."

"Xaphan?" Bryn was sitting backward in the boat, facing him, taking a break from the endless paddling.

He felt as if they'd been at it for a century, and she had to feel it more than he did given that she didn't have his supercharged metabolism. But she insisted on doing her share and not simply riding as a passenger. He respected that, and he didn't argue.

Lokan maneuvered the boat to the river's shore and let the bow nose up on the rocky beach. He climbed out and offered Bryn his hand. She frowned in confusion.

"Stretch break." He took her hand and pulled her to her feet. Her head tipped back. Her eyes found his.

He had to fight the urge to wrap his arm around her waist and draw her close.

"If I sit in that boat for one more second," he said, "I'm going to turn to stone." Unfortunate word choice. Parts of him were already starting to get hard as stone.

Bryn looked away. "So who's Xaphan?"

"The keeper of the braziers that light the lakes of fire."

"Do you know him? Can he help us?"

"Yes to the first question. I had dealings with him over the years. There aren't many Underworld powers that I didn't have dialogue with as my father's emissary."

"What about the second question?"

"Maybe, to that one. But I think the more pertinent point is *would* he help us. That's an almost certain no. Xaphan isn't the type to do anything that doesn't benefit him directly. And I can't see a benefit to helping us."

"And his concubines? What are they?"

"Fire genies."

Her brows rose. "Your brother Mal sleeps with fire genies? Isn't that...dangerous?"

Lokan grinned, thinking of his brother and just how close to the edge he liked to skate. "Yeah," he said. "Yeah, it is. He likes to spice things up."

Bryn dipped her chin and stepped away.

"What?" he asked, certain that she wanted to say something, uncertain why she was holding back.

"Do you sleep with fire genies?" she blurted, and he realized she'd mistaken the cause of his grin. "I mean, it's not my business, and really, I shouldn't even ask—"

"No."

She drew a sharp breath.

"I'm not celibate, Bryn. I'd be a liar to say that I am, and I think we've pretty much agreed, no more lies. But I don't sleep with any skirt that walks past."

"You don't."

Was that a question or a statement? He wasn't sure. He shook his head and spread his hands. "You know I don't because you know where I am a lot of the time. How many nights have I spent on your couch?" He had. Not in the beginning, but later, as Dana got older and he and Bryn spent time together and fell into a routine. He'd slept on her couch more times than he could count, not because he had to. It was easy enough to open a portal and head to his own bed.

He'd slept on her couch because she'd offered it and because he hadn't wanted to leave. Because he'd liked knowing that his daughter was asleep in her bed in the same house, that he was there when she woke up in the morning, with her big blue eyes and her little girl laugh. He'd liked seeing Bryn in her purple flannel pajamas with her hair in pigtails. He'd liked feeling as though—

No, not going there.

Then something hit him: Bryn had *always been there.* He'd popped by unexpectedly, and she was there. He woke up in the morning, and she was there.

There'd been no bedmates for Bryn.

In that second, he realized that on some level he'd always known that. And that if it had been any other way, he would have been less than pleased.

Talk about a double standard. He hadn't claimed her for his own, but he would have lost it if anyone else had made that claim.

He bent and picked up a flat stone, weighed it in his hand, then sent it skipping across the glassy surface of the river. It jumped once, twice—

Just before it hit the third skip, a serpent's head broke the surface and swallowed the stone whole.

"Oooh," Bryn murmured, sounding like a deflating balloon. He couldn't blame her. That snake had been just about big enough to swallow the damn boat.

"There was never anyone else for you," he said, keeping his gaze on the water, not looking at her. Not daring to look at her because if he did, he'd pull her into his arms, put his mouth on hers. Claim her. "You never dated, not once in all these years."

"Wha—" She gave an incredulous laugh. Then sighed at the pretense. "No, there was no one." He bent, claimed another stone and skipped it. Another serpent surged from the depths. "Why do you sound so smugly pleased about that?" she asked.

"Because I am. Smugly pleased." He turned his head and looked at her then.

The breath left her in a rush. Her shields failed her, and her expression betrayed surprise, confusion and…something else he couldn't quite put his finger on. He thought it might be regret. Then she shut down completely. He'd seen her do that before. Often. She used it when she wanted to hold him at bay. When she wanted to tell him that something was off-limits. That *she* was off-limits.

He'd never consciously noticed that before. All these years, and he'd never realized that she kept an invisible wall between them, sharing their love of their daughter, but never really sharing anything of herself except the superficial. She let him scratch the surface, but she never showed him what was deep inside. He'd never noticed because he'd been so fucking self-absorbed. The thought shamed him.

Slowly, he reached out and pulled the covered

elastic from her hair. The dark strands fell over her shoulders and down her back.

"Do you remember the first time I did this?" he asked, his voice low and rough.

"Yes." The tip of her tongue darted along her lower lip.

"Do you remember what I said?"

"That it looks sexier down."

"It does." He leaned in. She leaned back.

He leaned in a little more, and this time, she stayed put, her entire body trembling. He inhaled, taking in the scent of her skin, her hair. She didn't move. Didn't breathe.

"Please," she whispered, and though he wanted to pretend she was pleading for his kiss, the truth was, he knew she was pleading for him to give her space.

He didn't move. His lips were inches from hers, and everything inside him demanded that he close the distance, take the kiss.

But everything about her begged him to back off.

So he did. He moved back far enough to look down at her and see the flicker of sadness in her eyes before she locked it down and hid it away.

"We need to get you out of here," she said. "That's what this is about, Lokan."

"Fine. And when we're out of here, Bryn, we have things to settle. I thought you were human, while I wasn't. That didn't make for a hell of a lot of possibilities."

"And there are still no possibilities, Lokan. None."

"Then why do you look so sad when you say that?"

"I'm—" She pursed her lips and gave a hard exhale, then turned to face the river and the flames in the distance. "We should go."

Yeah, they should. The sooner they got moving, the sooner they could jump through Osiris's hoops.

Lokan held the boat while she climbed back in, then joined her and sent the boat floating with a hard shove of his paddle.

"What do you know about the next gate?"

"The flames challenge the soul," she said, her tone solemn. "They seek any impurity and set alight those who are unworthy. The souls are judged."

Judged. That wasn't news to him, but suddenly, he saw the situation from an entirely new perspective. He set his paddle down and scooted forward, closing his hand around Bryn's wrist as she went to dip her oar. She paused and looked back at him over her shoulder.

"You're protected, right? Being a guide means you aren't subject to the rules. You take me on the path and stand by while I face the challenges, right?"

"Guides are generally protected."

Not enough of an answer. The vagueness set off alarms. "Bryn, are guides subject to judgment?"

"Not usually."

Fuck. "But this isn't usual, is it?"

That little hesitation told him she didn't want to say.

"Is it?"

"No. I'm not guiding a soul *into* the Underworld. I'm guiding one *out*. That means the rules are different. There's a price. I face what you face. I'm judged as you're judged."

"Judged as I'm judged? You mean that my purity, my worth, determine yours?" Something close to panic set in. He believed her soul was pure enough. He believed that if she faced the lake of fire, she would walk through the flames unscorched. He couldn't make that claim for himself, but that was fine. He could handle a little pain.

"Bryn, if I'm burned, I'll know pain, but I'll survive. I'll heal."

She wouldn't.

And the possibility that she would be judged by his deeds and not her own, that if he were found lacking she would burn, wasn't acceptable. "Tell me you're judged on your own merit."

"I—"

Lokan tightened his hold on her when she went to turn away. Her head jerked down, and she stared at his fingers where they curved around her wrist. Her skin was warm and soft and smooth, and he could feel the tension in her muscles.

"Bryn," he said, knowing there were more words he wanted to say, but unable to find them. Him. The negotiator. He couldn't figure out exactly what he wanted to say to her or how to say it. Because he was no longer the person he had been, and he hadn't yet quite figured out who it was that he'd become.

He had no right to drag her into his mire. Bad enough that she'd come looking for him, put herself in danger, left their daughter alone. He wasn't going to make it worse by laying his emo shit on her.

She lifted her head and met his gaze, and he saw a world of pain before she shuttered her expression.

They were closer to the gate now, and the backdrop of the screams of the damned as they were consumed by flame didn't exactly make this the ideal moment for baring his soul. So when she turned away, he let her go, hoping they made it through this and he'd have the chance to tell her—

What?

He didn't even know what it was he wanted to say.

"Do you think this journey is only about you?" Bryn asked, her voice pitched loud enough to carry back to him.

"No. It's about you, as well. And about Dana."

"It's about more than that. Osiris is letting you pass the Twelve Gates. He's offering you a way out. What do you think that does to the balance? He's putting a great deal at risk. If Sutekh chooses to challenge—"

"He won't," Lokan cut her off. "Sutekh played his card. He wanted my soul gone and my body available for him to inhabit."

A howl of agony carried through the gate and filled the pause in their conversation. She shivered.

"Why you? Why not take a human or another supernatural? Why did Sutekh want *you?*"

"Been wondering that myself, and I think I have it figured out. A human wouldn't do. Even if he managed to eradicate the mortal's soul, there was the problem of a god in a body that would age and die, or worse yet, Sutekh's power would consume any form he commandeered. But my half-god metabolism would balance the human half. He could possess my form without destroying it, and I don't age, so problem solved."

"What will stop him from going after you again?" Nothing. "What's to say he won't simply attack the second you step free of the Twelfth Gate and steal your body once more?" Again, nothing. Sutekh might well try again. It was a possibility that wasn't particularly appealing.

"I know what he's after now," Lokan said, offering what reassurance he could. "I'll be watching my back. And my brothers somehow got my body to me, which means they know now what he did. Their loyalty to him has to have been fragmented by this. Unless he wants to lose them altogether, he doesn't dare make a move against any one of us. He'll need to think of another option."

"Dana," she said, her voice shaking. Nice. His attempts at reassurance had only led her down a worse path. He really was shoving his foot in his mouth with frightening regularity.

"Not right now. She's a child. He won't want to be

trapped in a child's form. And she's mortal, at least for the moment. That means she can't host him, not in her current form."

For a long moment, she said nothing, and then, "Maybe there's another reason Sutekh won't come after you again. Maybe this has changed you. Maybe you aren't the same as you were."

"I'm not."

She nodded but said nothing more. He was left with the feeling that she knew something she wasn't saying, and she was just waiting for him to figure out what the hell it was.

AS THEY DREW ABREAST OF THE gate, Lokan said, "There are no sentries."

Bryn had noticed that lack, along with the absence of a name that should have been on the tip of her tongue.

"I don't think this is one of the Twelve Gates."

"Looks like a gate."

"Looks like an archway," she said. "But not necessarily a gate. If it were, I'd be crying blood and calling names."

"And you're not."

"I'm not."

"So it's a gateway, but not a Gate." He arched a brow. "Maybe a gateway *to* a Gate?"

They edged closer, and beyond the massive archway she could see a lake of brackish green water. Herbs floated on the surface, a tangle of stems and leaves, sending up the scent of thyme and sage and other things. Far less pleasant things. Asafetida, she thought, among others. And mingling with that, the smell of burning hair and flesh.

Flames and writhing human forms danced across the surface. She counted them. Twelve. And as one sank beneath the surface with a final, horrific scream, a soul that stood in an endless, snaking line on the shore took its first tentative step into the bubbling green stew.

For a second, she thought he would walk through. The waters only burned the wicked. Surely some of the souls waiting on the shore were pure.

With a rushing sound, flames erupted on his skin, and his agonized cries joined the other screams. Bryn's hands tightened on the oar, and she kept paddling, putting everything she had into each stroke, wanting to be quit of this place. It frightened her as the other challenges they'd faced had not. Maybe because this wasn't an actual gate, and no magical words or spells were coming to her. It was just her and Lokan and the fires of the damned.

But no matter how hard she paddled, the boat stayed exactly where it was, though a glance over her shoulder revealed that Lokan was working in synchrony with her. He looked up, caught her gaze and said, "We won't get through this way. We need to get out."

Understanding dawned, and with it, cold terror.

They needed to get out of the boat. They needed to swim the waters of the lake of fire.

"The line of souls…" There was no end in sight. Just an endless parade of souls. If they took their turn in that, she had no idea how long they would be trapped here.

"We aren't waiting for the line." He flashed a tight smile. Then he set his paddle down, vaulted the side of the boat and sank into the water.

Bryn's heart skidded to a stop in her chest.

He stood there, and for a moment nothing happened, and then something did. Sparks ignited at his fingertips, then raced along his arms toward his shoulders. His features twisted in a mask of pain, but he kept hold of the boat and began to push it toward the distant shore. His skin looked as if it was melting away. His breathing came in harsh, panting rasps, and Bryn realized they weren't moving.

Because of her. Because she was still in the boat.

No matter how hard he worked, they weren't going anywhere until she got in that lake.

Cold sweat drenched her, and she shook as though she had a fever of one hundred and four. Lokan's torso was engulfed in flame now, and he was grunting with each exhalation. She couldn't imagine the pain. Didn't have to imagine it. Because she was going to feel it.

She felt tears tracking down her cheeks, and fear almost paralyzed her. But she drew up a mental image of her daughter, the reason for everything she was doing here, and with a cry she forced herself over the side.

All around her, the screams of those being consumed by the fire roared and swelled.

She dug her fingers into the side of the boat, holding on tight. And she kicked hard, trying to help propel them forward.

Then a horrific thought slammed her. Lokan wasn't going to get out of the lake in one piece. Only those that the fire did not consume were permitted to go free. In that second, she realized that the fire hadn't touched her.

And then she realized why.

She'd instinctively torn her soul free, torn it in two as she had the night she and Dana ran from Jack. She'd surrounded herself in a bubble, a shield, and with that realization, she saw that her pitiable efforts to propel the boat forward were wasted. Her strength could be put to better use.

The agony that seized her was unrelenting, like saws hacking at her, knives stabbing her. But she forced herself to dig even deeper, to welcome the pain, to ride each wave as she forced the bubble of her soul wider, spreading it in a thin layer between Lokan and the fire.

He gasped, and then so did she, he in relief, she in pain. Because the heat, the horror, were transferred to her, the fire sparking and flaring on the protective bubble she'd formed with her ruptured soul.

"What the fuck are you doing?" he snarled. His

shirt hung in charred shreds, baring his torso and arms, the skin raw and burned. Stray sparks had left marks on one cheek and singed the ends of his hair. She didn't know what was hidden beneath the waterline. More burns. More agony.

"Saving...your...ass," she managed, the pain of holding her soul ripped in two stealing her words, her thoughts. The fire swelled, angry, hungry, trying to burn away all she was and leave her a charred husk. "Swim," she ordered.

His jaw clenched. His eyes sparked fury. But he swam.

Inch by agonizing inch, they made their way to the opposite shore. And the whole time, the flames of eternity lapped at her soul with tongues hot and red.

She couldn't bear it.

She couldn't do this.

"Bryn!" She could hear the pain in his tone, and she knew he suffered, more for her than himself. He didn't want her taking his pain. "Whatever the fuck you're doing, let it go. I'll heal. I'll survive."

But he couldn't know that for certain, and she couldn't risk that he was wrong. Whatever it took, he had to get through.

So she *could* do this. She would. There was no other choice.

Seconds felt like hours. All around them, the screams of those being consumed rose and fell, a horrific symphony.

"There." She gasped, even that one word almost draining whatever reserves she had. But it was enough. He turned his head, saw the gate through the wall of fire that rose before them and swam hard for it. Bryn clung to the boat, letting Lokan's efforts drag her forward.

Closer. Closer. The gate loomed before them, and she struggled to hold on to consciousness. Words came to her, and the voices inside her clamored for release. The urgency to speak the name, to lose herself, was nearly overwhelming, made all the more so by the pain that consumed her from both inside and out.

If she lost herself, her soul would ricochet back inside her body, and there would be no more protection for either of them.

Her eyes met Lokan's. She saw the reflection of the fire dancing there. And then the reflection of herself, tiny, as she was tiny in the face of the flames and the lake and the challenge of the Gates.

Then all she saw and heard was from far, far away, and she was in this place but not in this place, choice and control wrested from her grasp.

"Tchetbi." The word came out on a gasp at the same second as the protection of her soul tore away.

Lokan surged forward and grabbed hold of the back of her shirt and with a mighty heave he threw her into the boat at the same instant as they both yelled "Tchetbi."

The boat keeled to one side and almost tipped.

Dark and glistening, the coil of a massive serpent—far larger than any they had yet encountered—broke the surface, and she wanted to grab hold of the boat, an oar, Lokan...anything. But she was trapped inside herself, able to do nothing but fall with a thud into the bottom of the boat as the serpent dove deep and the boat slapped the water, sending geysers rising on both sides.

A wave of fire loomed over her, an inferno, heat such as she had never known. She screamed and screamed again, but no sound came out. She screamed inside her own mind as the wall of flame crashed down on her.

CHAPTER SIXTEEN

*I have come, that I may make a reckoning with
my body.*

—The Egyptian Book of Gates

Zugspitze Mountain, Germany

"DAE." ROXY SHRUGGED OFF HER guards and strode
across the cavernous room toward him. Her chin
dipped toward his hand where it curled around the
Matriarch's throat.

"I dunno," she said, "but choking your hostess
might fall under the heading of bad manners." Her
lush mouth curved in a smile. "You got here fast."

"You know the deal." He held her gaze, forcing
his tone to stay even, forcing himself not to grab her
and kiss her and stalk out of here with his mate in
tow. Because Roxy wouldn't take kindly to that. "If
you run, I will find you."

She rolled her eyes. "I didn't run. It was more of
a very strongly worded invitation that I couldn't resist." Her gaze shifted to the Matriarch's throat. "Let
go. They didn't come looking for a war, but at this
rate, you'll start one anyway."

She'd reached his side now, and she rested her palm flat on his chest. His pulse slammed hard as relief swamped him. She was here. Right here.

He looked up to see that Mal and Alastor had made it through the rift he'd created in the glass, and that Naphré and Calliope stood by his brothers' sides. No guards tried to stop them, which backed up Roxy's assertion that the Matriarchs weren't looking for war.

"See?" Roxy continued as she followed his gaze. "No one stopped me or them. There's no threat here."

"No threat?" He shot a look at Beset. "Why'd they put us in a cell?"

"To ensure that you were calm and unaggressive," Beset said.

"Yeah. That worked well."

Roxy stepped between them. "We need to work together."

"Together. With Aset." Disbelief dripped from his words, but he couldn't say them any other way. The idea of Sutekh's sons working with Aset's Daughters… He figured his brothers were thinking along the same lines when Alastor lifted a brow in silent commentary and Mal widened his eyes, then narrowed them, making his opinion clear.

But then, Sutekh's sons were *mated* to Aset's Daughters. Couldn't get much more together than that.

This whole situation was fucked to high hell.

"There is more here than your petty enmity. Everyone must work together," Beset replied, and only then did Dagan realize that she was at the opposite end of the room once more, seated on her wooden throne. "You are stronger than I expected, soul reaper. And less aggressive. I would have thought that if you placed your hands upon me, you would try to terminate my existence. My heart and soul would no doubt please your father."

"I'm not particularly interested in pleasing my father at the moment. And I've got no beef with you." Dagan tipped his head toward Roxy. "So long as she's good, you and me, we're good. You hurt her…" He gave a one-shouldered shrug.

"How very…primitive," Hathor said, her tone flat.

"Yeah. That's us. Primitive to the core. Now that we've got that laid out all nice and open," Mal said, "why don't you tell us what the hell is going on here?"

The Matriarchs said nothing.

"You said that we need to work together," Alastor said. "With everyone. Define everyone, if you please."

Maybe it was his nice manners. Or maybe it was the fact that he homed in on a specific question, but Alastor got what Dagan and Mal hadn't been able to. An answer.

"Aset, and her brother husband, Osiris, have an interest in the events and outcome of Lokan Krayl's murder," Hathor said.

"Political interest?" Dagan asked.

A beat of silence greeted his question. Then Amunet spoke. "Political, yes. But personal, as well." Her tone suggested that she'd rather eat nails than offer up that information, which begged the question, why offer it?

"Because we do not trust you or any of your kind, soul reaper." She answered the question he hadn't asked aloud. "Yet, you have earned a small measure of trust, each of you, with your recent actions. A conundrum." Though he couldn't see her face, or her eyes, the way she moved her head left him with the impression that she looked first at Roxy, then Naphré, then Calliope. "You protected them."

"Not for Aset," he said. "Not for anyone but ourselves. Losing Roxy—" he glanced at the others, making it clear he spoke for his brothers and their mates "—isn't an option."

"Honesty, and emotion, from Sutekh's seed. Surprising and unexpected."

"Why?" Alastor asked. "Because our father is a lying snake who murdered his own son? Are you thinking the apple does not fall far from the tree?" He paused, visibly mastering his emotions, and when he spoke again, his tone was cool and clipped. "These apples do."

Naphré pinned him with an implacable look and said, "These are the Matriarchs, Alastor. The elders of my kind. Please." But despite the pretty word, it wasn't a request. She was actually *telling* Alastor to behave.

The look Alastor gave her said that he'd comply, for now, and that retribution would come later. Naphré offered him the barest whisper of a smile.

"So what are we doing here?" Dagan asked. "Why kidnap our mates? Lure us here? I have no doubt you knew we were coming."

"We kidnapped no one," Beset said. "We offered protection lest your father try and use our Daughters as pawns in his game."

"Let's say we believe that. It still doesn't explain why you didn't release them once the meeting of allies was over."

"Because it isn't over," a new voice interjected. A man Dagan had never seen before stepped from the shadows. He was dark-haired, tall, with eyes an unusual shade of blue, icy pale, rimmed in navy. There was something off about those eyes. They were too bright, as though lit from behind. And when Dagan turned his head just a little, the image of the man wavered at the edges, as though heat was steaming off him in cold air. Or as though he wasn't really there.

He wasn't human, but Dagan couldn't read his energy signature and say exactly what type of supernatural he was. Not one Dagan had ever encountered before. He shot a glance at Mal and Alastor. A quick shake of the head was enough to tell him that neither of them could call it, either.

"The meeting's merely been relocated, minus a key player or two," the stranger continued. "And when the time is right, it will reconvene with all deities present."

"And what determines the right time?" Dagan asked.

"The return of Lokan Krayl."

The room was silent, so quiet he could hear the rush of his blood.

Lokan.

He hadn't dared to hope.

"You know something we don't?"

The stranger offered a tight smile. "I believe I do."

"And we're supposed to trust you because…?"

"Allow me to introduce myself. My name is Cahn Falconer and I'm here because we have a shared concern." He paused. "I'm your niece's uncle. On her mother's side. And I was wondering if any of you gentlemen might lend assistance to ensure that your father doesn't get his murderous hands on her."

Then his gaze slid to Roxy. "Roxy Tam?" His smile widened, making Dagan's hackles rise. "Dana's been asking for you."

The Underworld, The Twelve Gates of Osiris

BRYN OPENED HER EYES AND HELD perfectly still, expecting pain. But there was none.

She turned her head to see Lokan sitting on the ground some ten feet away, his back against a large boulder.

"Hey," she said. Croaked, actually. Her mouth and

throat felt as if she'd been eating cotton wadding, but other than that, she felt...okay.

Lokan pushed to his feet, and that's when she noticed what he was wearing. And what he wasn't wearing. Black pants and nothing else. No shirt. No shoes. Images flashed through her thoughts, along with imprinted sensations. She remembered the fire. She remembered the sound of his voice as he yelled her name and the feeling of being held against his chest, his arms strong and sure. She remembered curling her hands around his neck and holding on because he was the one solid thing in her careening world.

She'd felt safe. When had Lokan Krayl come to represent somewhere safe? When had she allowed herself to trust him that much?

Years ago, she realized. Somewhere along the line, she'd stopped seeing him as the enemy and started seeing him as her partner in raising their daughter, and she'd never thought about it, never analyzed it. It had just...been.

"What happened to your shoes?"

"Serpent got one," he said, his tone clipped. "Almost took my foot along with it. Didn't seem worthwhile to hang on to the other."

A serpent.

"And your shirt?" she asked.

"Fuel for the fires of damnation." He sounded tense. Angry.

Wrapping her arms around herself, she nodded,

then shot a look up the pebbled beach. The boat was there, unburned, unmarked. It looked exactly as it had when their journey began—a reed boat with curved bow and stern, marked with symbols of the Underworld.

"Not anxious to climb back aboard?" There was an edge to the question.

She gave a strangled laugh. "Not hardly."

Lokan rose and walked over until he stood directly before her. She stared at his bare feet, finding the sight strangely intimate. And far safer than looking at his bare chest.

He hunkered down, one hand dangling loosely between his spread thighs, the other holding a bottle of water out to her. She couldn't avoid looking at him then. His chest was solid and strong, leanly muscled. A narrow line of brown hair ran down the center of his belly. Her gaze followed that line down to the waistband of his pants.

She'd seen him shirtless more than once over the years when he'd stayed over on the couch. What was it about this moment that made her want to look her fill, made her want to lay her palms flat on his muscled chest and feel his heart beat? Was it because she'd come so close to losing him?

Or because she *would* lose him—and he would lose her—when his journey was done.

Closing her eyes, she took a slow breath, not sure what was wrong with her, but whatever it was, she didn't like it. She felt as if her walls had been scorched away and all that was left was raw emotion. Maybe nearly getting burned to ash did that to a girl.

She opened her eyes and took the open water bottle from him, then guzzled several swallows before he put his hand on hers and said, "Slowly," curt and short. She wondered what was eating him.

"Okay." She silently counted to three, then took a smaller sip. Her gaze slid back to his chest, then dipped to his leanly ridged belly.

"What happened to the tattoo?" she asked.

He glanced down, then up. "How'd you know about the tattoo?"

"Boone told me."

"Did he tell you the rest?"

He'd told her that Lokan had been skinned, the tattooed mark of Aset sent to his father as a kill trophy. Except it had been his father who'd done the killing and the whole kill trophy thing had been a ploy to divert suspicion. She'd felt sick as she'd listened to details about what Lokan had suffered. She hadn't known. All she'd known was that Lokan was dead.

"The tattoo got cut out." He sounded matter-of-fact, as if a knife slicing the flesh from his body was nothing out of the ordinary. "I healed. Part of my half-god metabolism. I heal quick."

"Is that why you're not burned?" She shuddered as a memory of the flames and the pain roared through her. Then she realized that her skin was unmarked, her clothing intact. As if a wall of flame hadn't engulfed her at all. "Why am *I* not burned?"

"Because the souls of the damned are consumed by flames." Again she heard the edge to his tone, as if he was biting out the words.

"Those flames tried to consume *us*," she said. "I saw it, felt it. The fire. I saw it everywhere. It was burning yours arms, your body…and mine. You healed that quickly? I healed that quickly?"

"No on both counts. I was on fire, but I wasn't consumed by the flame."

"Why do you sound angry about that?"

"Not about that." He took the water bottle from her, his fingers warm against hers. Very carefully, as though the task required his full and undivided attention, he set the bottle on the ground and screwed the lid on. Then he caught her chin between his thumb and forefinger and stared into her eyes. He was more than angry. She saw that now. He was practically vibrating with leashed fury.

"I wasn't consumed because *you* weren't consumed. You did something that protected me, shielded me, and that almost got you killed," he said, his voice low and controlled.

She shook her head. Tried to, anyway. But he was holding her chin, and all she could manage were tiny movements side to side. He was angry with her for shielding him?

"You fucking put your life at risk for me." Not so controlled anymore. "You think I want that? You think I need another load of guilt on my cart? Dana was taken by the Setnakhts because of me. I put my daughter in harm's way and I have to live with that. Now you're here, in this place where nothing and nowhere is safe." He stopped, yanked his hand away and dragged his fingers back through his hair. "I can barely stand to have you here—"

His words tore through her defenses, annihilated the last remnants of the wall she'd created around her emotions in order to be able to do what she had to do to see him through the Gates.

He could barely stand to have her here?

The pain she had expected earlier hit her now, not physical, but an agonizing shredding of her emotions and defenses. She felt as though she'd skidded across pavement and was left bleeding and scraped. She'd dammed everything up in a reservoir, neat and tidy and held in check. But now the chinks in the wall gave way, and everything surged free. All her anger and fear and pain and regret.

With a cry, she rolled away, pushed to her feet and stood there staring down at him, her breath coming in harsh, quick rasps. "Barely stand to have me here? I saved your ass. I ripped myself in two—"

He moved so fast, he was on her before she could even process that he wasn't on the ground anymore. He caught her arm and spun her to fully face him.

"Yeah, you saved my ass, and that's the problem. I don't want you in harm's way. I don't want you at risk. I don't want you here. I want you in your kitchen with our daughter baking cookies."

"You don't get a say." The words tore free, laced with all the pent-up desperation and rage and fear that she'd bottled up for so long. Did he think she wanted this? Did he think she would have chosen this path if there were any other way? "What makes you think you get a say? I—"

He yanked her against him and kissed her, hungry, insistent. And she kissed him back, pouring all her fear and pain into that kiss, her mouth open and eager, her teeth catching his lower lip, biting him even as her balled fists came up to slam against his chest. She wanted to hit him, hurt him, for dying and leaving her and Dana, for being Sutekh's son, for all the nights she'd lain awake with tears creeping from the corners of her eyes as she sent feelers into the Underworld searching for him, only to come back with nothing.

Catching her wrists, he yanked her hands down to her sides, and he took charge, took over, his kiss stealing her breath, her thoughts, her will. She felt cool stone at her back as he pinned her against a bolder, his weight heavy on her, the bulge between his legs insistent and hard.

His free hand roamed up and down her back, closing on her ass, then her thigh, then her ass again. His touch wasn't gentle or sweet. And she didn't want it to be.

Jerking her wrists from his grasp, she pressed her

palms to his chest, his heart pounding beneath her touch. Smooth skin. Solid muscle. He was exactly as she remembered from that long-ago night in Miami.

No.

He was harder, leaner. And the playfulness was gone.

This was hunger. This was need.

There were layers here that hadn't been there then, built over seven years on a foundation of care for their daughter. Then built with bricks made of tears and loss when she'd thought he was gone.

Tearing her mouth from his, she pressed her lips to his chest, over his heart. Then buried her teeth in his flesh. Marking him.

His fingers threaded through her hair, and he pulled her head back so he could claim her mouth once more. His tongue danced and parried with hers, his body pressed against her, ridges and angles fitting her curves.

Coming up on her toes, she molded herself against him. Even a molecule of air was too much space between them. She was only hunger and need. Too much clothes. Not enough skin.

She yanked her shirt off. Fumbled with her bra. Finally, the clasp gave.

"Fuck," he muttered, dragging his teeth along her throat. "So fucking sweet, Bryn." One hand slid down to her ass once more, drawing her tight so she could feel the press of his erection against her crotch, the other closed over her breast, his thumb teasing her nipple as she arched into his touch. "Fuck," he said again and dipped his head to take her nipple in his mouth and suck hard enough to send an electric jolt to her groin.

His hips pressed hard against hers, pinning her to the rock, leaving her hanging there on the very tips of her toes as he feasted on her breasts, moving back and forth until she was panting and writhing, every stroke of his tongue and scrape of his teeth on her sensitive flesh making her gasp and arch.

"Please. Lokan. Please. Please."

Tangling his hand in her hair, he drew her head back so he could kiss her exactly as he wanted to, wet and deep, lips and tongue and teeth.

She fumbled with his button, then his zipper, her fingers clumsy, her breath rasping in her throat. Her hands brushed the solid bulge of his erection. She shoved at his pants until they slid a few inches down his lean hips and his cock sprang free.

Lust rocked her, liquid and hot as she closed her fist around him, velvet skin and smooth heat. He jerked, the air leaving him in a hissing rush.

Then he worked her jeans down in sharp, quick jerks until they wadded at her knees. His mouth found her shoulder, her collarbone, the curve of her breast.

Panting, she yanked one leg out of her jeans, and didn't bother with the other because he was hooking his arms under her thighs and lifting her, positioning her, with her back on the rock and her legs

spread to circle around his hips, baring her to him.
He held her there as he brought the head of his cock
to her opening.

She was wet and ready. So ready.

He pushed into her, stretching her, opening her.
Then he drew back a little, and a cry tore from her
as with a hard thrust he filled her, the sensation almost too much.

Her head lolled back against the rock as he drove
into her, hard, deep thrusts that pinned her in place,
and all she could do was hold on and *feel*.

LOKAN SEATED HIMSELF TO THE hilt, gritting his teeth
against the pleasure, so sharp and pure he thought
he'd lose it and come right then. It wasn't the time
or the place to do this. It wasn't smart and it wasn't
careful. And he didn't care. All he could do was
drive hard into Bryn, feel the tight heat of her sheath
and the sting of her nails biting into his skin and the
pleasure of being inside her. Being exactly where he
wanted—*needed*—to be.

"So hot. So tight. Damn, you feel so good," he
murmured, burying his face in her neck.

He didn't know what the hell he was feeling.
He only knew that whatever it was, it steered him,
pushed him, made him crazy as he thrust deep. He'd
wanted her for too long, denying himself the right
to tell her or show her because he'd rather have the
easy camaraderie she offered than nothing at all. And
she'd made it clear that there were walls between

them. For over six years, she'd made it abundantly clear.

Well, damn the walls and damn the boundaries and damn the fact that she had some explaining to do about exactly why he couldn't have been in her bed this whole time. She was his. *His.* And he was claiming her now before one or both of them got annihilated and he never got the chance.

He hadn't let himself acknowledge how he felt until now. Until he'd seen that wall of fire engulf her, incinerate her, and he'd felt as if he'd rip the entire Underworld to shreds to get her free, see her safe. Hold her one more time.

They might not get out of here. Either one of them could be lost. Wasn't that a fucking wake-up call? He wasn't waiting for later to claim her.

She grabbed his hair and yanked his mouth back to hers, kissing him hard as his hips moved against hers, and the gorgeous heat of her held him tight, driving him. He didn't think, only let himself feel, her mouth, her breasts, her nails raking his skin. She moaned into his mouth and clung to him and thrust her hips in time with his.

His body shook. His head spun. He could think of nothing but her, nothing but Bryn. His. She was his. She always had been.

He thrust his hand between their bodies, found the slick, swollen heat of her clitoris and pressed.

Her nails dug deeper. Her eyes slammed shut. She breathed his name, over and over, low and thick, as she fell over the edge, her body clamping tight around him, her release claiming her.

A last hard thrust and he came in a crashing wave, his cock pulsing inside her as he held her tight against him.

And he had no intention of ever letting her go.

CHAPTER SEVENTEEN

This god cometh forth to this pylon, and he passeth in through it, and those gods who are in the secret place acclaim him.
—The Egyptian Book of Gates

BRYN CLUNG TO LOKAN, BARELY daring to breathe. He was warm and solid, and for this moment, he was hers. How was she supposed to let go? How was she supposed to lose him all over again?

Her heart twisted. She was *going* to lose him. There was no arguing that. She'd agreed to the price Osiris had negotiated with her brothers. He would let Lokan Krayl pass, but his guide would remain in the Underworld. A soul for a soul. There was no changing that.

Boone had had tears in his eyes when he'd told her. He'd begged her not to do it. He'd begged her to let him and Jack and Cahn try to protect Dana. And her.

But they all knew there was only one way for Bryn to keep her daughter safe. She needed to get Lokan home.

She stared at him now, at his sun-bright hair, all shaggy and wild, and his blue eyes staring down at her, as if he could see clear to her soul.

But he couldn't. And she needed to tell him. She needed to explain about the deal. He had a right to know that only one of them was going back. But how was she supposed to say that, especially now?

Dipping his head, he kissed her, slow and sweet, his lips lingering on hers. Then he gathered her in his arms and carried her to the river's edge.

"We can't eat or drink anything here," she said, staring at the smooth surface of the water, "but given that we've already taken a swim in the lake of fire, I'm guessing it's okay to bathe...."

"But?"

"Well, I'm just thinking about the snakes."

He laughed, a low, rough sound that reached inside her and twisted her in knots. "I'll keep you safe."

Burying her face in his neck, she nodded. "I know." She did. And she was counting on it, not for herself, but because she knew he'd move mountains to keep their daughter from harm, and that's what she needed him to do.

She was no match for Sutekh, but according to Boone, Lokan was. According to Boone, Lokan's death had changed him, and his rebirth would change him even more. Change him enough that he'd be a match for Sutekh, and his father wouldn't be able to best him again. She didn't see exactly how that was possible, and Boone had played the "less-you-know-the-better" card. It left her thinking that maybe he didn't know everything, either.

So while she wasn't completely in the dark, she wasn't exactly a font of information. One thing Boone had been clear about: Lokan had to discover the changes in himself on his own. She couldn't tell him even what little she knew.

For all her best intentions to move forward with only truth between them, she wasn't doing so well at that.

He waded into the water just deep enough to reach his chest, then he ran his hands along her limbs and her back, her belly. She returned the favor, washing him and enjoying the feel of tracing her hands along his thighs, his waist, his muscled back. He bore no scars from the ordeal he'd just suffered in the fire and no marks of having been skinned and butchered. Not on the outside.

"You're not the same," she said, wondering if her words would make him look hard at himself, make him aware of the changes.

He drew back and stared down at her, then tucked a strand of her hair back behind her ear. "No?"

She smiled, but she had the feeling he could see through it to the sadness that she tried to hide. "Your hair's a little longer," she said, then traced the tip of her finger from the corner of his eye to his temple. "Your expression a little harder."

But the changes went far deeper than that. She had to bite her lip to keep from blurting questions and suppositions, saying everything that flashed through her mind, because talking just to fill the silence—the terrible silence that attested to all he'd suffered—was something she didn't want to do to him.

Finally, he shrugged. "Something had to give."

She waited, both hoping and dreading that he would say more. But he didn't. He only stroked his hands over her skin, as if he couldn't get enough of touching her.

He kissed her and touched her, and finally, she caught his wrists and said, "We should go," even though the words were not the ones she wanted to say, and even though she wished they could stay in this intimate moment, though perhaps not in this place.

"Yeah." He kissed her once more, a kiss that was more than passion, then looped one arm around her waist and walked with her to where they'd left their clothes.

Once they were dressed, he handed her into the boat, then climbed in and tucked her against his side and said, "Try and sleep, Bryn. I'll keep watch."

She thought that she should protest. But the truth was, as soon as he told her to sleep, she felt bone tired, as if her limbs were jelly and her neck was filled with down.

"Talk to me, Bryn. Let me listen to you talk."

"Talk myself to sleep?"

"Hey, if it works…"

She laughed. But for once, she couldn't find a

single word to say. She knew he wanted to hear her talk about nothing at all, the sorts of things she'd ramble about as she mixed ingredients for cookies. But this might be the only quiet chance she had to tell him things he truly needed to know. About her. About Dana.

Lethargy tugged at her, but she forced herself to stay aware and awake. "Dana should be human at least until she hits puberty."

Beneath her cheek, his chest rose and fell. "Is that when your abilities surfaced?"

A dark laugh escaped her to echo off the cavern walls. "No. I was a late bloomer. They surfaced a few years before I found you. I got a terse and dry explanation from Boone. He told me what I was, and what my brothers expected from me."

He lifted a strand of her hair and let it run through his fingers. Then did it again and again. "The same brothers that you left my daughter with."

The words were harsh, but the tone wasn't. There was no accusation there, and she didn't doubt that he knew she'd made the only choice she could. She didn't blame him for being skeptical. Worried. And she appreciated that he didn't go on the attack. Expected it, actually, because that was the Lokan she'd known before he was killed.

"The very same," she said. "I can't keep Dana safe. Not from your father. And not from any other deity who might know about her now. But my brothers can. At least until you get back. You'll free her from them. You'll keep her from your father."

"And we'll all live happily ever after."

She craned her neck to look up at him. "Lokan—"

"I'll free her." There wasn't an iota of doubt in his voice. Again, her hair slid through his fingers. "Is that what you did? You got free?"

"It wasn't all bad, Lokan. But I needed to escape the life they planned for me. To be free of their control. Free to *live*."

"Yeah? How'd that turn out for you?" He offered a short, dry laugh, and she wondered if he was thinking of his own life. From what she understood, no matter what freedoms and powers they enjoyed, soul reapers were basically indentured to Sutekh.

"Not at all the way I expected." She tried to gather the words, the *right* words, but any way she said this, it was going to sound terrible. Because it *was* terrible. What she'd planned. What she'd done. The mess she'd made of things because she'd been a young girl who rebelled just like lots of young girls. Except those girls didn't turn out to be supernatural time bombs. They just turned out to be young and foolish.

"Bryn, tell me."

"It isn't pretty." She hesitated. "It doesn't exactly paint me in the most flattering light."

He dipped the paddle and leaned down to rest his chin lightly on her crown before straightening once more. She closed her eyes, wishing—

"Tell me anyway."

"I never knew my mother. She left as soon as I was born."

"She was a supernatural. A walker."

"Yes." This was hard. Too hard. She was going to have to bare every ugly truth about who she was and the choices she had made, every mistake and misstep. But if she didn't tell him, he'd go back unprepared, and Dana would suffer for that. "My brothers raised me."

"Your father?"

Oh, no. Not going there. That was a can of worms she definitely wasn't ready open. "Not in the picture."

"You once said that your brothers were quite a bit older than you."

"Around seventy-five years older."

He was quiet for a moment. "I saved them. Did you know that?"

"No. Yes. I mean, I didn't know until recently. Boone told me about the train right before I came here."

"You weren't born yet."

She laughed. "No. I really am twenty-seven, not a hundred. You know, when I was a kid, I never noticed that there was something off about my life or my brothers. They hired nannies to take care of me, and a slew of armed guards. I thought they were there to protect me from my brothers' enemies. The human kind. And they were. But they were also there to guard me from any supernatural threat."

She could feel his heart beating under her cheek where it rested against his chest, and she closed her eyes and listened to each lub-dub, thinking how good it felt to hear it, and how good it felt to be this close to him. She hadn't let herself acknowledge how much she'd longed for this, how much that night in Miami had been imprinted on her psyche.

"Go on," he said, bringing her back from the haze she'd been drifting in.

"As a kid, I never noticed that my older brothers were *always* in their late twenties. That's how old they were when I was five. That's how old they were when I was ten. By the time I hit fifteen, I teased them about the fact that they had a great plastic surgeon. By the time I was eighteen, I didn't tease them about it anymore because by that point, they'd filled me in about what I was."

She felt the tension creep into Lokan's muscles. "And they were using you by then. Bartering your skills for their gain."

Oddly, she felt the need to defend them. Which was a little crazy, because she'd spent years hating them, hating the restrictions they'd put on her. She'd spent every waking second waiting for the chance to set herself free. But then she'd had a daughter, and she'd seen some of their actions through different eyes.

"Not that I'm defending them, and not that I can bear the thought of that life for Dana, but I've come to understand that my brothers did some of what they did out of love." She gave a soft laugh. "Stupid brothers. You don't cage what you love."

Lokan was silent for a long moment. "No," he said. "You don't. But I get why they might have wanted to."

She sat up and looked into his eyes. "But you would never do that to Dana."

"No."

Of course, she knew that. But hearing it stated with such calm certainty made her feel as if he'd given her a gift. "I think that my working for my brothers really wasn't much different than you working for your father." Whoa. Bad choice of words. Working for his father had gotten him killed. "Or any different than you helping your brothers," she hastened to add.

"I had a choice," he said. "It doesn't sound like you did."

"*Did* you have a choice, Lokan? Did you really?" she asked softly.

He drew her back down against him. After a second, he said, "One story at a time. Let's stick with yours for now."

"In the beginning, it was almost…exciting. I did my duty, followed their orders, guided souls to the Underworld god they needed to cement an alliance with at that moment. I lived under their protection. Of course, what that really meant was their control.

"Then things changed. As I got older and more adept, the controls tightened until I was desperate.

Choking. I was never alone. Not for a second. Can you imagine what that's like? I had guards on me at all times." She swallowed. "Even in the bathroom. They said it was for my protection. Knowing what I know now, I think maybe, in part, it was. But at the time, all I saw was that I was a prisoner with no way out and no hope."

"Did they hurt you?" She could tell from the way he asked, that if they had, he'd hurt them.

"No. No, nothing like that. They coddled me and pampered me and locked me away from any threat or danger. Jack brought me gifts. All the time. Jewels. Clothes. Books. I had a kitchen that would make any five-star chef happy."

"Is that when you started baking?"

She nodded. "One of my guards pulled out ingredients in a desperate attempt to entertain me one day when I was having a teenage girl meltdown. It worked. After that, Jack had the kitchen done for me. I was a princess in a tower. Then they'd send me off to guide a soul they needed delivered for political gain. Then back into the ivory tower I'd go."

"You weren't in an ivory tower when I met you."

"I ran away."

"How? If they were that vigilant?"

"It never entered their minds that I might bolt. My keepers were there for protection, not detention. Once I realized that, I started digging. I knew I was a half sibling to my brothers. Same dad. Different mother. I knew my mother was gone. I'd never met her. I always assumed she died at my birth.

"One of my guards had been with me since I was little. I couldn't remember a time that he wasn't around. Gruff guy. Not very chatty. His name was Crandall Butcher. He taught me tricks about how to hide. How to survive. Just in case I ever needed them. I doubt he expected me to use them against my brothers. He's the one who told me about the way things were. My mother was what I am, and I was the price of her freedom. A walker to replace a walker."

He tightened his arm around her. "So how did you end up in Miami? What were you looking for that night?"

"You," she whispered, wishing it were true. But it wasn't. To her shame, she'd been looking for a male supernatural, *any* male supernatural, to father a child. She'd happened to be at that club only because Jack talked about it all the time and talked about how many supernaturals frequented it. Of course, the night she'd chosen to go there, there had been only Lokan.

"Flattering," Lokan said, his tone dry and faintly amused, "but we both know that's a stretch."

She took a breath and then said in a rush, "I ran. From Boone and Jack and Cahn. I planned it for months. I hid money away. I bought a fake identity. I did everything I could think of to pave the way.

When I went into—" She felt her cheeks heat in a flush. There was no delicate way to say this.

"Into?"

"I guess you could say I went into heat. Four times. The only four times that would ever happen in my life. Walkers have a short window of opportunity to reproduce. And when it's gone, it's gone. Most of the time, I searched for someone to mate." Frack, this was hard. She felt sick laying it out there like this, naked and ugly. She wasn't the same girl who had done those things, made those terrible mistakes.

Lokan must have sensed her distress, because he pressed a kiss to the top of her head and said, "You were a kid. Whatever you did, whatever choices you made, you were a kid. You know the saying…hindsight's twenty-twenty."

"Would you change anything from that night?" she blurted, then closed her eyes and sank her teeth into her lower lip, wondering what had possessed her to ask him that.

For what felt like an eternity, he said nothing at all, and then he said, "Yeah." Just that. She held her breath, waiting for him to explain, but he didn't. He only said, "Your story, Bryn. I'm waiting for the rest of it."

She rolled her lips inward and swiped her tongue over them. "I needed to mate. I wasn't good at it. I couldn't find a supernatural. I tried with a human, and nothing took. I didn't get pregnant. I found a

Topworld grunt with a low level supernatural buzz. He was so drunk he fell asleep before the deed was done." She swallowed and pushed his arm off, not tired anymore and not willing to take the coward's way. She sat up and stared at him as she said, "And then there was you. I got pregnant. I planned to hand the baby to my brothers just the way my mother had handed me. A trade. A replacement. They'd let me go then, and I would be free."

His pupils were dilated and dark, the only overt display of his emotion. She didn't know if she disgusted him. If he hated her. Despised her. Whatever he felt, it could never be as bad as the things she felt about herself.

LOKAN FELT AS IF HE'D BEEN slammed in the gut by a brick. Dana. His daughter. She'd been payment that Bryn had planned to give her brothers in exchange for her freedom.

Rage surged. Not at her. At them.

He choked it back. That wasn't who he was. He was the thinker, the calm one, the politician able to look at all angles and see the best path through the tangled maze. He grabbed that part of himself now and held on. Because that part was calmly pointing out that Bryn *hadn't* given Dana to her brothers. She'd kept her daughter with her, and she'd kept her safe. It had been Lokan who'd put Dana in danger because of who, and what, he was. And it was those same brothers who were currently the only thing standing between his daughter and Sutekh, his murderous father.

Bryn shook her head. "I had it all planned. Find a supernatural. Get pregnant. Leave the baby with my brothers and get the hell out of there, just like my mother did. I would have my own life. I wouldn't be a pawn."

She made a choked sound, laced with self-derision. "I thought it would be so easy. But my first three fertile times were a waste. It turned out that finding a supernatural wasn't so easy. The night I found you was the final night of my fourth fertile time. My last chance. You were it."

"Flattering," he murmured. Only he couldn't drum up any sarcasm to lace that observation. A part of him understood. Hey, he'd been the dutiful son, playing by the rules, doing everything Sutekh asked and expected of him. And look how that had turned out. His father had hacked him to bits, sent his soul to purgatory and tried to steal his reanimated body.

Bryn's story explained a great deal. But it didn't explain one big hole. He was a soul reaper, and soul reapers couldn't reproduce. So what exactly had happened that night in Miami? He'd suddenly developed magic sperm because Bryn was a walker? That made zero sense.

Over the years, he'd often wondered how he'd come to father Dana, but he'd thought Bryn was human, and he hadn't dared tell anyone about his daughter, so there'd been no one to ask.

One more big question to find an answer to once he got the hell out of here.

"I looked for you," he said. "After that night. And I had a hell of a time finding you. It's because your brothers kept you hidden?"

She nodded. "Hidden. In their vocabulary, that's the definition of safe."

"And when I found you, you'd escaped them."

"I thought so."

"Thought so?"

"Turns out, they knew where I was all along. Kept an eye on me from a distance. Jack said they learned their lesson too late, that they figured if they tried to approach me, I'd bolt. So they just left things alone, left me my freedom, waited for the day I'd decide to contact them."

"And that's one of the reasons you trust them to keep Dana safe now. Because they've changed."

"Yes. And because I've changed. I made mistakes, too. Did things I regret. I thought I would give birth to a daughter, hand her to my brothers and walk away. I never thought—" Bryn shook her head.

"You never thought you'd love her the way you do."

"No," she whispered.

"Neither did I." *And I never thought I'd love you.* He did. Love her.

How the hell had that happened? How had he

fallen in love with Bryn? *When* had he fallen for her? Thinking about it now, he realized that he'd looked forward to seeing her every time he visited his daughter. That he'd liked the way things evolved. Easy. Natural. Bryn never complained when he'd changed the schedule, not just coming by on Wednesday nights and every other Saturday. She hadn't uttered a word of complaint if he showed up on Fridays, too. Or Sundays. She'd just let him tag along to whatever she and Dana had planned.

In fact, she'd seemed happy to have him there. They'd been a...family.

He should tell her. He should say it.

She pressed the flat of her fingers to his lips and shook her head. "Don't," she said. "Don't say it."

But he figured she had no clue what it was he was going to say. She probably thought he was going to say something harsh about the story she'd shared. But he knew better than anyone about making the best choice when every path sucked shit. She'd done the best she could with a raw deal, and he respected that. Admired it.

He stroked her hair. This wasn't the moment to tell her about his newly recognized emotions, to land something like that on her when he could barely understand it himself. To risk that maybe she didn't feel quite that way in return.

He didn't think he could handle that so close on the heels of his father's betrayal. So, yeah, maybe he'd wait a bit before laying everything on the line.

CHAPTER EIGHTEEN

*His enemies are under his feet, the gods and
the spirits are before him; he is the enemy of
the dead and the damned among the beings
of the Duat, Osiris putteth under restraint his
enemies, he destroyeth them, and he perfor-
meth the slaughter of them.*

—The Egyptian Book of Gates

THEY MADE IT THROUGH THE FIFTH Gate, but no farther.
No matter how hard they paddled, the boat stayed
exactly where it was. Bryn glanced around, her gut
telling her that they were overlooking a step in the
process.

"There," she said, pointing to a rectangular
shadow that notched the stone wall of the cavern,
and as soon as she spotted it, the boat floated toward
it as though dragged by an unseen rope.

The shadow turned out to be a corridor that cut
into the stone, and at the end, Bryn could see the
outline of a door.

"Looks like the only way in is through there."

"You sure we should leave the river?" Lokan
asked.

No. She wasn't sure at all, but the instincts that guided her, the genetic memories of thousands of years, told her that if they wanted to move forward, they must first stop here. "I'm not sure we have a choice."

Lokan guided the boat to the shore, and as the bow beached, Bryn jumped out and dragged it up. In seconds he was beside her, his hands within inches of hers as he helped her. "I doubt it'll float away. There's no current," he pointed out.

"It would suck if we had to make a quick exit and got here to find that we had no way to run. I don't want to take that chance."

He laughed, the sound warm and rich, touching places inside her that were dangerous and best kept under lock and key. Then he turned his head, so close that she could feel his breath on her cheek, and his eyes met hers. "It isn't like this whole journey isn't one big damn risk."

It wasn't. Not for her. She already knew exactly where she'd be when it was over. Trapped here for eternity. The risk to her was that she'd miss him for that eternity, that she'd long for him and ache for the sound of his voice, his laugh. She'd already had a taste of that when she'd been Topworld and he'd been gone. Now, the heartbreak would be compounded by the loss of her daughter, as well.

She looked away.

"No risk, no reward," she said, and headed for the corridor with Lokan at her back. She closed her eyes and swallowed when he laced his fingers lightly through hers, as though this was some sort of stroll through a garden rather than a journey through a vile and dangerous place.

At the door, she paused. There was no handle, no lock, just a smooth, wooden surface, polished to a high sheen. For a second, she only stood there, waiting for the words and spells that would open it to come to her, and when nothing did, she sent a questioning look at Lokan. "Suggestions?"

With a shrug, he reached over her shoulder and pushed.

The door swung open, and she gave an incredulous laugh. They stepped through to find mammoth columns towering on either side of them, so tall that the tops disappeared into the darkness.

Lokan rested his hand against the nearest column, traced his fingers over the symbols etched there. Then he spun, searching the shadows. "There should be sentries. One by each column."

"You know this place?"

"I've been here before. This corridor leads to the Hall of Two Truths."

She didn't know what that was, yet a chill chased up her spine, as though in some hidden place in her thoughts, she *did* know. And what she knew frightened her. "When were you there?"

"When I was sent by my father to parley with Osiris."

"That must have been…interesting."

He made a sound that might have been either a laugh or a grunt. "Even enemies occasionally find themselves in need of conversation."

"Is that what you had with Osiris? Conversation?" She had the unsettling feeling that there was something dark here, something frightening.

His jaw clenched, and she thought that whatever memories he had of this place would be better left in the past.

"What is it that has you spooked?" she asked. "This can't be any worse than the rinse and repeat episodes of fire and snakes."

"It is. Bryn—"

But whatever he'd been about to say was lost when an unfamiliar voice, disembodied and terrifying, broke in. "You will be judged."

Bryn turned and squinted at the darkness, but little had changed. There was no one else there, just a vast space lined by monstrous columns, illuminated now by an eerie greenish light.

"Lokan Krayl may pass. But Lokan Krayl is dead," the voice intoned.

"Thanks for the update. Lokan Krayl *was* dead," Lokan said. "You might want to work on your tenses."

"You will be judged."

"Been there. Done that. I know the way this goes down."

Knowledge uncoiled in Bryn's gut, along with fear, because judgment in the Underworld was never a good thing. She didn't yet know exactly what was coming, but she knew it was going be anything but pleasant.

Lokan took Bryn's hand and led her along the path that slowly became illuminated before them, the greenish light eating the darkness, step by step, to show them the way. "This might end up a good thing," he said in an undertone, though he didn't sound as if he believed that. "Might end up being a shortcut. You let me do the talking. And the slice and dice."

"Slice and dice?" She didn't know what he was talking about, but something in his tone made her wary. He sounded angry and tense.

A rustling sound, like rat claws scrabbling at rock, made her turn. From the corner of her eye, she thought she saw a robed figure with glowing red eyes and the head of a jackal, but when she looked at the spot dead-on, there was nothing there. The sound repeated behind her, and she turned again with the same results.

"Sentries," Lokan murmured. "Just ignore them and keep moving. They aren't the scariest things down here."

Now wasn't that encouraging?

A massive stone staircase appeared out of the darkness to loom before them. Lokan froze, drawing her to a stop. On the landing stood a creature with the body of a man and the head of a jackal.

There was a flail tucked in the crook of his arm, and he held a golden ankh, the symbol of life.

"Anubis." Lokan offered a shallow bow, just enough to be a mark of respect without showing weakness or subordination. Bryn wasn't sure exactly how he managed that. Maybe lots of practice.

"Lokan Krayl." Anubis's voice reverberated in Bryn's thoughts. "You are not dead."

"But not quite alive, either," Lokan said.

Something shimmered at the corner of Bryn's eye, and she whirled toward it. A second deity was revealed sitting upon a throne of hammered gold. Bryn gasped as he turned his head and leveled her with fathomless dark eyes lined in kohl. His skin was green, his garb pure white, so bright it glowed. On his head was a white Atef crown with feathers on the sides, and he held a crook and a flail.

Lokan's hold on her hand tightened in warning. He offered a slightly deeper bow and said, "Son of Nut. Son of Geb. God of life. God of death. Osiris, I offer greetings and respect."

"Lokan Krayl, son of Sutekh." Osiris's tone was blank and cold, sending a chill arrowing to Bryn's heart. Then he turned his head toward her, and she knew he waited for her to speak.

It was her turn to squeeze Lokan's hand. "Greetings and respect Osiris, god of life, god of death. I am Brynja," she said, "Daughter of Izanami and Pinga and Daena. Daughter of Sekhmet, warrior goddess, protector of Pharaohs. Daughter of Valkyries and shinigamis."

"You are the guide."

"Yes." Silently, she willed him to say nothing more. This would be the worst possible moment for Osiris to reveal the deal her brothers had made with him, a deal that would see Bryn sealed here in his Territory forever.

The shadows behind Osiris shifted and moved, and Bryn couldn't stop herself from taking a step back as a massive creature, terrifying in both proportion and appearance, stepped forward.

"Ammut," she whispered. The Devourer. Bone Eater. Part lion, part hippopotamus, part crocodile, she was a monstrous demon, the embodiment of eternal destruction.

"I know your blood, daughter," Osiris said. She felt Lokan stiffen beside her at Osiris's use of that particular word. Yes, she was his daughter. She had the blood of Osiris mingling with all the others in her veins.

Lokan squeezed her hand. "I figured," he murmured. "Hard to have genetic memory guiding you through a god's territory if you don't have that god's genetics in your cells."

She exhaled in a rush. Trust Lokan to have picked up on that. Of course, she should have told him before now. When was she going to learn? She'd said no more lies, no more omissions, and here was something that should have been first on the list of revelations. But the truth was, she hadn't thought it would come up, hadn't thought it important until right now.

"Why do you guide Sutekh's son?" Osiris asked.

The question blindsided her and left her feeling sick. Dizzy. Boone had said the deal was struck. He'd said that Osiris had agreed to let Lokan have a try at the Twelve Gates, and in exchange, Bryn was to stay in Osiris's Territory, his pawn, a guide in his ranks.

So why was he asking her that question? He knew exactly why she was here.

Her heart pounded. Her mouth was dry. The wrong answer and all could be lost. "He comes not as Sutekh's son, but only a traveler through this place. I come as his guide."

Osiris gave nothing away, but her words must have included something he wanted to hear because he made a slow sweep of his hand, and a massive scale appeared before him.

"Lokan Krayl, you will be judged."

And then he gestured for them to approach.

"JUST OUT OF CURIOSITY," Lokan murmured in an undertone as they walked up the gleaming stairs. "Any other deities you're related to, Bryn? Are you a Daughter of Aset?"

"No. The Daughters of Aset are of the blood of Aset's biological daughters. And I'm not of that blood."

He believed her. She was telling the truth. But there was something she wasn't telling him, and with both Anubis and Osiris staring down at them, and the gold scale holding their fate, now wasn't the moment to press for answers. Maybe it was information she didn't want to reveal in front of them. He could understand that, so he let it drop.

One plate of the scale was empty. The other held a single gleaming white feather. "The feather of Ma'at," Lokan said to Bryn. "The feather of truth." He turned his head to look at her. "Do you know what this ceremony entails?"

Her face was pale, her dark eyes wide. And when she shook her head, he figured he could pretty much guarantee that before this was done, she was going to get even paler.

A glance at Anubis, then Osiris gave him no clues as to their thoughts. But he knew his own thoughts and his determination. Bryn wasn't going to pay for her passage with blood. He'd figure out a way to keep her from having to live through the coming agony. He didn't know a damn thing about guides and guiding, but he knew she shouldn't have to face judgment as he did.

"Has your declaration altered since you last walked this path?" Anubis asked, projecting the question into Lokan's thoughts, and if Bryn's frown was any indication, into hers, as well.

"The forty-two declarations of purity," Lokan explained. To speak them tainted by a lie was to invite immediate destruction. But telling the truth didn't guarantee safe passage. "My declaration is as it was when last I passed this way," he said. There was nothing to change or add. Getting murdered by his father didn't change the cumulative body of his own sins.

"The ceremony demands your Ib," Anubis said and held out the gold ankh, the symbol of life.

"I know the routine." He did. And he wasn't too fond of it.

The ankh fit smoothly in his palm, and as he lifted it, the dagger at the end was revealed, catching the light.

"Lokan?" Bryn sounded uneasy and afraid.

"It's fine," he said, not looking at her. Because she was afraid for him, and seeing that in her eyes was only going to make this harder. He stared at the scale and said in a low voice, "O great Osiris, I would ask a question."

"You have nothing to offer in exchange for an answer."

Good point. "If I pass these tests and return to my former self, I will be in a position to repay you."

"You will never return to your former self, Lokan Krayl. Did your guide not tell you that?"

The words knifed through him, and his gaze shot to Bryn. "What?"

"No," she said, shaking her head, looking panicky. "That isn't what it sounds like. You *can* return Topworld. You just won't ever be the same as you were. After what you've been through, did you think you would be? Did you think you'd go back to being

Sutekh's soul reaper, sitting at his right hand, being his ambassador? Would you even want to?"

Everything she said made sense. Everything she said was truth. But there was something else there, something he couldn't put his finger on. Something he felt as if he ought to know, *could* know, if he just reached for it.

He looked at Osiris. "So I can return Topworld. I just won't be who I was before."

Osiris inclined his head. "You may return if judgment falls in your favor."

"So in what ways will I be different? Will I be mortal?"

To his surprise, Osiris actually smiled. "No, Lokan Krayl. You will never be mortal."

Anubis's voice reverberated in his skull, cutting short any further dialogue. "Proceed, or forfeit the right to be judged."

"What about Bryn? Does she need to do this?"

"She does not."

Relief was candy sweet.

"That was the answer I sought. I thank you for that."

He flipped the dagger in his grip, so the blade pointed toward his chest. He rested the thumb and index finger of his left hand on his fourth and fifth ribs.

He'd done this before, as Sutekh's ambassador, but then, all his heart had been required to prove was no malicious intent toward Osiris. This was different. This time, he really did have to prove purity and goodness. He'd laugh if the situation wasn't so dire.

His gaze found Bryn's. She was shaking, her eyes wide, pupils dilated. He offered a reassuring smile, then plunged the blade between his fingers, cutting through skin and muscle and fascia. His breath rushed through his lips on a harsh exhale. Damn, that hurt.

She cried out, and her fingers clenched into tight fists as she took a half step toward him. He shook his head, and she froze, drew a deep breath, stepped back. Yeah, that was his Bryn, soft and sweet and warm as a chocolate chip cookie, tough as hell when she had to be.

Blood ran in rivulets down his chest and dripped to the floor, each drop hitting the stone with an audible *plop.* He flipped the dagger once more and offered it hilt first to Anubis, who took it and wiped it on his own robe.

Bryn was sinking her teeth into her lip so hard she drew blood.

Using both hands, Lokan curled his fingers around his fourth and fifth ribs and spread them wide. The sound of cartilage snapping echoed like a shot. The pain was horrific, compounded by the knowledge of Bryn's horror and distress. But he'd done this before, with only Sutekh's whim riding on it. He could do it again now that it was his life riding on it.

He reached his right hand inside his chest, closed his fingers around his heart, felt it pulse and twitch as he yanked it free. His blood sprayed in an arc, hitting the scale, the floor, Anubis. And Bryn's shoes.

She gasped but held her place. Then she shocked the hell out of him, reaching out to hold the empty plate of the scale steady as he set his heart on it to be weighed. It lay there, still beating, sloshing blood onto the gold plate.

The side with his heart on it sank low, the weight of a lifetime of dark deeds dragging it down. Then it rose, slowly inching up. Then dipped again.

From the shadows behind Osiris, Ammut the Devourer stepped forward, jagged rows of crocodile teeth bared and ready to eat his soul.

"No." Bryn gasped and made to step between them. He threw an arm up across her chest, blocking her path.

Dizziness clutched him and spun him around. Or maybe the room was spinning. He couldn't say. He only knew there was nothing for him to grab hold of, nothing to save him. Memories ran through his mind like grains of sand, dark and bloody memories. And then there was one that froze and held, like a snapshot.

A cold and bitter wind. Two people, a woman and a man, and two little girls. He saw them in the water, and again on the ice. Then three little boys, with eyes blue and bright.

Then he was back before the scale, on his knees, head bowed. One palm was flat against the floor, the other pressed to his chest. Blood leaked between his fingers. Pain leaked through every cell.

But the plate of the scale was empty. And the hole in his chest was sealed.

He had been judged.

And he'd passed. Somehow, he'd passed.

Bryn fell to her knees beside him, thrust her shoulder under his arm and rose as he staggered to his feet to stand before Anubis and Osiris. Ammut was gone, swallowed by the shadows.

Then Lokan realized how different this scenario was than the times he'd come here as his father's ambassador. Those times, there had been only the scale and Anubis. He'd had to pass this point in order to be able to get in and see Osiris.

Why the differences this time? The judging process had been deeper. Darker. And why had Osiris been waiting for him?

Because this time *was* different. He wasn't just trying to get in to see Osiris. He was trying to pass through the entirety of the Twelve Gates and rise with the sun. Different process for a different outcome.

He turned toward Osiris. "So that's it. We're done. I've been judged and since I'm still standing here, that means I've been deemed worthy. I get to pass." He tipped his head toward Bryn. "And her."

"You may pass," Osiris said.

But Lokan had had too many years sitting by his father's side and being sent out as emissary and negotiator to fall for that. "Your use of the word *you,* is that singular or plural?"

Osiris blinked. In all the years Lokan had been dealing with him, he'd never seen the lord of death betray even that small hint of emotion. But today, he'd blinked, and earlier, he'd smiled. He had to wonder at it now, and for a second he tensed, wary and watchful.

"You may both pass."

"Thank you," Lokan said and meant it. He bowed, low enough to show respect without weakness or subservience. "A boon, if I may ask."

"You may ask, with no guarantee that I will grant it."

"Having been through the Hall of Two Truths more than once, I know you can move things along. I know that Bryn and I don't need to go back to that boat, that you can send us out through a different path."

Beside him, Bryn gasped, and he wasn't sure why. He couldn't imagine she wanted to go back to the endless river and the Gates and the serpents. "Lokan—"

"I can," Osiris said, looking at him intently. "Is that truly what you wish, a more direct and shorter route?"

Odd question. As if he'd want to fight lakes of fire and serpents and be tailed by Apophis for another seven Gates.

"Depends on the price. I seem to be running on

empty at the moment." He pulled his pockets inside out, his hands leaving smears of blood. His blood.

"The price has been paid in advance," Osiris said, and his gaze flicked to Bryn.

For a second, panic clogged Lokan's throat. Not Bryn. She wasn't the price. She couldn't be. He opened his mouth, but before he could say anything, Osiris continued. "You may both proceed to the final hour of the Duat."

The final hour. The Twelfth hour. And the final gate. Good news. Which left Lokan wondering why Bryn was trembling beside him, her skin cold, her lips blue.

And why unease was squirming in his gut like maggots on rotting meat.

CHAPTER NINETEEN

They it is who guard this hidden gate of Ament,
and they pass onwards in the following of this
god.

—The Egyptian Book of Gates

THEY STOOD IN A CORRIDOR SWEPT by flame, the entire length notched by alcoves. No river. No pebbled
beach. No cavern. Just a towering ceiling and block
walls, and a floor that went on and on in a straight
line without end. One moment, they had been standing before Osiris, and the next they were here, just
the two of them.

Bryn wondered if this was what Lokan had had in
mind when he'd asked Osiris to detour them around
the Gates. She thought he might have been angling
for a direct return to the Topworld. But that would
have been too easy.

And she wouldn't have been able to go with him.

Part of her was glad that they didn't have to face
the trials of the untried Gates. Part of her bitterly regretted the time she would not have with Lokan.

A surge of flame roared down the hallway, narrowly missing them as Lokan grabbed her arm and dragged her into the nearest alcove. It was shallow and dark, and she was pressed close against him, chest to chest.

"You're pale." He studied her, focused, intent. "And you're shaking." He dug around in his pocket and came up with some white-and-red mint candies that she'd seen in the backpack Boone had sent. "Here. Sugar might put some color back in your cheeks."

"Is a sugar hit your answer for everything?" she asked, trying for normalcy and suspecting she was failing.

He waggled his brows, clearly in a good humor after their success in the Hall of Two Truths. "Not everything."

The smile he offered made her heart catch. Then flames roared down the corridor again, and he pulled her deeper into the alcove, bracing his arm between her and the fire.

Bryn tried to summon what she hoped passed for a smile. "I'm glad to be rid of the boat," she said, "but I'm getting very sick of fire."

"I'll take you skiing in the Alps when we get back. You and Dana. You've never been a fan of snow, but I think this experience might change your mind."

Skiing in the Alps. An impossible dream, but she nodded anyway because her throat felt too tight to answer, and what would she say? Lie? Tell him that yes, the Alps would be lovely? They *would* be lovely, but she wouldn't be with him and Dana when they went.

"Dana would like that." She dipped her head and stared at the floor, the candy dissolving on her tongue, minty and sweet.

Lokan hooked his index finger under her chin and lifted her face. Then he leaned in and pressed his mouth to hers. She opened her lips, inviting him in, treasuring the feel of his mouth on hers and his hard body pressed tight against her own.

This might be their last kiss. This might be the last private moment she had with him, and she'd left so many things unsaid.

She leaned toward him when he drew back, her lips clinging to his. She wanted to remember the taste of him, the feel of his mouth on hers and his arms around her. The smell of his skin. The way he looked at her and listened to her, as though for that moment she was the only person in the world. As though what she had to say really mattered, even if she was just listing ingredients or chattering about Dana's day at the park.

From the first night she'd met him, he'd *listened.*

That mattered so much to her, to the girl inside her who had never been asked what she wanted or listened to when she spoke.

He cupped her cheeks and stared down at her, his pupils dilated in the dim light, surrounded by a rim of denim-blue. Laying her fingers along his jaw, she memorized his features. The tiny bump at the bridge of his nose. The way his lips curled up ever so slightly at the corners. The faint new lines that fanned from his eyes.

This moment would have to last her an eternity.

She remembered the first time she had seen him. She remembered the look on his face the first time he'd seen Dana. She remembered so many things.

And she needed *him* to remember one immensely important thing.

She needed to say it. She needed him to know. She didn't know if there would be another moment that offered this chance.

"Lokan, I love you," she whispered and came up on her toes to press her mouth to his. She tasted the salt of her own tears and the warmth of his mouth, and when she drew away and he made to speak, she pressed her fingers to his lips, willing him to let her finish.

"I love you. I will love you for eternity. I need you to know that. I need you to know that the choices I made were the best I could manage at the time. Don't—" She broke off and took a deep breath. "Don't hate me for my mistakes."

He caught her wrist and turned her palm and pressed a kiss there, his eyes locked on hers. "If you don't hate me for mine."

He knew something was wrong. She could see it in his eyes. He just didn't know what it was and she couldn't bear to tell him. Not now. Not yet.

"Bryn—"

"No. Please. Let me finish. I need to finish. I think I've loved you all along. But trust comes hard to me. Giving up any part of myself, even harder. I've made so many mistakes and I couldn't take the chance that you would be another. Because it wasn't just me anymore. I didn't want to take the chance that I would do something wrong, and things between us would sour, and Dana would suffer for that. But now I need you to know." She lifted her shoulders in a shrug because she didn't know what else to do, what else to say. "I love you."

He cupped his hand around her neck and dragged her against him with one quick yank. She was in his arms, chest to chest, the beat of his heart in time with hers.

The world fell away. There was only the two of them there in that kiss. No Underworld. No danger. No lies and omissions. Just her and Lokan. For the last time.

Her hands roamed his body as he kissed her. He was still shirtless, and she was glad for that, for the feel of his warm, naked skin beneath her palms.

The kiss was lush and deep and she poured her heart and soul into him, into letting him feel what she felt, letting him know the song in her heart. This, she could send back with him, a last shining memory, just as she would keep this memory here with her.

Her hands dipped to his waist and she undid the button there, then his zipper. And then she sank to her knees before him, wanting this so much.

She licked the line of muscle that disappeared
into his waistband, then tipped her head back and
looked up at him. His eyes weren't cool denim-blue
anymore. They'd darkened to the gray of a winter
sky. She licked him again, her tongue tracing lower.
His smile tightened. His eyes darkened even more.
His fingers twined through her hair.

The bulge of his erection teased her, tempted her,
and she dragged his pants down, setting the length of
his cock free. She licked him there, from the base of
his shaft to the tip. His smile disappeared; his breath
hitched; his fingers fisted tight in her hair.

A coil of heat spiraled to the pit of her belly, his
desire feeding hers.

Her tongue darted out to swirl around the head,
then she sucked him deep. He was hard and thick.
She couldn't take the whole of him in.

She grazed her teeth lightly all the way along his
shaft, dragging a slow hiss of pleasure from him. The
sound stroked her senses, making her ache. She took
him as deep as she could, wanting more, wanting to
swallow him whole.

His hips arched in a smooth pumping grind as he
filled her mouth, his pleasure heightening hers.

"Fuck," he snarled and dragged himself free, then
sank down until they were kneeling, face-to-face.
He kissed her, hunger and power stealing her breath,
making her liquid with need.

His fingers worked her button, her zipper, the me-
tallic rasp loud in the quiet. He dragged her pants

down over her hips, her thighs. An awkward scuffle and twist and she kicked them free, naked from the waist down, wet, ready.

Sinking back so his buttocks rested on his heels, he shoved his fly open a little wider, his cock standing thick and heavy. He hauled her forward, his mouth finding hers once more, his hands warm and sure as he brought her above him, positioning her thighs on either side of his.

One hand slid between them, his fingers finding her slick folds. She gasped as he stroked her, sliding one, then two fingers inside. He moved his hand in a teasing glide until she was rocking against him, gasping his name with each touch.

She was on fire. She was electricity and heat. And he was the switch.

"Bryn," he murmured against her lips. "So beautiful. So hot. So fucking sweet."

She was shaking as he cupped her ass and lifted her, then pulled her down onto the head of his cock. She felt stretched and filled as he pushed at her opening, and then he surged up and slid fully inside.

The feel of him was so good, so right. She trembled and cried out, her entire body consumed by each thrust. She buried her face in his shoulder. She bared her teeth and bit him, tasting salt and man. The feelings he was pulling from her were too deep, too strong, sex and love and fear that she was losing him, that in too short a time he would be gone.

Hold on to this moment. That's what she needed to do.

So she held on to him and rode him, his muscles hard under her hands, his cock thick velvet inside her.

He moved and she moved, drawing back to hold his gaze, the two of them in a perfect dance, their bodies working as one, their eyes locked on each other.

So good. He felt so good.

And it wasn't until he stroked his thumb along her cheek, then brought her tears to her lips that she realized she was crying. She sucked his thumb into her mouth, tasting salt, then she sank her teeth into him, and he grunted and surged deeper inside her.

His hands moved to her hips, gripping her hard as he rocked up, down, up again, the tempo faster, each stroke harder. Her fingers dug into his shoulders. Her thighs tightened on his.

The pressure built until it was too keen, too sharp, and she was gasping and crying out, her body wound so tight she thought it would snap.

His hand slid to her breast, his fingers brushing her nipple.

"Now," he gritted and tightened his fingers on her nipple. "Come for me, Bryn. Right now."

She did. With a scream, she shattered, her release rushing through her limbs, her spine arched, her head flung back.

His fingers convulsed, digging into her hip, her

breast. His body convulsed, shuddering beneath her. He came with her name on his lips, a low, dark moan.

Letting her head fall forward until her forehead rested on his shoulder, she struggled to catch her breath, to bring herself back from the place he'd taken her. She didn't know how long she rested there, but after a time, she realized that she was running her hands up and down his back in slow, lazy strokes, and that he was doing the same to her, as though neither of them could bear to stop touching the other.

"I'm sorry for being such a watering pot. Seems like I've cried more on this journey than in all the years I've known you put together," she whispered against his skin. She didn't want that to taint his memory of this moment. She didn't want him to remember her crying.

"Bryn," he said. "Look at me."

She did. She looked at him and *saw* him, saw everything about him. Not just the surface, so handsome, but everything inside. And she knew. In that second she knew, even before he gave her the words.

"I love you, Bryn. I love everything about you. The tears. The chatter. The strength." He smiled. "The cookies."

She took a shaky breath. *Now.* She needed to tell him now.

But the words wouldn't come. She couldn't bear to spoil this perfect moment.

He must have seen something in her eyes because he said, "I know you're afraid. I know you think you won't be able to guide me through. But we've faced the worst of it. There's only this last Gate, and then I rise with the sun. I'm not staying here. I'm coming back. I *will* walk the Earth once more." He kissed her again. "And I love you."

She nodded and forced words past her tears. "I know. I know." She did. Everything he said was true. He *would* get free of here. He *would* make it to the Topworld once more.

But she couldn't go with him. When he rose with the sun, he would be alone.

"No snakes. That's promising," Lokan said as they walked the corridor. They passed pairs of double-headed sentries, each clutching a staff. On one head was a glowing disk, on the other a scarab beetle.

Bryn's hand was cold in his. He figured he understood the reasons for that. This was the final Gate, the final step, but not the final challenge. Once they were free of the Underworld, there were still her brothers to face. They'd want to hold on to Dana. Of that, he had no doubt. And he and Bryn wanted their daughter back.

But he had brothers of his own, and if push came to shove, he'd start a war over his daughter.

He only hoped push didn't come to shove. He didn't want to do that to Bryn. Despite her estrangement from her brothers, and despite what they'd done to her, he had the feeling that she still loved them. Besides, she'd said something about them realizing their mistakes and mending their ways and knowing where she was all along but choosing to respect her privacy. He hoped that was true. But hoping wasn't the same as believing.

If it wasn't true he'd just have to dig deep, find the skills he'd learned at Sutekh's side and use them to negotiate an acceptable truce.

"What will you do about your father?" Bryn asked, her voice tense and low.

Now, wasn't that the question? "I don't know. I can't go back. But unless I can find another deity to take me on, I can't go anywhere else. It's a problem." Her hand twitched in his. "One I'll solve, Bryn. Every problem has a solution." True enough. Except he might not like the solution very much, because in order to guarantee his continued survival, he just might end up back in the family business. Wouldn't that be a barrel of fun? Working for the father who'd already murdered him once, spending every second of every day wondering what betrayal he was planning next.

Nothing personal. Business is business. He could almost hear Sutekh's voice in his head.

"What if you didn't need to find another deity to accept you? What if you could just…I don't know… exist on your own?"

He laughed. "Nice dream, but impossible. I need allegiance to a Territory. Either Sutekh's or someone else's. The cease-fire agreement doesn't allow for independent contractors in the Underworld. No deity affiliation means no go."

She stopped and turned to face him, and she was about to say something when a ball of fire rolled down the corridor toward them. He grabbed her and spun her into an alcove, the heat blanketing them. Once it passed, he stepped out and drew her along, their fingers intertwined.

"I have a question for you," he said. "Why did Boone help me?"

"Didn't he tell you?"

"Yeah, but I don't trust that he was completely honest. Let's say I buy into the idea of a debt repaid." To Underworlders—to supernaturals of any kind— debts had value. "And let's say I buy into the idea that Boone did it for you because you're his sister. There are still a lot of holes in that story." Boone had put his sister at risk, and Lokan wasn't one hundred percent convinced that there weren't a whole hell of a lot of layers under the icing of this particular cake.

But the answers he wanted weren't forthcoming because Bryn said, "We're here," and he turned to find that the corridor was at an end.

Lokan did a double take. An instant ago, there had been only an endless hallway. Now, there was an end to the hallway and two doors, each guarded by a monstrous serpent that stood on its tail. "More snakes," he said.

"Sebi," Bryn said and gestured at one of the doors, then gestured at the other and said, "Reri."

Her fingers tightened on Lokan's and her eyes met his. "I love you," she whispered. "And I love my daughter. Remember that when you're tempted to hate me."

He didn't like the sound of that. "What—"

The serpents rose up, and the smell of sulfur was strong in the air. Here was the source of the flames that had harried them all the way along the corridor. And it looked as if they were about to spit fire once more.

"Speak the names. Now," Bryn ordered, her voice tense.

Together, they spoke the names. "Sebi. Reri."

The snakes eased down, and together, both doors swung open.

Bryn lurched forward and pressed her lips to his in a clumsy kiss. He figured she must be elated. He knew he was feeling pretty good himself. They'd made it this far. They'd completed the journey. All that was left was for them to walk through the doors and board the bark of the sun that would carry them into day. Through the open doors, he could see the first pink-and-gold hint of sunrise.

"Does it matter which door we take?" he asked, his throat dry, his pulse racing.

She was trembling, her jaw set, her eyes wide as she shook her head. "No. Go ahead."

Alarms went off in his head. Something was wrong. "You first," he said and took a step back toward her, away from the serpent and the open door.

With a cry, Bryn launched herself at his legs, throwing her weight against him and sending him tumbling backward. Only the unexpectedness of her actions gave her the edge, and he fell back through the doorway while she remained in the corridor, curled on the floor, sobbing.

"What the fuck?" he snarled and pushed to his feet, then tried to step through the threshold to get back to her. But he couldn't. His way was blocked, and the door was slowly swinging shut. "Bryn," he yelled and tried to shove his foot and then his hands in the doorway. But no part of him could pass through. "Bryn," he roared.

"I'm sorry." She lifted her head, and her gaze met his through the narrowing crack in the door. She stretched out one hand toward him, their fingers almost touching as he stretched his toward her. "I am the price. I'm sorry."

And then the door slammed shut.

CHAPTER TWENTY

This is the secret Circle of the Duat, wherein this great god is born, when he maketh his appearance in Nu, and taketh up his place in the body of Nut.

—The Egyptian Book of Gates

"Bryn!" Lokan pressed his palms against the door and roared her name. But no matter how many times he slammed his fists against it, no matter how many times he dragged his fingers around the perimeter looking for a crack, no matter that tears wet his cheeks, he couldn't get the damn door open once more. "I can't leave you here. I can't just walk away."

She didn't want that. Couldn't want it. What she wanted was to get back to Dana. What she wanted was to stay with him.

And she wasn't going to get either of those things.

Because she was on the wrong side of the door. How many times during this journey had she told him there was no going back?

"The door is sealed, Lokan Krayl."

He knew that. He fucking knew that. Dropping

his forehead against the wood, he tried to get his emotions under control. Tried to rally. To face what came next.

Logic was his enemy. Because logic told him he couldn't just stand here and mourn. He needed to get free of the Underworld. He needed to rescue his daughter. Only then could he figure out a way to come back, a way to get Bryn back. He had to believe there was a chance even when everything inside him told him there wasn't. Damn. Damn. He wanted to hit something. Kill something. Rip a beating heart from a torn chest and feel the blood spray his cheeks. He wanted to let the primitive pain inside him out.

Instead, he turned and faced the room.

On either side of him were more serpents, smaller than the ones in the corridor had been. Not cobras. Asps.

"She is gone."

Nice. A talking snake. Telling him exactly what he didn't want to hear. But there was something odd about both serpents. When he turned his head and caught sight of them from the corner of his eye, they shimmered and danced and changed forms. Not serpents. Women, he thought, though he couldn't get a clear enough view to say with any certainty.

But the voice. He knew that voice.

He turned his head, looking past her instead of at her, and for an instant a woman stood before him in place of the snake. She had night-black hair and a face both lovely and arresting. Her features were bold and strong, her dark eyes outlined in kohl, her mouth lush. She was dressed in a diaphanous gown of white, shot with silver thread, and when she moved, the cloth and her hair and even the air around her appeared to move with her. She was beauty and grace, and he knew her.

"Aset." Sister/wife of Osiris. Mother of Horus. Progenitor of all Daughters of Aset and the Asetian Guard.

She was Sutekh's enemy, and until his death, she had been Lokan's.

Now, she was the last boundary between him and freedom. And she was possibly the one who could salvage this mess.

"Oh, Aset," he said, his voice rough as gravel, "give me that which I ask. Return to me what is most precious."

Tinkling laughter, it danced through the air all around him. Like water. Like chimes in the wind. But sad, somehow. As though she knew his pain.

He turned his head as she became an asp once more, trying to see the form of Aset, but he saw only the serpent, her scales shiny brown-black.

"Most precious?" she asked. "What is that, Lokan Krayl? Answer me. Tell me. Is it your life? Your daughter's life? The lives of your brothers? What is most precious? What gift do you beg? Or perhaps it is vengeance you crave."

All that and more.

Anger and regret choked him, sitting like a lump

of cold porridge in his throat. His daughter. Bryn. His brothers. Himself. Revenge against Sutekh.

A list of many things. Was there some significance to the order of priorities? They flowed through his mind in that order. Was that how he ranked them now? With only Dana standing before Bryn in his heart?

"I don't want to leave her here," he said, certain of that.

"There is a price for your life. A sacrifice that must be made," Aset replied. Her voice sounded as if it came from all around him. In front, behind, above, below. He spun a full circle, ending up facing forward once more. "One soul may go, and one must stay. Will you stay here and send her back?"

"Yes."

"Then all she has done and suffered will be for naught. Sutekh will find her. He will find your daughter. Brynja is no match for him. He will take what he wills and leave only decimation behind."

He knew that. He couldn't argue a word of it. Because for centuries, he had been the decimation Sutekh sent to those who crossed him.

"I'm no match for him. He killed me once already."

"With your agreement."

True. Because he'd traded his life for his daughter's. Who was to say he wouldn't find himself in exactly that position all over again? The possibility bubbled and hissed like molten lead inside him.

"Regardless, the question is irrelevant," Aset said. "The choice was made before she ever came here. Brynja knew the price."

He felt as though Ammut the Devourer had taken a bite out of his chest, clear to his heart. It was on the tip of his tongue to call Aset a liar, but he held back the words.

Because as much as he wanted to rant against her assertion, he knew it to be true. There had been hints all along, and he just hadn't wanted to see them.

"Is there nothing you can do?" His mind spun the possibilities on a wheel and came up with only tangled threads. "She is of Izanami's line. And Pinga's. Maybe even yours," he threw out there, offering a desperate gambit, though Bryn had said she was no Daughter of Aset.

"She is the child of all, the descendant of many." But something in the seconds that ticked past before Aset replied made him think there was some link between her and Bryn. Then it hit him. Bryn was of Osiris's blood. Aset was his mate. That meant that she *had* to be Aset's line. But not a Daughter...

"Horus," he said. "Bryn is your son's daughter."

Aset inclined her head. "She is of Horus's line."

Which meant her brothers were of Horus's line. His thoughts spun. He'd known Horus had four sons, advisers of pharaohs and kings, but he'd never followed where that line led.

All considerations for another day. On this day, his focus was leaving here with Bryn at his side.

"You have your blood, O Aset. You have your power, O Aset. You have your magic, O Aset. In this moment, you have all the power. You are here, and the many who claim lineage to Bryn are not." He paused, fighting against the panic that surged. He couldn't bear to leave her here. To never see her, hold her, kiss her. To rob their daughter of her mother. "You are here and they are not."

"I cannot."

"Surely there is one deity who will claim her."

"One deity has," Aset replied. "Osiris has claimed her. She will guide souls through the Gates. It is done. It is written."

He gritted his teeth and held her gaze, and when he spoke once more his voice was a hollow rasp. "My father used dark magic to briefly possess a human form. He and his followers skinned me alive. And with each cut of the blades, I stared straight ahead. He hacked the limbs from my body, one by one, and I held back the screams, only knowing I had traded my life for something far more important." The life of his daughter. He swallowed, then continued. "I never begged. I was murdered, my soul banished to a hellish place, a null zone. And I never begged. But now—" slowly, he sank to his knees, and his voice broke "—now I'm begging you, O Aset. Set Bryn free. Let me take her back. Let her live."

Aset said nothing for so long he thought she would not reply. When she finally spoke, her voice was soft. And sad.

"I have no power in this, Lokan Krayl. I cannot return your love to you. But I can return you to the daughter you created together. I can return you, and in her you will see her mother. In her, you will be comforted as I was comforted by my son Horus when his father, Osiris, was taken from me."

Taken from her by Sutekh, Lokan's father. The agony of loss had come full circle.

Her words tore at him. He was going back. He would be what he had been before. A demigod. A soul reaper in his father's—his murderer's—army. Immortal. Invincible. But Osiris was right. He could never *truly* be what he had been before because without Bryn, he could never be whole.

What Bryn had sacrificed for him…the sacrifice she had chosen for their daughter. It killed him to know that there was no other way.

"Why do you believe this of me? Why do you believe I am the only one who can keep the jackals at bay, the only one who can keep my father from taking my daughter's life and sending her soul to a null zone as he did to me? He killed me. He stole my body. What makes you think I can stop him from doing the same to her?"

Aset gave an incredulous laugh. "You do not know? You truly do not know?"

"Know what?" he snarled. "Damn, I'm getting tired of subterfuge."

"Your entire life was subterfuge."

"Was. Past tense."

She strode toward him, her eyes black as onyx, her dark hair swaying, the folds of her diaphanous white dress undulating as she moved. She was beauty and grace, and she was being far kinder to him, the son of her enemy, than he had a right to expect. Sutekh had hacked her husband, Osiris, to pieces, stolen his life, left her heartbroken.

He'd heard the story a thousand times, but until now he'd never understood what she'd been through.

She laid her hand on his back, a gentle touch. "Accept. Mourn. If you fight, it will only bring you pain. You have a daughter to live for." He tipped his head and looked up at her, his throat clogged. Tears. He wanted to cry. He wanted to strike and beat something to a pulp. Not her, but…something. Someone. His father. In the end, it was Sutekh who was responsible for all of this.

"I can't go back to him. I can't be his ambassador or his soldier. I can't reap souls and carry them to him to feed what he is. So what happens now? Is there even a way for me to choose another path?"

She stared at him for what felt like an eternity, and he waited, certain she would tell him something monumental. But in the end, she only turned away and gestured at the boat of glowing gold that waited.

Of course. It had to be a boat.

CHAPTER TWENTY-ONE

The hidden abode is in darkness,
so that the transformations of this god
may take place.

—The Egyptian Book of Gates

BRYN CRIED OUT, RIBBONS OF pain sluicing through her as she tried to pull her soul free and send it after Lokan. She knew she couldn't join him. She'd known it all along. But she wanted to see him safe, to know that he made it, that the final step of his journey was complete. That their daughter would be safe.

But though her soul tore free, it could not pass the Gate. She said the name again and again, but the doors were shut to her and she could not pass.

"Enough."

Lifting her head, she blinked against the veil of tears and saw Osiris standing before her.

"Is he gone?" she asked, unable to hold the words back, though Osiris owed her no answer.

And he offered none, only stared down at her without words or expression.

"Rise," he said.

She did, pushing up onto all fours, then forcing herself to her feet. She had chosen this. She had agreed to this. She would not lie on the floor like a discarded rag.

Rising to her full height, she filled her lungs and waited for Osiris's instructions. She had no idea what would be expected of her now.

"Behold," he said. And then he turned and drew his hand before him.

Bryn gasped and stumbled back a step as a vista opened before her. There was Lokan, in a boat. She expected to see him sailing for the dawn, but he wasn't. He was in a tunnel, dark and dank. The river was still, and he paddled, alone.

"No," she said. "He was supposed to go free. He faced the Gates. He passed all the tests."

"He must face the demon, Apophis," Osiris said.

Bryn's heart hung like a chunk of lead in her breast. Apophis. Evil incarnate.

"How—" She surged forward, hands outstretched, but the image wavered and disappeared, only to re-appear several feet away.

Behind the boat, the water parted to reveal the coils of a massive serpent as it dove to the depths. Lokan was looking forward, not back. He didn't know the snake was there, had no way to know as it slid through the dark water, silent and deadly.

Bryn's heart slammed against her ribs, and she couldn't still the instinct to cry out, to reach out. All she succeeded in doing was to make the image disappear again, then reappear once more farther along the corridor. Forcing herself to keep still, she wrapped her arms around her waist and held tight, her heart in her throat.

The serpent's head broke the surface directly in front of the boat, sending up waves as tall as houses. It reared up and up, towering over Lokan, fangs white and sharp, red eyes glowing. Fat droplets of water flew off it in all directions.

Lokan brought his paddle up in a two-handed grip, his stance defensive.

Apophis's jaw unhinged; his prey was in sight.

With a roar, Lokan surged forward, with only the paddle for a weapon.

A paddle against a demon god fueled by evil and the drive for chaos. Lokan could not win. He could not survive.

"Help him." Bryn spun to face Osiris, who only turned his head to look at her, vital seconds ticking past.

Then he said, "I cannot. This, he must face alone."

Bryn sank her nails into her palms, barely aware of the sting. To her horror, the serpent descended, its head twice as long as the boat, its gaze fixed on Lokan. He ducked and came up from below, slamming the underside of Apophis's jaw. But the snake kept coming.

Everything in her screamed for her to go to him, to find a way to get to him, to stand by his side. Again, she pulled her soul free, but Osiris turned to her, his expression solemn, and said, "You must not. He must prove himself to be what he is meant to be. You must not interfere." He paused. "You cannot interfere."

Bryn's soul snapped back with enough force to send her stumbling. Panting, she slammed her hands against the wall, struggling for balance, then turned to watch the tableau unfold.

Again, the snake struck, incredibly fast. Lokan ducked and rolled and the snake's jaws closed on the middle of the boat, snapping it in two. The first half, the serpent flung against the cavern wall with a twist of its head. Then it turned to the remaining half, the half that Lokan clung to.

His paddle was lost. The stern tipped up, the jagged, broken middle sinking into the inky depths.

Bryn didn't move, didn't breathe, her chest so tight she thought her ribs would snap.

The remains of the boat slid down and down until the curved end disappeared beneath the surface. And Lokan disappeared with it.

LOKAN DOVE BENEATH THE BOAT, using it as a shield. Apophis's coils surged and twisted as the snake searched the depths for him.

Nice of Aset to warn him that he'd be facing the demon snake on the way out.

Maybe that was the point. No forewarning. No chance to prepare. Some sort of test of his right to follow the sun into day.

His lungs screamed. His heart pounded. And still, he held himself beneath the shattered husk of the boat.

The massive girth of Apophis's body slid past. Then his tail. Lokan knew he had only seconds before the demon snake rounded for another pass.

He needed a plan and he needed it now. He'd already lost Bryn. He couldn't allow his daughter to be robbed of both her parents.

He had no weapon. He had no way to fight this evil. Fuck, he'd need an army—

An army.

He remembered the cordon of souls and the rowers telling him they were here for him. *Him.*

How many times over the centuries had his father told him that a leader leads? He had learned from a master. It was time to put his lessons to use.

With powerful kicks, he surged upward, his head and torso breaking the surface as he roared. "I call upon the souls of the dead. I call upon the souls locked in the Duat. *Behold, to me belong these words of power, from whomever they are with. Fleeter than greyhounds, quicker than a shadow—otherwise said, quicker than a shadow.* I call the souls of the Duat to me."

The water churned and boiled, and he saw Apophis coming toward him, red eyes glowing beneath the water.

"To me," Lokan roared.

All around him the water surged in bubbling geysers, and the shore filled with blue light. The souls of the dead came as they were called, wielding magical nets, gathering his power and the power of the Duat, leashing the chaos that Apophis carried and turning it to order.

Apophis struck, mouth open, razor sharp teeth bared.

Lokan wrapped his arms around one of Apophis's massive teeth and hung there. As the serpent rose above the water, Lokan was carried with him, whipped to and fro, the demon snake struggling to dislodge him.

"To me belong these words of power. Come to me."

His hands were slick from the water and the serpent's venom. His gut churned. His pulse raced so hard and fast he could hear only the roar of his own blood rushing in his ears.

Apophis whipped his head to one side, and Lokan's grip slipped. One hand fell away, and he hung there, high above the surface of the water. The serpent tossed its head to the opposite side, and Lokan's hand slid along its fang, lower. Lower. He gripped as hard as he could, but couldn't hold on.

His fingers tore free. He flew through the air for what felt like forever, then he slammed against rock. Pain ricocheted up his arm from his wrist.

He slid down the cavern wall and onto a ledge, a grunt of agony pulling free as he landed on his injured wrist. His hand hung limp and useless, jagged ends of bone protruding through his torn flesh. And above him, Apophis reared.

With an unholy yell, he pushed himself to his feet and forced everything he had into thoughts of a strike. A killing blow. He fed his rage and pain and the horror of leaving Bryn behind into his need to destroy the demon snake.

Below him, the blue light surged and grew stronger. *His* light focused and magnified by a thousand souls.

He staggered to the edge. The heads of a thousand souls rocked back, and their eyes turned to him, expectant, revering. He dug into whatever reserves of power he had. He visualized a net made of bands of fire, the same bands of fire he had used to tether darksouls for nearly three hundred years.

They danced and wove, and the eyes of the army turned from him to the snake. The hands of his army rose, with filaments of light connecting them. Then the light wove strands, a net of magic and power, and together they held the demon snake back.

Panting, Lokan hung his head, trying to get his breath. The light faded. The cavern grew dark once more. And then the way out became clear.

Not a boat at all.

Kheper. A scarab beetle, vessel of the sun.

Bleeding, battered, Lokan dragged himself down the wall of the cavern, inch by torturous inch, his damaged wrist cradled against his belly. Then he dragged himself onto the golden back of the beetle and hung there as he went forth into day, carrying pain and regret and confusion with him.

But his heart, he left behind in the darkness of death's night.

CHAPTER TWENTY-TWO

Evil is the doom which hath been decreed for
you before my father. It is you who have com-
mitted sins, and who have wrought iniquity in
the Great Hall; your corruptible bodies shall
be cut in pieces, and your souls shall have no
existence, and ye shall never again see Ra.
—The Egyptian Book of Gates

LOKAN TOSSED THE KEYS TO THE valet and strode
around the hood of the Porsche. The sun was hot on
his skin, and he took a second to tilt his face to it.
He'd be a fool to ignore the gift he'd been given. A
second chance at life.

It had taken him longer than he would have liked
to get here. He hadn't been able to choose where the
day brought him. Given the choice, he'd have come
to Dana straightaway. Searched for his brothers.
Brought reinforcements with him.

But nothing ever went according to plan. He'd
been dropped, bloody and bruised and clad only in
a pair of ragged and torn khakis, in the middle of the
fucking Mediterranean Sea, his energy stores so low

that his best efforts to summon a portal had carried him only as far as land.

Actually, he was surprised he'd even been able to accomplish that. He shouldn't have, not given the fact that he'd eaten only protein bars, some candy and the single meal Boone had fed him in months and months. He was running on empty.

But he felt... He didn't quite know how to describe it. He'd healed too fast, his cuts and abrasions, and even the fractured wrist he'd suffered when Apophis had thrown him against the cavern wall, gone within minutes of hitting land.

All soul reapers healed quickly. But not that fast. Especially when he'd been starved and drained for months. Not to mention dead.

And there were other things. Odd things. He'd reached for his brothers. He should be able to sense them. But they weren't there. He couldn't find them, and he didn't want to acknowledge the cold terror that lurked at the edges of his thoughts, the fear that they were dead as he had been dead. Killed by Sutekh. Could Sutekh have done that? Killed them all? The thought was acid burning in his gut.

But he needed a calm head to face Boone. And he had a feeling that Bryn's other brothers would be here, as well.

Bryn.

He swallowed against the fist that closed around his heart as he thought about her. That fist was there every second of every day. Sometimes tighter. Sometimes it let up just a little. But the pain never really went away.

He paused and tipped his head back, studying the black glass face of the Luxor. Time to hold his daughter in his arms. And he would cut down anyone who tried to stop him.

Spells and wards touched him with icy fingers. They were things that might have given him pause before. The politician he'd been wouldn't have wanted to ruffle feathers. He'd have taken an alternate route, talked his way inside.

Fuck that.

He strode to the hidden door at the side of the pyramid. When it didn't open under his touch, his fist shot through the glass. His power shot through the wards, frying them like faulty wiring.

That was new. An added benefit of having come back from the dead?

He strode down the hall that he'd followed Boone through the last time he'd been here. He stalked through the deserted, darkened club. When he reached the first set of leather-covered metal doors, he paused just long enough to rest his fingers on the surface and feel it, cool and smooth beneath his touch.

Then he curled his fingers into the minuscule gap at its edge and tore the thing off.

"You're paying for that. And the glass you smashed."

He spun to find Boone leaning against the bar, watching him.

"Not a problem. Where's Dana?"

"Safe."

That one word was like salt rubbed in a gaping wound.

"I want to see her. Now."

Boone nodded. "This way."

Lokan was beside him in three strides. He caught Boone's arm in an inexorable grip. "You fuck with me," he said softly, "and I will annihilate you."

"I don't doubt it, my friend." Boone glanced down. Blue fire sparked off Lokan's fingertips and ran along Boone's arm.

The smell of burned cloth and then burned skin wafted upward.

Lokan jerked his hand back and his gaze shot to Boone's. Except Boone didn't look surprised. Which was funny, given that Lokan was shocked as hell. That wasn't a soul reaper ability, that whole blue light/fire thing. But it looked as if it was *his* ability now.

"Dana is well," Boone assured him and led the way through the double set of doors that Lokan had passed through last time he was here. Except this time, the second door didn't open to a room but to stairs that descended into the bowels of the earth. "We created a dimensional box for her, and we recruited guards to remain inside, protecting her and entertaining her."

"Guards?"

"The woman who retrieved your daughter from the Setnakhts—"

"Roxy Tam, right?"

"Yes. She agreed to join our efforts. Dana was asking for her. Apparently Bryn taught her that if everything blew to high hell, Dana was to contact Roxy."

The sound of Bryn's name on Boone's lips hurt. So Lokan focused on his daughter, thought only of Dana and what Boone was explaining because thinking about Bryn was like gutting himself with a dull knife.

"You said guards. Plural."

Boone glanced back and nodded. "Two other Daughters of Aset joined her. Naphré Kurata and Calliope Kane."

"Should I know those names?" He didn't, but he almost felt as though he ought to.

"Perhaps not," Boone said and began to descend the stairs. "Not yet, anyway."

Lokan could feel spells and wards growing stronger with each step he took. They touched him with damp, cloying tongues of magic. So, not wards of pure light, but spells woven with darkness.

"Who set these wards?" he asked.

"The Matriarchs."

Lokan stopped dead. "The Matriarchs. You're talking about the top dogs of the Asetian Guard."

Boone stopped a few stairs down and turned to look at him. "I am. They have a vested interest."

"In my daughter?" He crossed his arms over his chest. "Explain. And while you're at it, tell me exactly what I'm going to find in this dimensional box. I'm not much one for surprises."

"So you've said before." Boone offered the faintest hint of a smile. "You will find your daughter, hale and hearty. You'll find the Daughters of Aset that I've already told you about. You'll find luxury and entertainments we provided to keep Dana busy." He paused. "And you'll find your brothers."

"My brothers." Maybe that was why he'd been unable to pick up on their emotions. Because they weren't in the same dimension as him. He hadn't been able to reach them when he'd been in the null zone, either, and he'd tried. Damn, he'd tried. Then another thought struck. "My brothers. In a box with three Daughters of Aset."

"One of whom also happens to be the granddaughter of Izanami-no-mikoto."

"Right. Okay. And you kept them from killing each other, how?"

Boone smiled, a cat with a full bowl of cream. "You'll see." And turning, he led the way down and down and down.

"So how does this work?" Lokan asked when they got to the bottom. "I just walk through into the box?"

"No." It wasn't Boone who answered. He lifted his

head and saw two other men, familiar, but not. They
looked like Boone and a little like Bryn if he stared
hard enough. So he stopped staring hard enough because seeing her in them was too painful.

One guy was wearing jeans and biker boots and
several silver hoops in each ear. The other was
dressed in khakis and a shirt that stretched tight
across his chest and shoulders and hung a bit loose
at the waist.

"Jack." The first guy offered his hand. Lokan took
it, consciously holding back the fire that had singed
Boone earlier. The second guy shook his hand and
introduced himself as Cahn.

Lokan had mixed feelings. These were Dana's
uncles, Bryn's brothers. The same brothers who had
used her and held her prisoner and sent her to the
Underworld to stay there forever. The same uncles
who might challenge him and try to keep Dana for
their own purposes. He didn't trust them. But he also
owed them. Because they'd kept Dana safe. Somehow, they'd even wrangled the Asetian Guard into
helping and convinced his brothers to work with their
enemies. All for Dana's sake.

Which told him that whatever their flaws, they
were persuasive bastards, and *that* he counted as a
virtue.

Behind the three Falconer brothers, the air undulated and curved, as though the wall and the door
were an illusion. Lokan could see the limits of the

dimensional box. It struck him that he hadn't been able to do that the last time he and Boone had met.

"I want to see her."

Boone nodded. "We need to bring them out in layers. Dana will be last."

Lokan stared straight ahead, every nerve alight. He felt as if electricity danced off his skin, as if he was going to spark and go up in flames.

"You, uh, might want to rein that in," Jack said, with a nod at Lokan.

"What?" He glanced down to see blue sparks dancing off his skin. He had no explanation for it. It was just something he'd brought back with him into the day.

He'd rather have brought Bryn.

No. Not going there. He would not think about her. He would think only about Dana right now.

The air before him shimmered and bent, and a man walked through, then another, then a third.

Lokan couldn't breathe, couldn't move. And if the expression on Dae's face was any indication, he was feeling pretty much the same way.

"Fuck. Me. Raw," Dae rasped, then surged forward to grab Lokan in a bear hug. He lifted him clear off the ground, then set him on his feet. Then punched him in the gut.

Except his fist never connected. It stopped an inch away, held there by an unseen force.

"Damn," Mal muttered as Dae drew back his hand and shook it out, as though he'd actually connected

with something. Then Mal must have decided he
didn't care because he shouldered Dae aside and gave
Lokan a similar hug.

And then it was Alastor's turn. He strode forward
and stopped directly in front of Lokan. His eyes were
shadowed, his mouth grim. "You bloody arse. You
saved my life. You kept me sane. Then you sod off
and get yourself killed. You lie to us. You neglect to
tell us we have a niece. Then you resurrect yourself
like a bloody—" He shook his head, and to Lokan's
horror, he could swear he saw a sheen of moisture
in his brother's eyes.

Then Alastor slung an arm over Lokan's shoulder
and drew him in for a hug.

Lokan looked at each of them in turn. "Thank
you," he said.

"For what?" Dae asked.

"For helping to keep my daughter safe. For working with your enemies to do it."

"Enemies?" Mal asked and shot a look at Boone.

"The Asetian Guard. Boone said they've been in
there with you." He jutted his chin toward the doorway his brothers had just passed through.

"The Ase—" Dae broke off and laughed. Which
had Lokan staring at him in surprise, because Dae
laughing was a rare and unusual thing.

Alastor turned and held out his hand, and a woman
stepped through and came to his side. Came to stand
against Alastor's side, close enough to stick, and she

looped her arm around his waist. She was beautiful. Dark hair cut in a sleek bob, dark eyes, athletic figure.

And she was looking at Alastor as if he hung the freakin' moon.

"Izanami's granddaughter?" Lokan asked with a sharp look at Boone.

"Many generations removed," the woman replied. "Naphré Kurata," she said and stepped forward to shake his hand.

"You're a Daughter of Aset," Lokan said, feeling like his world had tipped on its axis.

"Yes."

"And you're Alastor's—" He shot a confused glance at his brother, having no idea what he was supposed to say.

"Mate," Alastor supplied with an un-Alastorlike grin.

Mate. It was a term Alastor usually applied to his brothers, other soul reapers, even random companions. But in this case, Lokan was pretty sure the relationship wasn't random. Alastor had a mate.

Lokan had a sudden flash of himself asking Boone how he'd kept his brothers and the Daughters of Aset from killing each other.

His gaze shot to Dagan, then Mal. "Don't tell me—"

Two more women stepped through the doorway. The one on the left had skin that was creamy and pale, her hair almost black, hanging in a straight, thick curtain halfway down her back. Her cat eyes glowed green, accented by dark lashes. There was an air of cool control about her, and Lokan was startled when she moved to Mal's side.

"This is Calli," Mal said.

"Calliope Kane," she offered, her voice smooth and cultured.

Then his attention shifted to the last woman. She was all sass and swagger, dark-skinned, with brown-black ringlets that tumbled over her shoulders and bronze-green eyes. She stepped to Dagan's side and cocked a hip.

"Roxy Tam?" Lokan asked.

"That'd be me."

This was the woman who had saved Dana from the Setnakhts. "I owe you a debt. You were there for my daughter and my—for Bryn, when I couldn't be."

Her brows rose. "No debt, Lokan. That's what family's for."

Family. His brothers had family. Mates. Daughters of Aset. Sutekh's enemies.

"How—" he started to ask, then just shook his head. If he started firing questions, he wouldn't stop. He wanted to ask how Sutekh had taken all of this. How his brothers could bear to be in the same room as their father after what he had done. If there were repercussions. Who had taken over as second-in-command with both Lokan and Gahiji dead.

So many questions, with only one that truly mattered at the moment.

His gaze returned to the doorway, and he felt as if he was going to jump out of his skin.

And then there she was, his baby, his little girl, her hair in pigtails with pink bows. And she was hugging Flopsy against her chest.

"Daddy!"

He fell to his knees and opened his arms, then closed them around her as she flung herself against him, her fingers clutching his neck, her face against his chest. He buried his face in little girl hair.

"Daddy. Daddy, Daddy."

There were no words for what he felt, no way to describe the emotion pounding through him.

Raising his head, he met Boone's gaze. He'd thought he'd have to fight for her. He'd expected to storm the bastion. He hadn't expected capitulation and...tears in Boone's eyes.

"My sister?" Boone asked, and Lokan heard the world of pain in that question.

He couldn't answer. Not with words. He could only shake his head.

Gone. She was gone, and she was never coming back, and he was supposed to find a way to live with that.

Dana was patting his shoulder, little girl pats. "I knew you would come back," she said. "Mommy was sad. She cried. But I knew."

Lokan just held her. He had run through a thousand options in his head, trying to figure out the way to tell his daughter that her mother was never coming back, and he hadn't been able to find the right words. There were no right words.

"Did you see me?" Dana asked, pulling back and pressing her palms to his cheeks, holding his head steady as she stared at him. "Did you see me? I was quiet. Mommy didn't even know I was there. But I saw you. I saw the long line and the boat." She frowned. "But the man in the boat scared me. And the spiders."

Lokan stared at her, stunned. She was describing a scene he had lived while he was trapped in the null zone. There had been a bloodred river and a boat and ferryman whose skeletal hands had been covered in spiders. Dana had seen that...how?

This wasn't the conversation he'd planned to have the first time he saw her after so damned long. But plans changed. Around the room, everyone was still and quiet, watching, listening.

Then Lokan locked eyes with Boone, and he had the feeling they were on the same page.

Dana had been to the null zone. Which meant she was exactly like Bryn.

"I'm sure you were very quiet," he said, thinking about how he'd thought he'd seen Bryn there in the Underworld, but her eyes and her hair had been the wrong color. Now he got it. It was because she hadn't been alone. The image he'd seen had been a union of Bryn and Dana. His daughter's eyes. Bryn's face. They'd gone to the Underworld together, looking for him. And they'd found him, but they hadn't been able to make contact.

He had a million questions to ask her, but he wasn't asking them in front of Boone and Jack and Cahn. Just because they'd helped free Lokan didn't mean they were trustworthy.

All he knew was that they'd used Bryn for years, until she'd escaped their control. And Lokan was never going to give them the chance to use Dana.

"I wouldn't," Boone said.

"What are you, a mind reader?" Lokan asked.

Boone shook his head. "Just good at guessing and reading expressions. I figure you're thinking what I'd be thinking if I were in your place." He crossed his arms over his chest. "I learned my lesson years ago. I figured the best way to prove that to Bryn was to leave her be, to let her have the life she wanted."

"You knew where she was all along."

"Yeah. And we kept an eye on her. Checked on her from time to time." He paused, his expression dark. "And now my sister is gone and I'll never have the chance to make amends."

"Did you know about me?" Lokan asked, suspecting he already knew the answer.

"Yes." Then Boone shocked the hell out of him when he said, "We knew what she wanted. We sent her to find you."

Lokan stared at him, thinking about Bryn telling him Jack had frequented the club they'd met at and Jack's assertion that supernaturals hung out there. Then he thought about a few nights after he'd met Bryn, when Mal had insisted he'd never made plans to meet Lokan in Miami. He'd never worried overmuch about an explanation for that. But now he had one, and it sure as hell wasn't anything he'd expected.

Lokan drew Dana tight against his chest, holding her as if he'd never let her go. Because he wouldn't.

"Lokan..." Dae's voice, wary and concerned.

He turned to meet his brother's gaze and found the concern in his voice mirrored in his eyes.

And then he realized why. He and Dana were surrounded by light. Blue light that danced and curled like flames. Except it didn't burn them. It surrounded them, warmed them, protected them.

Dae spread his hands in question, but Lokan didn't have answers.

He knew he'd come back different than he had been. Osiris had said as much.

But exactly what had he come back as?

CHAPTER TWENTY-THREE

*The blood of Aset. The blood of Sutekh.
And the God will pass the Twelve Gates
and walk the Earth once more.*

The Underworld, The River Styx

"LET ME GUESS," LOKAN SAID. "A boat."

"You got a better way to get across the River Styx?" Dagan asked.

Mal and Alastor were both looking at him questioningly. His brother's mates—*his brother's mates;* that was going to take some getting used to—had agreed to stay behind and return to the dimensional box with Bryn's brothers in order to keep Dana safe while Lokan went to the Underworld, to the far side of the River Styx to face his father before a tribunal of his father's peers.

Not that there was anything Lokan could do to Sutekh. But making sure that the other powerful deities were fully aware of his perfidy was a solid plan. According to Dae, they'd all witnessed Sutekh's attempt to reanimate Lokan's body and steal it. But having Lokan's side of the story out there might garner him an offer to join the ranks of another deity.

Not likely, but possible, and Lokan was willing to try for possible because going back to Sutekh was a horror he did not want to have to face.

He had to wonder…if he could convince Osiris to take him on, would he have a chance at seeing Bryn? The thought brought equal parts agony and hope.

When he closed his eyes, he could almost see her face, almost hear her voice. So he closed them now and let the memories wash over him, wishing—

No sense wishing.

Opening his eyes, he pushed those thoughts away. They hurt too much. He wondered if the time would come that they didn't. He wondered if, like his human brother Richard, Bryn would become a soft-edged memory that he hauled out and touched, then folded away.

The boat was massive, the wood stained dark with age. There were no seats or slats to sit upon, so they all stood, while a hooded and silent boatman used a long wooden pole to steer their course. Lokan glanced at the boatman's hands, just to be sure they weren't denuded of flesh, the bones held together by the webs of a thousand spiders.

It was hard to shake the memory of the things he had experienced in the null zone. A skeletal boatman was the least of them.

They neared the midpoint of the river. The water surged upward in an enormous geyser, towering over them. Then it erupted into a wall of flame and unbearable heat.

Flame. Heat. All that was missing was a damn snake.

Lokan made a sharp gesture, and the flames snuffed, leaving only the smooth face of the river before them.

"Better," he said, then lifted his head to find his brothers staring at him. He even had the feeling the boatman was looking at him in surprise, though his face was obscured by his cowl. "What?"

"Did you do that?" Dagan asked.

Lokan laughed. "Right. Like I could still the river of fire. Coincidence."

"Hmm."

"I feel like we're making a habit of crossing the River Styx," Mal said, and when Lokan turned to look at him, he explained. "We were just here for the meeting of allies."

"There aren't a lot of choices," Lokan said. The far side of the River Styx was a crossroads, a neutral zone. The most powerful players of the Underworld weren't allowed to go Topworld. They couldn't cross borders into each others' Territories. So this was one of the few places they could meet face-to-face, rather than through emissaries.

"No hostages?" Lokan asked. Usually a meeting like this involved a complicated arrangement for the exchange of hostages, and setting that up could take time.

Alastor shook his head. "Sutekh killed his own son. That puts a bit of a spin on things."

Lokan could see his point. If Sutekh would sink to murdering his son, then no hostage was safe.

"Which means there are no guarantees that all the players will show," he said.

"They'll show." Dae pinned him with a look, gray eyes cold and flat. "You did the inviting. None of them will want to miss the fireworks when you and the old ma—" He broke off and his jaw clenched. "When you and Sutekh face off."

Lokan wasn't so sure there were going to be any fireworks. However powerful his rage and hate, he was still his father's subject. He wasn't an Underworld god; he couldn't take on Sutekh as an equal. And that ate at him like a cancer because he wanted vengeance for what had been done to him and what had been taken from him. Bryn. If Sutekh hadn't killed him, she'd still be baking cookies in her damned kitchen.

Missing her was a knife in his heart, a whip flaying his soul.

The boat beached on the far shore, and Lokan was out before the craft stopped moving.

They weren't the first ones there.

Lokan did a slow scan of the faces of those who stood on the shore. There was Asmodeus, with a phalanx of female warriors standing at his back. The demon of lust inclined his head to Lokan, then offered his hand. Surprising. Last Lokan had heard, Asmodeus was allied with Sutekh.

"You look well," Asmodeus said, grasping Lokan's wrist as Lokan grasped his. There was an odd sizzle between them, an electric charge that sparked up Lokan's arm. He shoved it away, sent it back. Asmodeus jerked, and his eyes widened. "What—" He cut himself off, and his mouth drew taut, leaving Lokan wondering what the hell was going on. "Good to see you," Asmodeus finished, and he actually sounded as if he meant it.

Lokan turned to see that Alastor was greeting a tiny, delicate woman dressed completely in white. No part of her was visible. Not her hands or face. The cloth draped her completely.

As he approached, Lokan's path was blocked by eight creatures who stepped between him and the woman in white. At first glance, one might think they were draped in gray velvet. In fact, they were clothed in undulating layers of living spiders and centipedes and maggots that writhed and crawled over their skin and into any orifice.

They were the Shikome, guards and associates of the woman in white. Izanami-no-mikoto. Naphré Kurata's progenitor. Izanami said something to Alastor, then moved toward Lokan, all regal grace and elegance. As she passed Mal, she stopped, turned her head toward him, and said, "It blooms still."

Mal offered a shrug in the face of Lokan's questioning glance. "I brought her flowers."

"To Yomi?" Lokan had been there as Sutekh's ambassador. There was no way flowers would bloom in Izanami's realm. There was no light.

"Moonflowers," Mal clarified.

Alastor stepped forward and faced Izanami. He shot a glance at Lokan, his expression troubled, then he bowed low and said, "Izanami-no-mikoto, grandmother of my mate, and so, my grandmother, I beseech you, implore you. Take my brother into your realm. Do not send him back to serve my father, my brother's murderer."

The other gods stopped talking and Lokan could feel all eyes on them. His gaze met Alastor's, and he saw that Alastor bled for him. But he couldn't *feel* him. Lokan had lost his ability to connect with his brothers' emotions. And he knew they could no longer sense him. He'd noticed that before, but he'd made excuses. In Vegas, he'd told himself it was because they were in the dimensional box and he wasn't. Not so. There was some sort of barrier between them. The three of them could still feel each other, but he was the odd man out.

One more change that had happened when he was returned to the living. One more price he'd paid for what Sutekh had done to him.

But link or no link, Alastor clearly recognized his agony, knew what torture it would be to return to Sutekh's ranks. So he was trying to fix it. Control it. Wasn't that just like Alastor?

Izanami turned to Lokan, and he thought she would simply decline Alastor's request. Instead, she reached out and laid a cloth-draped hand on his arm. The same thing that had happened with Asmodeus happened with her, the weird electrical spark chasing through him, only this time, it was even stronger.

She dropped her hand, turned to Alastor and said, "I cannot." And the Shikome closed ranks around her, sealing her off from view.

"What the fuck?" Dagan asked.

"Nicely put," Alastor said, frowning as he stared after Izanami.

So it went as they made their way to an open spot on the shore. Lokan spoke with a few lesser gods, those he had had pleasant dealings with as Sutekh's ambassador. With each one in turn, he hinted at becoming one of their legion.

Each one touched him as Asmodeus and Izanami had, and each one declined.

At length, another boat arrived. This one carried Aset. Lokan stopped and watched as she descended from the barge, her white gown flowing with each step, her night-dark hair cascading down her back. The sight of her was like a knife digging deep into a freshly healed wound. It made him think of the final Gate and the door closing with Bryn on one side and him on the other.

Directly behind her was a man with the head of a falcon, his body tall and lean and muscled. As Lokan watched, the shape of the head changed, and he became a man, handsome, dark-haired, dark-eyed. He was Horus, Aset's son, conceived when she brought her husband/brother Osiris back from the dead long enough to give her a child.

Then came Osiris, majestic, regal.

"Didn't expect to see him here. He didn't come to the meeting of allies," Mal murmured.

Lokan wasn't surprised. Osiris was known to cleave to his domain, to leave it only when he must.

For some reason, he felt this meeting was a must.

And that, Lokan did wonder at.

Then Osiris turned and stared out at the water, his expression laced with hate. Lokan didn't need to turn to know what he was looking at.

Sutekh had arrived.

SUTEKH HAD COME WITH ONLY A single soul reaper to accompany him. Kai Warin, his new second-in-command.

Lokan knew Kai. He liked him. That made it all the worse to see him standing by Sutekh's side. As if he had a choice. It was that or annihilation, and from what his brothers had told him, Lokan figured Kai now had quite a bit to live for. He was mated to the daughter of Asmodeus. Yet another interesting bit of information; Lokan hadn't even known that Asmodeus *had* a daughter.

He focused his thoughts and turned. No more putting it off. He'd avoided looking at his father as he'd made the rounds of the other deities, because he hadn't been certain that he could control the rage and pain.

Now he did look at him, locking the destructive emotions behind an impenetrable wall, putting on a mask of calm indifference. Today, Sutekh had chosen to wear the guise of humanity, to take on the fair coloring of three of his four sons. For the moment, Sutekh looked like a mixture of Dagan and Alastor and Lokan, and that burned Lokan's ass.

But he didn't show it. He wasn't about to offer Sutekh even that small edge.

"Begin," Sutekh ordered and made a languid gesture in Lokan's direction. As though Lokan were a supplicant looking for a favor. As though Sutekh wasn't the betrayer. The monster. The killer.

Anger sluiced through him, for everything Sutekh had done. Most of all for Bryn. For the sacrifice she'd been forced to make because of Sutekh's treachery. And with anger came the sparking fire that had come back with him from the Twelve Gates.

He felt it in his bones, in his tissues and organs, in his cells. And he couldn't control it, couldn't stop the flare of light that rose up and surrounded him.

"Begin?" he asked, his voice whisper soft. "What would you have me begin? A narration of your betrayals? A litany of your sins?"

Sutekh stared at him, eyes soulless and flat. "Is that not one of the first things I taught you, Lokan? A body of sin stands on its own merit."

"Merit implies worth." Lokan took a slow breath, forced himself to stay calm, to deny Sutekh the taste of his rage and pain. His father fed off those things, except...

Except, he didn't look as if he was enjoying this confrontation. He didn't look as if he was pulling anything from Lokan's emotions.

Which made no sense. The only beings exempt from Sutekh's parasitic nature were—

He froze and spun to face Aset, turning his back on his father, facing his father's enemy. Then he looked to Osiris, who watched him with a calm and detached expression.

In five strides, he reached Osiris and stood before him.

"What was it you said to me when I was judged against the feather of Ma'at?" he rasped.

"I said many things, Lokan Krayl."

"You did, but one thing in particular. About what I would be once I passed the Twelfth Gate."

Osiris inclined his head and intoned. "You will never return to your former self, Lokan Krayl." The exact words he had said once before.

Only now, they held new meaning.

Lokan could feel the eyes of all those assembled burning holes in his back, but he didn't turn, didn't look at them.

Extending his hand toward Osiris, he asked, "May I?"

Again, Osiris inclined his head and stretched out his arm, taking Lokan's hand in his. The same electric spark he'd experienced with the other deities tore through him. Stronger. With each one he touched, he felt it more, until it grew and swelled and repelled him. The power of it tore his hand from Osiris's grasp, repelling him three feet back.

His gaze shot to Dae, then Alastor, then Mal.

This was crazy. What he was thinking here was crazy.

"The cease-fire pact," he said. "It doesn't allow gods into each others' Territories." He spun back to Osiris and continued. "Does it repel them from touching each other? Like magnets?"

"In the beginning, it did. We each needed to learn to master it. We can tolerate each other well enough now to clasp hands if we must."

Panting, he turned back to Dagan. "The prophesy. The one we talked about. The one about combining the blood. Tell it to me." The words came out in a rush, because if he didn't get them out quickly, he wouldn't get them out at all. What he was thinking was too crazy, too impossible to be considered. But he was considering it.

"The blood of Aset," Dae said. "The blood of Sutekh." Lokan turned back toward his father and watched his face as Dagan finished. "And the God will pass the Twelve Gates and walk the Earth once more."

"You thought it was you," Lokan said, his tone diamond hard. "You thought to kill me and use my body and walk beneath the sun. You thought the prophesy was about you."

He felt his brothers step up at his back, facing his father with him, risking everything.

"But it was never about you." He lifted his hands, and the flames of power erupted from his skin, consuming him, consuming his brothers, holding them all in a bubble of power.

"It was about me. I am the god who passed the Twelve Gates. I am the god who walks the Earth once more."

For the first time in his existence, he saw his father display emotion. Shock. Dismay. Then cunning.

Around them, murmurs of shock and awe grew and swelled.

"Lokan Krayl," Sutekh said over the din, his voice even and smooth. "Let us make an alliance."

"SOULS ARE OWED IN REPARATION," Osiris intoned once the pandemonium had died down. He turned to Lokan and said, "Choose. He breached the pact. He acted against another deity—"

"He was not a deity when I acted against him," Sutekh interjected. "He was my subject. My property. Mine to dispose of as I willed it."

"He was your *son*," Mal said at the same moment

that Alastor stepped forward and held up a finger. "Actually, no," Alastor said. His tone was icy cold, utterly controlled. No hint of his emotions leaked into his words. "You are the deity who made the ruling about the passage of time. You are the one who claimed that time in the human realm and in the other Territories has no meaning. Hence, your claim of a timeline as defense is arguable."

"Claim your souls," Osiris said to Lokan.

"My souls? What do you mean?"

"Your father must forfeit to make amends for his acts. The cease-fire demands it. He cannot act against another god without repercussion." Osiris offered a tight smile. "Even a lesser god who must now learn his way."

"So I'm a god with little power and no Territory?" Lokan asked, stalling for time as he silently weighed and measured his options.

"You have the Territory of Lokan Krayl. You survived that which was the null zone. It is now yours to build into a home."

Lokan stared at him, a single horrible thought bubbling to the surface. If he was an Underworld deity now, did that mean... "Am I trapped here in the Underworld, like—" *Like you're all trapped in the Underworld.* Maybe that wasn't the best question to ask.

"You are the god who walks the Earth once more," Aset said.

Lokan heard what she said, and what she didn't.

He was the *only* Underworld god who could go Top-world. Oh, Sutekh had managed it for a short span when he'd taken over a human form the night he killed Lokan. But he hadn't been able to hold that form for long, and it had taken him millennia to amass the energy to do even that. He wasn't going to be able to carry out a repeat performance anytime soon.

"You are a vital ally for all," Aset continued, the mistress of understatement. A valuable ally? He was unique among them. More than valuable. He was one of a kind. "I myself will be glad to meet with you and build an alliance as soon as you have chosen your reparation from your father."

An alliance. With Aset. Whose daughters were mated to his brothers.

His gaze shot back to Osiris. "How many souls?"

"Betrayal. Murder. Theft of your body. Three heinous crimes to be paid with three souls." Osiris pinned Sutekh with a hard look. "Souls that will be your right hand and the guard at your front and at your back. Souls who will owe allegiance to you and no other. Choose wisely."

Lokan could swear he saw Sutekh flinch.

"Can you think of three such souls, Lokan Krayl?"

"Yeah, I can." He looked first to Dae, asking the silent question, leaving the choice to his brother. Dagan stepped to his side.

Sutekh made a sound of denial and stepped forward. Lokan swore he saw pain flash across his father's face.

"I made the choice to sacrifice one son in order to gain something of great value. I do not choose to lose all," Sutekh said. There was no inflection to the words. They were flat as a Kansas prairie, but by saying them at all, Sutekh betrayed himself. Whether it was due to genuine affection or simply the need to control what he saw as his, Sutekh didn't want to lose his remaining sons.

Lokan turned his face away and repeated the silent exchange with Alastor and Mal, and when each of them stood by his side, he turned back to Sutekh and said, "These souls I claim from you, a penalty, a penance. These souls are mine. Dagan Krayl. Alastor Krayl. Malthus Krayl." And with those words, Sutekh lost not one, but all four of his sons.

For a millisecond, Lokan felt the satisfaction of vengeance delivered. And then the feeling fizzled, and he was left with the knowledge that it wasn't enough. The desire to make his father pay had sustained him for so long, and yet that victory, now achieved, rang hollow. There was still a giant hole in his heart, his soul. An empty place that could never be filled.

"Wait," Osiris said. "There is one more crime that must be addressed. The theft of your mate whose loss may be laid at Sutekh's feet."

The words knifed deep. The loss of his mate. *Bryn.*

"Another soul, Lokan Krayl."

Lokan's chest rose and fell in ragged breaths. His gaze slid to Kai Warin. A political choice. Kai was mated to Asmodeus's daughter. If Kai switched allegiance, so too might his father-in-law. And Lokan knew Kai had helped his brothers, supplying information and risking his own neck.

But he wouldn't demand. Instead, he held Kai's gaze and let him choose.

Kai glanced at Asmodeus, but Lokan didn't see the demon of lust's response because he stood staring straight ahead, his thoughts whirling as he tried to assimilate everything that was coming to pass.

Then Kai stepped up beside Dagan.

"This soul I claim from you, a penalty, a penance. This soul is mine. Kai Warin," Lokan said.

Short of killing Sutekh—an impossibility—stealing his sons was sweet payback. Stealing his second-in-command, the cherry on top. But it was a sundae Lokan couldn't fully enjoy.

Bryn.

"We're done," he said to Sutekh.

His father stared at him, then inclined his head. Sutekh was still the most powerful of the Underworld deities. Nothing could change that. But Lokan had something he didn't. The ability to go Topworld. Out of all of them, he was the only god who could.

But what he didn't have was Bryn.

He swallowed and turned away, the momentary glow of achieving his revenge snuffed like a match.

Because what he wanted most was Bryn. And what he wanted most, he wasn't going to get.

"Lokan Krayl," Osiris said. "One moment."

Lokan turned back to him, putting on his game face. Here it began, the negotiating, the alliances, the never-ending politics. Had he truly loved this once upon a time? Had he truly thought it was a high?

Maybe he could learn to love it again. Maybe it could fill some of the massive hole inside him.

"Before witnesses, I offer an alliance," Osiris said. "I offer my hand in friendship—" he paused, and Lokan could swear he smiled "—although given your as-yet-unharnessed power, you will forgive me if I offer something in its stead…perhaps a soul, a token of my sincere interest in furthering our association."

The breath left Lokan in a rush. A soul.

Sheer will alone kept him from grabbing hold of Osiris and demanding that he spell out what was on his mind. He couldn't mean—

"Claim your soul, Lokan Krayl," Osiris said softly, "and you will be in my graces and I in yours."

"In your debt," Lokan corrected, waiting for the hammer to drop, waiting for him to say any soul but Bryn's.

"The enemy of my enemy is my friend."

And there it was, a seed of hope, uncoiling in his heart. "Any soul?"

"Is there one in particular you wish?" He waved languidly at the boat he had arrived in.

Lokan's heart stopped, then started again with a sharp lurch. Bryn stood there looking exactly as she had the last time he saw her. Love shone in her eyes, a beacon in the darkness. She stepped forward, then stopped short, as though yanked back by a tether.

"She cannot come unless you claim her."

Claim her. Make her his. Hold her in his arms once more.

His throat was so tight, he had to force the words free, his first attempt coming out as a croak. His second attempt better.

"This soul I claim from you, a token of alliance. This soul is mine. Brynja, daughter of the Underworld." His. She was his.

The words had barely left his lips before she was leaping out of the boat, tearing across the beach toward him. And then she was in his arms, talking, talking, and though the rushing in his ears prevented him from hearing her words, the sound of her voice washed over him, through him, as it had in his memories, the sound that had sustained him in his darkest moments.

He yanked her against him and lowered his head. His mouth was on hers and hers on his. She was kissing him and clinging to him and she was warm and real.

She was here. She wasn't gone.

"You died for me," he rasped. "Now you're going to live for me. For me and Dana."

So much to say. So much to tell her.

But pressing her palms to his cheeks as she stared into his eyes, she said the only thing that mattered. "I love you, Lokan Krayl."

* * * * *

From a dazzling new voice in paranormal romance…

STEPHANIE CHONG

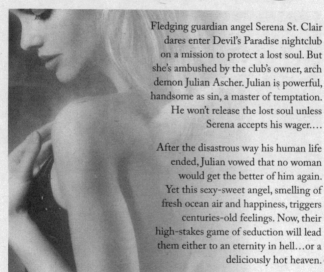

Fledgling guardian angel Serena St. Clair dares enter Devil's Paradise nightclub on a mission to protect a lost soul. But she's ambushed by the club's owner, arch demon Julian Ascher. Julian is powerful, handsome as sin, a master of temptation. He won't release the lost soul unless Serena accepts his wager.…

After the disastrous way his human life ended, Julian vowed that no woman would get the better of him again. Yet this sexy-sweet angel, smelling of fresh ocean air and happiness, triggers centuries-old feelings. Now, their high-stakes game of seduction will lead them either to an eternity in hell…or a deliciously hot heaven.

WHERE DEMONS FEAR TO TREAD

Available wherever books are sold.

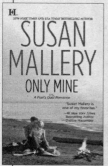
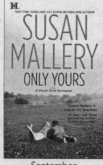

Too much of a good thing...

**A fun and feisty new romance
from *USA TODAY* bestselling author**

VICTORIA DAHL

With her long ponytail and sparkling green eyes, Tessa Donovan
looks more like the girl next door than a businesswoman—or
a heartbreaker. Which may explain why Detective Luke Asher
barely notices her when he arrives to investigate a break-in
at her family's brewery....

GOOD GiRLS Don't

Available now.

REQUEST YOUR FREE BOOKS!

2 FREE NOVELS FROM THE PARANORMAL ROMANCE COLLECTION PLUS 2 FREE GIFTS!

YES! Please send me 2 FREE novels from the Paranormal Romance Collection and my 2 FREE gifts (gifts are worth about $10). After receiving them, if I don't wish to receive any more books, I can return the shipping statement marked "cancel." If I don't cancel, I will receive 4 brand-new novels every month and be billed just $21.42 in the U.S. or $23.46 in Canada. That's a saving of at least 21% off the cover price of all 4 books. It's quite a bargain! Shipping and handling is just 50¢ per book in the U.S. and 75¢ per book in Canada.* I understand that accepting the 2 free books and gifts places me under no obligation to buy anything. I can always return a shipment and cancel at any time. Even if I never buy another book, the two free books and gifts are mine to keep forever.

237/337 HDN FEL2

Name	(PLEASE PRINT)
Address	Apt. #
City	State/Prov.	Zip/Postal Code

Signature (if under 18, a parent or guardian must sign)

Mail to the **Reader Service:**
IN U.S.A.: P.O. Box 1867, Buffalo, NY 14240-1867
IN CANADA: P.O. Box 609, Fort Erie, Ontario L2A 5X3

Not valid for current subscribers to the Paranormal Romance Collection or Harlequin® Nocturne™ books.

Want to try two free books from another line?
Call 1-800-873-8635 or visit www.ReaderService.com.

* Terms and prices subject to change without notice. Prices do not include applicable taxes. Sales tax applicable in N.Y. Canadian residents will be charged applicable taxes. Offer not valid in Quebec. This offer is limited to one order per household. All orders subject to credit approval. Credit or debit balances in a customer's account(s) may be offset by any other outstanding balance owed by or to the customer. Please allow 4 to 6 weeks for delivery. Offer available while quantities last.

Your Privacy—The Reader Service is committed to protecting your privacy. Our Privacy Policy is available online at www.ReaderService.com or upon request from the Reader Service.

We make a portion of our mailing list available to reputable third parties that offer products we believe may interest you. If you prefer that we not exchange your name with third parties, or if you wish to clarify or modify your communication preferences, please visit us at www.ReaderService.com/consumerschoice or write to us at Reader Service Preference Service, P.O. Box 9062, Buffalo, NY 14269. Include your complete name and address.

EVE SILVER

77484	SINS OF THE FLESH	___ $7.99 U.S.	___ $9.99 CAN.
77483	SINS OF THE SOUL	___ $7.99 U.S.	___ $9.99 CAN.
77482	SINS OF THE HEART	___ $7.99 U.S.	___ $9.99 CAN.

(limited quantities available)

TOTAL AMOUNT	$ _____
POSTAGE & HANDLING	$ _____
($1.00 FOR 1 BOOK, 50¢ for each additional)	
APPLICABLE TAXES*	$ _____
TOTAL PAYABLE	$ _____

(check or money order—please do not send cash)

To order, complete this form and send it, along with a check or money order for the total above, payable to HQN Books, to: **In the U.S.:** 3010 Walden Avenue, P.O. Box 9077, Buffalo, NY 14269-9077; **In Canada:** P.O. Box 636, Fort Erie, Ontario, L2A 5X3.

Name: _____
Address: _____ City: _____
State/Prov.: _____ Zip/Postal Code: _____
Account Number (if applicable): _____

075 CSAS

*New York residents remit applicable sales taxes.
*Canadian residents remit applicable GST and provincial taxes.

HARLEQUIN®
www.Harlequin.com

PHES0911BL